CHILDREN GAIA

RICHARD LEE BYERS

author:	richard lee byers
cover artist:	steve prescott
series editors:	eric griffin
	john h. steele
	stewart wieck
copyeditor:	jeanée ledoux
graphic designer:	aaron voss
art director:	richard thomas

More information and previews available at
white–wolf.com/clannovels

ISBN: 1-58846-812-7
First Edition: March 2002
Printed in Canada.

White Wolf Publishing
735 Park North Boulevard, Suite 128
Clarkston, GA 30021
www.white-wolf.com/fiction

CHILDREN OF GAIA

RICHARD LEE BYERS

Chapter One

Cries Havoc stood on the wooden bridge and looked over the guardrail at the rocks jutting from the water at the bottom of the ravine. When first venturing outdoors, he had reflexively, unthinkingly pulled down his cap to cover the small, curved horns protruding from his brow, but he needn't have bothered, any more than he needed to maintain the puny, hairless guise that was less natural for him than his towering Crinos half-man/half-wolf form. No human was watching, only Luna, a sickle shining white in the night sky. But a Homid body had one advantage. It was fragile.

He wondered how the final moment would feel. Would it be like flying? He hoped he would finally feel *something*.

Something rumbled at the west end of the bridge, the side opposite the decrepit tourist cabins and other civilized amenities, where except for a few man-made trails, the Appalachian woods were pure and unscarred. To the ears of a werewolf, that growl conveyed, as plainly as any human speech, *What are you doing?* Cries Havoc wasn't alone after all. It was just that his dull Homid nose and ears hadn't detected the approach of a Garou in another form.

He turned to see a large, gray wolf dissolve upward into a figure scarcely less primal. John North Wind's Son was a young, powerfully built Amerind clad only in a pair of tattered jeans. A raven tattoo spread its wings across his chest, and atop that image dangled a fetish, a crystal—or something—that looked like an icicle strung on a leather thong. The warrior wore his black hair in a braid and carried a flint-pointed, feather-bedizened spear in his hand.

"Hi," said Cries Havoc. "I was just admiring the view. And thinking."

"Don't bullshit me, packmate." North Wind's Son came closer. Even though he was now in human form, the planks of the old weathered bridge declined to creak beneath his naked feet. "I know *what* you were thinking, and you've got to snap out of it. I realize it's hard—"

"No, you don't," said Cries Havoc. "No offense, but you don't really know anything about it. You think I care what happened. I don't. I only sort of wish I cared. And that's worse."

"You didn't act this way back in New York."

Cries Havoc pondered how best to explain. Off in the forest, an owl hooted.

"I think," said Cries Havoc at last, "that for a while after Antonine and Julia pulled me out of the coma, I was in shock. People told me I'd lost some of my memories and with them, a piece of my spirit, and I figured it was bad, but at first I didn't realize just how big a hole the winged Bane put in me. Gradually, though, I've come to feel just how… raped and broken I really am."

North Wind's Son frowned. "You still walk. And talk. And change shape. You remember the Silver River Pack and our mission. You don't seem all that messed up to me."

"I'm a Child of Gaia. A peacemaker. A teacher. And I *was* a Galliard, a lorekeeper and bard, and I used my stories to further the mission of my tribe. Without them and the gifts spirits grant Moon-singers,

I'm pretty much nothing at all. Empty. Definitely not up to helping the rest of the pack fulfill some heroic prophecy."

"But we're trying to get you fixed. You can't just quit on us! Hell, I'm Wendigo tribe. I hate all you damn white people." He grinned to show it was a joke. "And I'm sticking around."

Cries Havoc sighed. "Like I said, you can't understand. It's hard to have nothing on the inside. It seems like it would be easier to just *be* nothing, period. Especially when there isn't any hope."

"There's always hope. Do you know the tale of Laughs-at-Pine-Cones?"

"Of course."

North Wind's Son continued just as if Cries Havoc had replied in the negative. "Laughs-at-Pine-Cones lived at the end of the first age of the world. Of course, he didn't know it was the end. All the time he was growing up, the Triat were in harmony, and the earth, though it could be hard and dangerous, was clean. Laughs-at-Pine-Cones had no reason to think things would ever change.

"But if he could have looked inside the secret heart of existence, he would have seen the start of a major fuck-up, which still threatens the world to this day.

"The Weaver was proud, stupidly proud, and it decided it wasn't going to live in balance with the Wyld anymore. The first spider wanted its rules and logic to control everything. It wanted to push the Wyld's magic and mystery right out of the world, even though that was the power that gave its creations life.

"So what the spider did was trap the Wyrm in its web. Because the Wyrm was like a cop enforcing the balance between the Weaver and the Wyld, and the Weaver figured that with the Great Serpent out of the picture, it could beat the Wyld down.

"Well, we all know how that worked out. The Wyrm suffered in the web so much that it eventually went crazy. Sometime after that, it figured out how to reach out and touch the world even though it was still stuck inside, and by then, it didn't care about balancing the Weaver and the Wyld. All it wanted to do was get even with the whole universe for the bad thing that had happened to it. Which it would accomplish by spreading pain and corruption.

"The first thing the snake did was call its old servants into its presence. Up to that point, they'd just been preservers of balance. Kind of gray and boring. But the Wyrm turned them into monsters who were ready, willing and able to rip up Creation for him. These evil spirits were the first Banes. The serpent gave them a pep talk, I guess, and turned them loose on the world.

"And that was very bad news for the Garou and the humans they watched over. At least today, the Garou know to watch out for the Wyrm and its helpers. Back then, in those first few terrible days, they didn't. The Banes caught them with their pants down.

"Including Laughs-at-Pine-Cones. He was a mighty warrior, the protector of his sept, but the Banes played him for a fool. Three of them, called Smashes-to-Dust, Burns-to-Ash, and Rots Away, came to him in the guise of tired travelers, and he gave them the hospitality of his lodge. They thanked him by jumping him while he slept, and they did more than kill him.

As you might figure from their names, they completely destroyed his body.

"Still, Laughs-at-Pine-Cones had such a strong spirit that it refused to pass into the beyond. It held onto this world, but not because it was afraid of death. Laughs-at-Pine-Cones was never afraid of anything. He stuck around because he understood what the Banes were going to do next. They were going to range through the forest, destroying everything he loved and everyone who looked to him for protection.

"But without a body, what could he do about it? Nothing but give a silent howl of rage.

"And even though Laughs-at-Pine Cones himself could hardly believe it, that ghostly yell was enough. Somehow the spirits of the forest heard him, and together they built a new body to hold his soul. The oak and the redwood gave their strongest branches to make his bones. The ground gave mud to be his flesh. The river gave water for his blood and a big oyster to make a heart. The rock gave moss to be his fur. The bramble gave thorns for teeth and claws, and two round berries for eyes.

"When the spirits finished, Laughs-at-Pine-Cones rose from the place of his death, hunted down Smashes-to-Dust, Burns-to-Ash and Rots Away, and did to them what they'd done to him. And *they* weren't able to come back.

"Afterward he traveled from one sept to the next, warning all the Garou of the coming of the Banes. Some people say we only survived those first few dangerous weeks because of him and the fact that he wouldn't give up."

Cries Havoc shook his head. "You told that very badly. The tone was inconsistent, and you rushed through all the best parts."

"I'm sure you could've done better."

"No. I couldn't. The words would tangle and die in my throat."

"Whatever. Will you just come off the damn bridge?"

"All right." He didn't know why he should, but he guessed that he would.

Chapter Two

Storm-Eye stalked through the shadowy spaces between the nasty little cabins, which reeked of kerosene heating oil and other unnatural human smells. She was wearing the wolf body into which she had been born, and which she always chose whenever possible. If any non-Garou with his inadequate senses noticed her at all, he would probably mistake her for a stray dog, and if by some chance he did recognize her for what she was, well, that would really be his problem, not hers.

She wished she was still on the west side of the gorge, where the world was more or less as it ought to be. But though she had learned considerable respect for her packmates, she still didn't quite trust werewolves who were neither of the Red Talon tribe nor even lupus breed to keep watch over this temporary lair as diligently as they ought. Well, maybe North Wind's Son, but as far as she knew, the Wendigo was still off in the forest hunting his own supper.

Around the corner, gravel crunched. Storm-Eye slunk forward until the night breeze brought her Julia Spencer's scent. Reassured, she trotted forward to greet her packmate, then faltered in dismay.

Julia was wearing her own preferred form, which is to say, she looked human. The Glass Walker was slim and fair skinned, with incomprehensible layers of tight-looking clothing, and hair which, for some mad reason, she tousled and tangled deliberately. Storm-Eye had overheard a man at a gas station call the other werewolf "hot, but classy"; she herself was no judge of what rendered a human female attractive.

Julia had the hard little bag she called a *suitcase* in her hand, and she was headed for the rented car. Her guilty flinch made her intent even more unmistakable.

Nonetheless, Storm-Eye, using the Garou language of growl and posture, felt compelled to ask, *What are you doing?*

"I don't want to be selfish about it," Julia said in what Storm-Eye had recently learned was an *English accent*, "but as I recall, I'm the only one who even wanted to hire the minivan. It's on my credit card, and besides, I think that except for maybe North Wind's Son, the rest of you don't even know how to drive it."

No one cares about the Weaver's rolling box. But you can't desert the pack.

Julia sighed. "I wish you wouldn't put it that way. I love you and the others, and it's been a grand adventure. But it's over."

Storm-Eye reluctantly shifted to Homid shape, not because she doubted her ability to communicate as a wolf, but because she thought the citified Glass Walker might be more receptive to persuasions issuing from a human mouth.

At once, she became more aware of her blind eye. It never bothered her in Lupus or Crinos form, but now that she was half-deaf and virtually noseless, it seemed much more of an impediment

The cold air of early spring raised gooseflesh on her furless and vulnerable skin. Her packmates had purchased garments for her and coaxed her into attuning them to herself, but she loathed them and shed them whenever she could. She swore she could feel them binding and itching even after she changed form and they allegedly disappeared. Only her fetishes, the gun barrel bent around her forearm and the cat skull hanging around her neck, were truly tolerable.

"Good lord," said Julia, "you're the answer to a voyeur's prayers."

Storm-Eye didn't know what that meant, but she sensed that, like much of what humans and human-born Garou said, it was irrelevant. "You can't leave. Cries Havoc needs you."

"And I'd crawl through silver razor blades to help him if I could, but it's just not possible. The magic compass led us in circles, we finally wound up in this charming tourist destination, and then the wretched thing evaporated. Maybe it was glitched, or maybe the Record Keeper didn't want to meet with us. Antonine warned us that could happen.

"Either way," Julia continued, "it amounts to the same thing: game over. We didn't reach the Emerald City, we didn't see the Wizard, and we can't obtain the ruby slippers. We might as well go home to our various septs."

"Antonine told us that the pack which formed around Cries Havoc would be needed to destroy Jo'cllath'mattric."

"We took direction from Antonine before, and look where it got us. Cries Havoc had his spirit torn apart and the Silver River Pack ended up labeled a bunch of incompetent losers."

"We killed the Tisza River spirit. It was a great victory. Fools cannot rob us of our pride."

"Speak for yourself. Look, Antonine isn't one of us. The Stargazers opted out of the Garou Nation and the struggle against the Wyrm a while ago. Maybe we should have consulted one of our own oracles. All I know is, I'm not doing anybody any good sitting around Nowhere, North Carolina, USA."

"I am the alpha of our pack, and you must follow my commands in war. So says the Litany, our law."

"Rubbish. The war's in Serbia. I'll be a lot closer to the front lines, and better able to work for the good of the cause, back in London."

"I…" Storm-Eye had rarely participated in this sort of cunningly parsed babble, and she felt as if the Glass Walker Theurge had conjured up some Weaver spirits to spin a web of words around her.

"War or peace," the Red Talon continued, "I am still your alpha, and you cannot leave while this is true. You have to challenge me and oust me from the role to disobey. If not, I will tear you apart if you try to go." Storm-Eye took a single step forward. "You know I can do it, city wolf."

Julia's painted lips pulled back to show her puny white human teeth. "No, I don't know it, but if you want a challenge, here it is: beat me at gamecraft and I'll give you my throat."

Storm-Eye hesitated, something she almost never had occasion to do when ranging the wilderness in wolf form as Gaia intended. As alpha, she had the right to choose the contest. She could demand a clash of fang and claw instead of a game of riddles or something similar. From a tactical standpoint, it was obviously the right move.

Yet the Red Talon sensed that even though she was the leader, and she and Julia were comrades, in one respect, the Glass Walker looked down on her.

She believed a homid from the city must surely be far, far cleverer than a lupus from the forest. And indeed, deep in Storm-Eye's mind, a timid voice she had rarely heard whispered that Julia might well be right. The Red Talon had a feeling that if she wanted to command her packmate's absolute loyalty and quash her rebellious impulses for good and all, she would have to meet her on her favored ground.

"Gamecraft it is," she said.

Julia narrowed her eyes in surprise. "Really? Well, fine then. What shall we play?"

"Rock-paper-scissors!" a brash young voice declared.

Startled but determined not to show it, Storm-Eye turned to see that Carlita, or Big Sis, as she liked to be called, had walked up out of the darkness on her blind side. In Homid form, Big Sis was a skinny teenager with dark, expressive eyes, an impish smile, and long, black hair she tucked up under a baseball cap. A member of the Bone Gnawer tribe, she too was a city wolf, but even a Red Talon could see the difference between her and Julia. The adolescent's clothes were loose, floppy and somehow didn't seem to match. She'd mentioned she bought them at *Goodwill*, whatever that was.

"Rock-paper-scissors!" Big Sis repeated.

"That's not a game of skill," Julia answered. "It's pure luck."

"It is not!"

"Stop," said Storm-Eye. "I don't know this game. Tell me what it is."

Big Sis explained, and once the alpha understood, she decided that *rock-paper-scissors* might validly be considered a game of wits, for a player won by outguessing his opponent. She also liked its simplicity, which might make it difficult for Julia to use convoluted Glass Walker thinking to trip her up.

"That's it," Storm-Eye said. "That is the contest."

Julia shrugged. "Fine. At least it won't take all night."

Big Sis said, "I'll give you guys the count to three."

Storm-Eye and the Glass Walker raised their fists.

"One." Big Sis spoke louder than seemed necessary.

Storm-Eye's mind raced. What to pick? Her inclination was rock, the one article that was natural, not man-made, but wasn't that exactly what Julia would expect?

"Two."

If Julia anticipated rock, she would put down paper. So Storm-Eye ought to counter with scissors. Unless—

"Three!"

Storm-Eye jerked her hand down and showed two fingers. Julia kept her fist closed. The Red Talon felt a sick, sinking feeling in her belly. The city wolf had been one step ahead of her. She had produced a rock to break her opponent's scissors and made herself the new alpha, with every right in the world to leave and break up the pack.

Julia looked at Storm-Eye's hand and sighed, "Damn. But all right, fair enough. I'll go put this away." She hefted her suitcase and walked back toward her cabin.

Storm-Eye stared after her in astonishment. She could only conclude that the Glass Walker had looked at her play and seen paper instead of rock. But how was it possible?

"Hey, boss," said Big Sis, "if you want to like, tell me I'm a genius or anything, I won't fight it."

"Did you do that?" asked Storm-Eye.

"Someone has to be the trickster around here."

"You are not Ragabash," Storm-Eye said. "You are Philodox. A Half Moon, a judge, like me."

"Yeah, but the whole Half Moon gig is about balance, right?" Carlita slipped another of her endless array of processed bonbons from her jacket, unwrapped it and popped it into her mouth. "And this Silver River Pack of ours is getting caught up in the gloom and doom without a Ragabash, so I figured I'd step in."

"You are renouncing your moon-sign?" The idea almost turned Storm-Eye's stomach. It happened occasionally among the Twelve Tribes, but she thought it disgraceful.

"No way, boss." Another pause, another candy. "I'm a judge, all right, but I just figure you've got the wise-and-serious Philodox angle pretty well covered. I've picked up a few grifter tricks here and there, so this seems like the right play. You know, for the pack."

Storm-Eye didn't say anything for a full minute, just kept her gaze fixed on Carlita. Then she did a very unwolflike thing: she smiled. "You are wiser than you think, Big Sis."

"Yeah, yeah, save it for the awards speech."

Storm-Eye decided not to inquire about just what *that* was for now. "But I have never heard of a Gift, even among Ragabash, that could affect Julia like that."

Children of Gaia

"Hey, Julia's not the only one who can talk to a spirit every once in a while. One of Uktena's fish Gafflings helped me out. For a second, it was able to make Julia see what she wanted to see."

"I don't understand. She wanted to win and go home."

Big Sis grinned. "The rest of us weren't raised by wolves. Wake up and smell the ambivalence." She winked and walked away.

Storm-Eye melted back into wolf form, but the transformation didn't resolve her own ambivalence. Since Big Sis had cheated on her behalf, the only honorable thing to do was go and tell Julia that, in fact, she was the victor.

Yet the trick had preserved the pack to fulfill Antonine's prophecies, to heal Cries Havoc and destroy the enemy in Europe. Wasn't that more important?

Storm-Eye decided it was, but she wasn't happy about it. She prowled about in a foul mood deploring the shabby compromises implicit in existence outside her own tribe until North Wind's Son came running up to the cabins.

"Where is everyone?" he asked. "There's something you all should see."

Chapter Three

Hands resting on the guardrail with its splinters and peeling paint, Cries Havoc stood at the center of the bridge and peered north, which was to say, upstream. At the point where the watercourse and ravine snaked west, there gleamed a pearly haze. At first glance, a viewer might mistake it for a mass of luminous mist, but soon he would discern that it was somehow even vaguer and less substantial, as if the air itself was putting forth a feeble phosphorescence.

The Child of Gaia had wondered if, when he beheld it, his emotions would return in a great surge, even if it was only for a moment. They didn't. He still felt numb and hollow.

"Cries Havoc and I had turned in," said North Wind's Son, "but I couldn't sleep, so I got up again and drifted back here. That was when I saw it." He pointed with his spear.

"It's beautiful," said Big Sis. A stray lock of black hair had escaped from under her cap. "But what is it? Witch? Lorekeeper?"

"I don't know," said Julia, sounding too preoccupied to resent being called *witch*. She repeatedly tapped the screen of her handheld computer with a metal stylus.

"Me either," said Cries Havoc. "Maybe it isn't anything, just an optical illusion."

Don't be stupid, said Storm-Eye in the language of growl, yelp and posture. In wolf form, she had a red blaze, gray in the darkness, on her chest. *It is a sign*.

"I agree," said Julia, closing the plastic tablet that was her machine. The latch clicked. "But a sign of what?"

"The Record Keeper sent it," said North Wind's Son.

"You may be right," the English werewolf replied, "but still, what does it signify? Is it supposed to tell us how to fix Cries Havoc? It's just a white glow, for mercy's sake."

In recent days, Cries Havoc's thoughts had moved slowly, reluctantly, like a sullen mule that saw no reason to drag the cart of reason another step. Now his mind surprised him by grinding forth at least the semblance of an idea.

"Maybe we aren't seeing everything we're supposed to see. Maybe we need to get closer to it."

"That's possible," said Julia. "Let's try." Her body flowing, her computer shrinking to nothing, her clothing seemingly transforming to mottled brown and black fur, she dropped to all fours. The spirits who bonded her clothing and fetish to her, regardless of shape, saved her a fortune in designer suits alone.

Cries Havoc, Big Sis and North Wind's Son followed her lead and transformed as well. In a moment, no human figures remained on the bridge, only a quintet of wolves, one still wearing the curved horns that marked him as metis, inbred, in every guise.

For the ram-horned storyteller, the last traces of color bled out of the benighted world, and a symphony of new sensory impressions arose to take their place. He caught countless scents, including the robust, healthy smells of his companions, individual and distinct as their human faces. He could hear the slap and gurgle of the current far below him and the bark of a fox far to the west.

Cries Havoc had always taken a private pleasure in the moment when his perceptions shifted along with his external form. He noticed he no longer felt that, either.

Storm-Eye loped off the west end of the bridge, then northward toward the glow. Cries Havoc and the rest of the pack followed.

Up ahead was a wooden stairway descending to the creek bed. Storm-Eye disdained it in favor of a series of rock outcroppings projecting from the steeply sloping wall of the ravine. A human could have negotiated them, but slowly and cautiously. Their claws clicking on the stone, the werewolves bounded from one almost-level spot to the next nearly as quickly as they could run across open ground. In seconds, they were racing along on the talus beside the stream.

Cries Havoc noticed a curious thing. As the pack approached, the luminous haze became dimmer, less real, until a few strides before they could reach it, it disappeared altogether.

He wished he felt disappointed, but he didn't. Although perhaps the core of him grew a shade more numb and dead than before.

I don't understand, said North Wind's Son. As a wolf, he was larger than most, his fur an almost uniform gray. *Where did it go?*

It was never here, said Cries Havoc. *It was just a trick of the moonlight, maybe shining through a mist of spray from the creek.*

Shameful, said Storm-Eye. *You are all blind.* With a jerk of her head, she bade them look around the

Children of Gaia

Chapter Four

The Bane stared down in consternation. The wolves were running away!

The Garou hadn't sensed the spirit of corruption lurking behind an oak at the top of the ravine. It was careful, it was high above and downwind of them, and the excited pack was preoccupied with the strange, milky glow.

In fact, as far as the Bane could tell, during all their time at the resort, the werewolves had never once suspected its presence as it spied and nibbled on them from the shelter of its puppet. It had hidden itself so cunningly that even the Glass Walker Theurge, whose birthright it was to treat with the unseen, had remained oblivious.

Secure in its anonymity, the Bane had felt rather smug, but the events of the last few minutes had stripped away its complacency. None of this was supposed to happen. The members of the Silver River Pack were meant to stay put, to bicker and despair until such time as their foe consented to take their pain away.

One thing was sure, the Bane wasn't particularly eager to follow them into the hills. True, it had crippled their Galliard, but the rest of them, fighting together, had bested it, indeed, had come nearer than they knew to killing it outright. The Wyrm spirit liked sniping away at them from cover much, much more than it liked the prospect of another open confrontation.

Yet it knew it had to follow. That was why Great and Terrible Jo'cllath'mattric had bade it follow them to America, to watch them and hinder them as required. The Bane also realized it had no chance of keeping up with a werewolf pack in the wild while weighted down with its current shell. It would have to discard Howard Pierce, vacationing produce manager for a chain grocery and lover of college basketball, and walk naked in the world of coarse matter once more.

But before the spirit of corruption vacated the premises, it drank down what was left of Howard's mind. He was thin gruel, not the sort of stuff the Bane needed to sustain itself. But by consuming the human, it both covered its tracks and took out its irritation on a victim conveniently at hand.

When the Bane finished its repast, it terminated the possession. It crawled out of Howard's flesh and brain. And, crouched in the Penumbra, the mirror world of spirit where it had ever been, it pulled a thick, black taproot out of the human's mind. Deprived of his operator, Howard swayed and fell backward on his butt. He screwed up his face and began to bawl.

Happily, Jane Pierce would never have to see her husband in this deplorable condition. Just yesterday, the Bane had strangled her, sliced her up and put the pieces in the refrigerator in their cabin, just for something to do.

As the spirit rose, it noticed that in the final moments of the possession, a bit of his power must have leaked out through Howard's hand resting on the trunk of the oak, for the bark was already subtly discolored. In time, it would likely rot, fall off, and leave an ugly, oozing sore in the sapwood. Because every living thing had a need to remember, even the cells of an oak.

The Bane spread its wings and took flight, pursuing the Garou down the ravine. Howard's sobs followed it into the night.

Chapter Five

Cries Havoc climbed up the slope to the ledge from which North Wind's Son had said he was going to spy out the lay of the land. This far from any sign of human civilization, the Child of Gaia wore his Crinos form, striding on two legs but half again as tall as a man, with the dark fur, fangs and claws of a beast, and crowned, of course, with the curling ram's horns of his tainted birth.

His senses were animal-keen as well, and he caught North Wind's Son's scent before he was within sight of him. It was different than it had ever been before, tinged with a sharp, almost metallic unpleasantness that might have been illness or fear.

Despite his withered emotions, Cries Havoc felt a pang of concern. He took the last few paces at a run.

When the Galliard broke though the last maples, North Wind's Son was crouched in human form just where he'd said he'd be, contemplating a vista of sunlit wooded mountains and valleys. In certain shaded spots, patches of snow still speckled the ground, mementos of the hard winter just concluded.

Everything looked all right until, the icicle fetish sliding across his raven tattoo, North Wind's Son turned his head. The young Amerind's dark eyes were glazed and perplexed, and after a moment Cries Havoc was shocked to discern that his friend didn't seem to recognize him.

The Silver River Pack had followed the ever-receding glow all through the first night, only to lose it in the light of dawn. Thinking, hoping they had gone as far as required, they searched the area where the shining had last appeared, and found nothing.

At that point, Cries Havoc had been all but certain they were the victims of a bizarre and inexplicable prank perpetrated by Antonine, the Record Keeper or perhaps Gaia Herself, but it had also occurred to him that maybe, just maybe the glow would return with the night. He'd suggested the pack stay and see, his companions had agreed, and sure enough, the pearly sheen had revealed itself just as the first stars appeared in the darkening sky.

In the days that followed, the werewolves chased the glow deeper and deeper into the Appalachians, traveling in lupus form by night, sleeping and hunting rabbits, opossum and deer by day. While loping along, first down the creek bed and later, when the light abandoned that convenient avenue, across the ridges and dales, the Garou occasionally sighted a lone shack on a distant slope, or a tiny settlement nestled in a hollow, but for the most part, the land showed little sign of the presence of humankind.

For Cries Havoc, the trek was a dim but persistent aggravation.

The vegetation was only just beginning to sprout tender green shoots and buds, yet prior to his crippling, he would, as a Child of Gaia, in tune with the earth, have sensed the roaring vitality about to quicken every twig and branch. Actually, he still could smell and feel it, but where the perception would once have half-intoxicated him, now it meant nothing at all.

But that was his problem. He'd thought that at least North Wind's Son and Storm-Eye would enjoy escaping the cities and highways, and for a while, that seemed to be the case. Gradually, though, all four of his packmates fell prey to a certain irritability and distractedness. Cries Havoc had assumed it was because they were impatient for the journey to end or were finally coming to believe that it was pointless.

Now, however, he wondered if there was more to it and thought himself a fool for not considering the possibility before this.

"North Wind's Son," the storyteller said, "what's the matter? Don't you know me?"

The Wendigo shook his head. "I…should…"

"I'm Cries Havoc," the storyteller said, "your packmate. We're all traveling though the mountains to find a cure for me."

North Wind's Son gave a start, and the dullness left his eyes. "Yeah! Yeah, of course! I'm sorry."

"You don't have to be sorry, but what just happened? Were you napping? I've heard that sometimes, when people seem to wake, their brain doesn't wake all at once, and then they're confused for a minute or two."

Actually, he had heard that about humans. He had never known a werewolf to suffer the problem.

"No," said the warrior, "I wasn't asleep. Something just came over me, and I'm not sure how to describe it. I think I knew most everything I've always known, all the basic facts, but suddenly, they didn't fit together. Did you ever look at something, a drawing, maybe, and for an instant, even though you really do see it, you can't tell what it is? Then you notice a detail that makes it make sense."

Cries Havoc nodded. "The detail that gives you context, or the right perspective. Yes, I know what you mean."

"Well, it was like that. When I turned around and saw you, I recognized you, but I didn't. I couldn't come up with your name. Then, when I heard it, everything was clear again. I don't know, maybe I'm exhausted from all this running up and down the hills." He smiled. "That's a hell of a thing for a big, tough Wendigo Ahroun to have to admit, isn't it, when the 'city wolves' are still going strong?"

"I'm not sure that's really the problem," Cries Havoc said. "What if—?

Big Sis tramped out of the maples, her long, baggy coat flapping about the tops of her tattered sneakers. "Julia wants us," she said. "I don't know what the deal is, but judging from the look on her face, it probably sucks."

North Wind's Son looked at Cries Havoc. "You were about to say something."

"It can wait a minute," the Child of Gaia replied. "I might as well say it to everyone at once."

"Suit yourself," said North Wind's Son, rising. He and Cries Havoc followed the girl back down the mountainside toward the hidden glade where the pack was lying up till nightfall.

Chapter Six

Julia knew she was a walking disaster. Even though she had done her traveling in wolf form, her designer suit was rumpled and grass stained, her styled hair ratty and snarled and her body so sweaty and undeodorized that even a human could have smelled it.

Fifteen minutes ago, she'd been regretting it. Then she decided to start her computer, her fetish, and what she thereby discovered wiped vanity from her mind.

"My computer has a GPS. Do you all know what that is?" she asked.

No, said Storm-Eye, sitting on the ground in lupus shape.

"I believe it tells you your longitude and latitude," said Cries Havoc, squatting in Crinos form, "your precise geographical position." To Julia, his huge, bristling, devil-eared guise was of course unremarkable, one aspect of a friend. But she could never quite forget that viewed from a human perspective, he would seem Grendel born again.

What is the point of such a thing? Storm-Eye asked. *We know where we are. Or are you lost, city wolf?*

"Of course not," said Julia. Because her machine was equipped with a GPS. "Please, just listen. Once my computer figures out our location, it can pull up a map of our environs." She gave her companions a speculative glance.

"We're with you so far," said Big Sis. Her ratty old coat covering her like a blanket, the Bone Gnawer lay on her side with one arm crooked to prop her head.

"Good," said Julia. "Now, I've plotted our progress for the last couple nights." She showed them the little color screen. "You can see the ghost light has been leading us in about as straight a line as the terrain will allow."

Yes, said Storm-Eye without bothering to look at the screen. Apparently she just knew. Maybe, thought Julia, they all did, except for her.

"All right," the Glass Walker continued, "now, pretty much any high-end portable computer—even some mobile phones—could do this. But this isn't a normal computer, it's also a fetish, and sometimes, when conditions are optimal, the spirits within it can locate fields of Wyrm energy, gatherings of Banes and such, in its immediate vicinity. Conditions were good this afternoon. Look at this."

She pressed a key, and a black blot appeared directly in front of the arrow of dots.

Everyone seemed taken aback, even Storm-Eye. "Damn," said North Wind's Son, "is that what I think it is?"

"I'm afraid so," Julia said. She looked at Storm-Eye. "I know we haven't smelled or laid eyes on them yet—"

You are our Theurge, said the alpha, *and a good one, as I have seen. If you say a Wyrmhole is there, a Wyrmhole is there.*

"I remember one idea we had," Big Sis said wryly, "was that maybe the glow just wanted to lead us into trouble."

"It's even worse than you think," Cries Havoc said. Usually, since his crippling, his speech had a flatness to it. It still did, but with a reluctance, a shame, perhaps, underneath.

"What do you mean?" Julia asked.

"Do you know how you've all seemed distracted from time to time," the storyteller asked, "or irritable, like you had a burr stuck under your tail?"

"Hey," said Big Sis, sitting up, "we've got stuff on our minds. Serbia. Our home septs. So what if we space out once in a while?"

"A few minutes ago," said Cries Havoc, "North Wind's Son was more than 'spaced out.' He was disoriented. He didn't know my name. Has anyone else had an episode of outright confusion?"

Julia hesitated. Up to now, she'd kept her *episode* to herself because she hadn't thought it was important and because it wasn't the kind of thing that any werewolf would care to admit. But perhaps she needed to acknowledge it.

"Last night," she said, "for a second or two, I didn't know why we were traveling. But it was only for a moment, and I was tired."

"Something kind of like that happened to me," said Big Sis, frowning:

I haven't gone out of my head, Storm-Eye said, *but I have forgotten little things, and I have not understood why tiny vexations make me so angry. Cries Havoc, if we are all afflicted, what does it mean?*

"Isn't it obvious?" said the storyteller, his eyes lowered. "What happened to me is happening to you, only a little bit at a time. As my sickness has progressed, it's started to attack my packmates. Maybe it's a sort of Wyrm virus, and I've infected you. Maybe it's just a...wrongness leaking out of the holes in my

Children of Gaia

spirit and picking holes in you. I hope that's it, because then you can stop the damage just by getting away from me."

For a second, the others were silent. Julia wondered if any of them was composing angry recriminations in his head or would switch to Crinos shape, the form of rage, and attack.

Then Storm-Eye said, quite matter-of-factly, *If we all have caught your sickness, that gives us all the more reason to find the cure.*

"Agreed," Julia said.

"But there's no way to find it," Cries Havoc said.

Don't start whining again, snarled Storm-Eye. *We've been through this already. We follow the light.*

"But now we *know* it's leading us into what amounts to an ambush," said Cries Havoc.

"Maybe it's another test," said North Wind's Son.

"The test theory sucks," said Big Sis. "But to hell with it, I'm not afraid to go onto Wyrm turf. We did it before, and we killed a shitload of Banes."

As we will do again, said Storm-Eye. *When Cries Havoc regains his voice, he will make a tale of it.*

The Child of Gaia looked at his packmates. "This is wrong. It's stupid. But...thank you."

It might turn out to be stupid, Julia thought. If they all really were ill with Cries Havoc's sickness, if it made them dazed or even just a little slow in the midst of battle, the plan could turn out to be very stupid indeed.

Chapter Seven

The most unsettling thing, Cries Havoc thought, was that it all smelled and looked fine, just a moonlit stand of pines on a rolling piece of land, the cool night air pungent with their sharp perfume, the ground carpeted with their dry discarded needles. He hadn't seen many Wyrmholes up close—at least not that he remembered—but they were usually clearly unfriendly, blighted places. Still, any werewolf, born to defend Gaia, would feel the aura of corruption here. It made the bones ache, the skin crawl beneath the fur, and the white haze shone in the midst of it like mockery incarnate.

The Silver River Pack members had all skulked onto the tainted ground in wolfman form. They were darting silently from one patch of cover to the next, moving and hiding with a facility astonishing in creatures so huge. Yet even so, they had no expectation whatsoever that they would succeed in crossing the Wyrm's domain unopposed.

"There are just too many Banes to count about," said Julia, who'd been peeking into the spirit world. "And they're strong here. I recommend we stay on this side of the Gauntlet rather than fight them in the Penumbra, where they're at home. They'll all be able to take on a physical shape here, most likely, but I think we'll have better luck taking on their physical shells instead of the spirits themselves."

"That won't kill them, though?" John North Wind's Son was readying his spear, the tension of the moment starting to feed his warrior's rage.

"No, just send them into a deep slumber. They'll probably come back, but not for a good while."

"Lions and tigers and bears, oh my," Big Sis breathed. In Crinos shape, she was long limbed, skinny by Garou standards, but she moved with a confidence that might make even the fiercest Ahroun warrior think twice about challenging her. She carried an ivory dagger, carved from the fang of some huge Wyrm abomination, in her furry hand.

Storm-Eye had taken the lead. She turned, exposing the blaze on her chest and the cat skull on a leather string swinging on top of it, and gestured fiercely for silence. Big Sis lowered her eyes in apology and acquiescence.

These people are all going to die for no reason at all, Cries Havoc thought.

To his surprise, a vestige of the old, lost Cries Havoc, that vital, passionate Garou who had had his spirit gutted in Serbia, responded to the despairing thought. *Yes, your friends will die if you don't watch their backs, or if you fall apart and they have to try to take care of you. So do what they told you: stop whining and get your head in the game!*

Suddenly, instantly, the ground split beneath Storm-Eye's feet. Along with a shower of pine needles, she fell into the hole, and rows of sharp, pointed rocks arranged in rows like teeth began to close on her.

North Wind's Son lunged forward and jammed his spear between the earthen jaws. Had it been an ordinary weapon, the fetish surely would have snapped under the strain, but it didn't. It held.

Fangs bared, Storm-Eye tried to climb out of the Bane's maw, but she didn't make it. It looked as if her feet were stuck to the bottom of the pit. Sleek and somehow elegant even in the form of rage, Julia stooped and grabbed the Red Talon by the forearm to pull her out.

It was then that four more Banes, these more or less humanoid, stepped from the spirit world into the physical one. They silently materialized behind North Wind's Son and Julia, obviously intending to jump the Garou while they were busy with the entity possessing or nestled in the soil.

Cries Havoc and Big Sis roared and sprang at the creatures, who spun around to face them. The Galliard wound up confronting two of the Banes. One looked and smelled like a bloated corpse, with its guts leaking from a rip in its belly. The other sported scales and a swelling hood that would have done a cobra proud.

Seemingly without any prompting, lengths of glistening bowel shot out of the first one's wound. They weren't one continuous conduit as true intestines would be. They were more like clumps of eels, each plump, slimy strand terminating in a round, fanged maw resembling a lamprey's.

Stretching insanely, the guts snatched hold of Cries Havoc by biting, coiling around his limbs or both. The sucking mouths incised hot circles of pain as the teeth chewed at him, striving to embed themselves more deeply.

The cobra man rushed in to finish off the Child of Gaia. His jaw shifted back and forth, unhinging itself, and then dropped at least twelve inches. The Bane's material form bore the long, curved fangs Cries Havoc would have expected, but it also began to drool a squirming, continuous stream of pale grubs and insects with the thick stink of puke.

The Bane grabbed hold of Cries Havoc's right forearm. Roaring, the Garou tore the limb free of the snake man's hands and the loops of guts as well. At once, he slashed at the serpent creature, but he was too slow. The malignant spirit jumped back, and the werewolf's claws, which should have torn the horror's head from its shoulders, only sheared away a part of its face. The mad, dark eyes remained intact, and the damage almost certainly was insufficient to stop a Bane.

Cries Havoc ripped at the coils of gut. He shredded one of them, but the rest released him and, writhing this way and that, jerked back beyond his reach. The two Banes started to circle, searching for the moment when one would be in position to attack from behind.

The Galliard reached inside himself for that berserk fury that was the birthright of every Garou and as often as not his salvation in battle. He couldn't find it. It had rotted away with the rest of his emotions.

He didn't have a chance, then. The Bane back in Serbia had for all extents and purposes killed him, and he might as well let these two finish the job.

No! No, damn it, he wouldn't roll over and die. Maybe if he had come to the killing ground alone, but he hadn't. And he *did* have a chance. Even without the Wyld's gift of godlike fury, he still possessed all the combat skills his teachers had hammered into him, honed by years of battles against the Wyrm.

Feigning confusion, he gave the reptilian Bane his back, because he reckoned that one would be easier to kill quickly, after which he could spin back around to deal with the other. In turning, he glimpsed Big Sis beckoning with her gory dagger, taunting her opponents. She looked like she was having fun. Some of the cobra man's disgorged vermin crawled over his feet, biting and stinging, but it was easy to ignore them. The pain was insignificant compared to the fierce throbbing of the ragged circular wounds higher up.

The cobra man was probably trying to be stealthy, but a werewolf's ear could easily catch a footfall whispering in the fallen pine needles. Cries Havoc spun and struck, and the Bane was right where he had estimated it would be. His talons tore through muscle, shattered ribs and mangled a lung.

Even that might not be enough. His claws still buried in the snake man's chest cavity, Cries Havoc had no difficulty yanking his enemy closer. Showering the spirit's vile living vomit about, he lifted the Bane over his head and bit out several vertebrae of its spine. The snake creature's meat, blood and bone tasted cold and putrid, but under the circumstances, he didn't mind. At least he could spit out the nasty stuff.

He whirled and thrust the cobra man's corpse forward like a shield. The mangled body blocked out the lengths of gut that were just about to sink their rings of gnashing fangs into him.

Cries Havoc charged, squashing the mock intestines against the dead-looking Bane, driving the spirit backward. After two staggering steps, the Bane fell down. Still clinging to his shredded, bloody, makeshift armor, the Child dived on top of his supine foe and landed precisely as he'd intended. The corpse was still hindering the writhing guts, but it left the

Children of Gaia

spirit's bruised-looking, deliquescing head exposed. Cries Havoc pulped it with a single sweep of his arm.

After that, without the rage to pull him up and on to another enemy, the werewolf tried to stay still for just a moment and take a breath. At once he caught a whiff of a different foulness, one he hadn't smelled before, and wrenched himself around. A leprous Bane was lunging at him with what seemed to be a silently vibrating bone chainsaw in its upraised hands. Cries Havoc barely managed to dodge the spirit's first swing, then ripped it apart before it could take another.

An important lesson, that: keep moving. He scrambled up and surveyed the battlefield.

The woods now swarmed with Banes, no two alike but all horrible, like escapees from a Bosch painting of hell. Fortunately, they hadn't yet succeeded in taking down any of the Garou. Storm-Eye's feet and legs were bloody, but at least she'd made it out of the dirt creature's jaws, and she was tearing into its allies with a snarling, slavering, seemingly reckless savagery. Fighting almost as aggressively, North Wind's Son speared one foe after another. Big Sis continued to mock the Banes while displaying a rare knack for dirty tricks and low blows. Julia flickered in and out of sight, visible one instant, gone the next, dancing back and forth between the Umbra and the world of matter with an ease remarkable even in a Theurge. When she reappeared, it was generally to strike down an enemy from behind. Some of the unclean spirits tried to chase her, to step sideways through the Gauntlet whenever she did, but even they couldn't keep up with her.

A pine suddenly blurred and became a hundred-armed ogre of gnarled and rotting wood. The Bane bent over to club the oblivious Big Sis, and Cries Havoc lunged to intercept it. He scrambled and dodged through the lashing branches until he reached the trunk, then clawed away chunks until the spirit's woody home abruptly exploded into scraps and splinters. The battle paused for a second as everyone, Garou and Wyrm minion alike, cringed and shielded his face from the flying debris.

Cries Havoc dashed closer to his packmates so that he could protect their flanks, and they his. After that, he lost all track of time as the Banes came and came and came until it seemed they always had and always would. He was almost startled when, as suddenly as they had begun their assault, they stopped.

It didn't mean the Garou had cleansed the wood. Far from it. Cries Havoc could smell and hear plenty more Banes slinking through the trees. But the pack had killed the first wave and, in so doing, won the opportunity to run on a little farther.

Cries Havoc looked for the white glow, and for an instant something twisted in the cold, dead core of him. The shining was gone. He had been right all along. It had led the pack to the slaughter and, its task accomplished, disappeared.

Then he realized that during the fighting, he had gotten himself turned around. The ground was irregular—it lay on a mountainside—and in its totality was sloped. The werewolves had been traveling down the grade, and he was looking up. He wheeled and the silver light gleamed at him from a spot perhaps fifty yards ahead.

Children of Gaia

"Let's go," he said, and the pack dashed on.

He soon decided that following the light across that poisoned earth was the hardest thing he'd ever done. Occasionally the Garou managed to lope a few strides without having to fight for them, but soon enough, more Banes charged out of the dark to waylay them. Sometimes the spirits were neither too strong nor too many, and the werewolves were able to slaughter them more or less on the fly. But often enough the pack found itself bogged down, outnumbered, surrounded, and had to battle frantically to rip its way out of the trap.

By now, they all bore bloody wounds, yet they were all still able to run and fight. To come so far without a loss was a triumph, and the others rejoiced in it. Between melees, Cries Havoc could see their pride in their bearing and the fierce light in their eyes. He himself felt nothing but the blunt determination to see them safely off the killing ground.

They tore their way through two more skirmishes, and then, as the slope steepened, an unexpected vista stretched out before them, a long aisle running down through the pines with the ghostly sheen floating, waiting, at the end. The ground was still sickeningly tainted, but Cries Havoc couldn't smell or otherwise detect any Banes lurking down there. Maybe the Wyrm minions hadn't believed that the werewolves could possibly get this far. Maybe the abominations that normally lurked hereabouts had all moved farther up the slope to make sure they would get a chance at the kill.

They were coming back now. Cries Havoc could hear a horde of them rushing down the mountain.

But he thought his long-legged packmates could keep ahead of the deformed creatures, and if so, they might all live to see the dawn.

He bayed, urging his comrades on, and they ran with all their flagging strength. The incline challenged their balance even as it quickened their stride. Cries Havoc's horns caught on a low-hanging branch and snapped it off. The wind brought him the scent of fresh water somewhere up ahead. A stream, perhaps.

The Child of Gaia was bounding along between Big Sis and Julia. When he glanced at one or the other of them, he saw that, despite their fatigue, each had found new vitality in the prospect of escape. The Bone Gnawer's mouth stretched in a wicked grin. Had she been in Homid form and so possessed of clothing, Cries Havoc could have imagined her stopping long enough to moon the Banes. As always, the Glass Walker was more reserved, but her smile bespoke satisfaction and perhaps a touch of relief.

Evidently craving a glimpse of the Banes lumbering futilely along behind, Big Sis grabbed hold of a sapling and used it to spin herself around to face uphill. "Shit!" she cried. She howled, a discordant screech that brought her packmates staggering to a halt.

Cries Havoc turned to see what had distressed her. He went rigid with dismay. Storm-Eye was standing motionless some distance back up the slope. Evidently, in their headlong flight, none of the Garou had noticed her stopping. But the onrushing Banes saw her. Indeed, they had nearly reached her.

The Child of Gaia could hardly believe it. Of all of them, Storm-Eye with her iron will and straightforward manner of thought seemed the least vulnerable to mental dysfunction. She had even said she hadn't experienced the same sort of lapses as the rest. Yet there she stood entranced.

The worst part was how far behind her packmates had left her. Garou might be stronger and faster than humans, but they couldn't possibly dash all the way back uphill in time to keep the Banes from slaughtering her.

"You can't have her," Julia growled. Cries Havoc turned and saw the English werewolf extract her small computer from a pouch that seemed to have adapted to her Crinos shape. She rapidly tapped the screen with the points of her claws.

Half a dozen gleaming crystal snowflakes, each a foot across, materialized in the air above and around Storm-Eye. It took Cries Havoc a moment to realize that the perfect, intricate, seemingly inorganic things were Weaver spirits, different in form but similar in kind to the clockwork spiders the pack had encountered before. Julia had compelled them to manifest themselves and do her bidding.

As the Banes drew near, the snowflakes silently discharged thin shafts of bluish light. Whenever one of the beams touched a minion of the Wyrm, the abomination froze in place, bound in that stasis that some believed was the Weaver's ultimate goal for all the world.

Julia closed her computer and slipped it back into its pouch. The werewolves charged back up the slope.

They were running flat out, but after a moment, Cries Havoc felt as if they were floundering through quicksand, because he could see that Storm-Eye was still going to die. The Weaver spirits were mounting a formidable defense, but they could only paralyze one foe at a time, and they shattered into sparkling motes when something hit them hard enough. They weren't quite able to hold back all the Banes. A scabrous cyclops darted inside their circle and raised her claws to tear Storm-Eye apart. The Garou were still too far away to close with the abomination in time to prevent it.

North Wind's Son halted, pulled back his spear, and threw it, so quickly it seemed impossible that he could have aimed. Yet the lance plunged into the cyclops's burly neck and out the other side. The Bane collapsed.

The werewolves raced on, and some of the Wyrm spirits ran to meet them. Cries Havoc knew that he and his packmates would have to break through them quickly if they were to form around Storm-Eye and keep her safe.

The two groups slammed together. The Child of Gaia slashed at the mass of Banes in front of him, scarcely even perceiving them as individuals. They were just a wall he had to demolish. He carved his way into it one stride and one maiming at a time.

The Banes shrieked and gibbered, raising a hideous cacophony. Cries Havoc didn't know how he made out Julia's cry amid the din, but he did. She was down on all fours with two dwarfish horrors clambering over her and stabbing with rusty little knives. He ripped them off her, lifted to her feet, and turned back around just in time to keep a shapeless ragged sheet of a thing from wrapping a slimy flap of itself around his head.

He killed that Bane and another and then he was through. He glanced about. His friends had made it through as well. He, North Wind's Son, and Julia took up positions among the three surviving crystal stars. Big Sis scrambled inside the perimeter to Storm-Eye. She started yelling in the lupus's face and shaking her.

After that, the werewolves on the front line made their most difficult stand yet. Cries Havoc's wounds throbbed, and fatigue weighted his limbs. During one of those rare moments when the onslaught slackened, he thought how odd it was to fight side by side with Weaver spirits, by nature inimical to Garou and any other children of the Wyld. But he was grateful for their presence. Constrained by Julia's will, the snowflakes—they were down to two now—showed no sign of wanting to shine one of their azure beams at their allies.

As the seconds passed, the Galliard took a fresh wound, then another. He gasped for breath, and it occurred to him that if he just stopped fighting, the Banes would swarm over him, and the pain and grinding weariness would end an instant later. As before, he shoved the shameful thought away.

The last surviving snowflake shattered. Then, behind him, he heard a change in Big Sis's ranted pleas and demands. Now they were all growls and yips, fragmentary, and utterly bestial. A human wouldn't perceive them as language at all. Cries Havoc risked a glance around and saw that, as he'd assumed, the Bone Gnawer had shifted from Crinos to pure wolf shape.

He didn't know why that should make a difference, but it did. Giving a start, Storm-Eye woke.

She threw back her head and howled, a furious cry that might have been directed as much at her own humiliating stupor as the Banes arrayed before her. Then she lunged into the fight. Big Sis changed back to Crinos form and did the same.

In a minute, it became apparent to Cries Havoc that the Bone Gnawer and Red Talon, who were neither as bloodied nor fatigued as their three packmates, were turning the tide of battle. The Banes knew it, too. After a few more frenzied exchanges, the surviving Wyrm-spawn turned and ran, probably to collect reinforcements for yet another attack.

"I have a proposal." Julia was wheezing. Blood matted her soft, lustrous fur, and quite a bit of it was her own. "Let's not kill any more Banes tonight. Let's save some for next time."

Clutching at her forearm, trying to stanch the flow from a particularly ugly wound, Big Sis grinned. "Wuss! But come to think of it, maybe we could use a little break."

Storm-Eye pointed. "The white light. Let us follow while we can."

"Just let me get my spear," said North Wind's Son. He pulled it from the cyclops's corpse, and then the pack ran on.

The grade leveled out once more. The werewolves broke through a final stand of trees, and then Cries Havoc faltered.

It wasn't a stream he'd smelled. It was a lake. The luminous haze floated above the center of the black water, then disappeared, but not in the same way as before. It seemed to dive beneath the surface, glowing there for an instant before plunging even deeper.

Children of Gaia

"Shit," said Big Sis, and Cries Havoc reckoned he knew why. When it came to running, jumping, climbing, lifting or any form of ritual combat, the puniest runt of a werewolf could put any Olympic gold medallist to shame. But by and large, the Garou didn't do a lot of swimming. It was entirely possible that some of his friends had never learned to do it at all.

Chapter Eight

"This is a good sign," said Storm-Eye, not betraying a hint of uncertainty as she stared out over the lake.

"Of course," said Julia ironically. "I'm sure we all appreciate what a promising development it truly is."

"It *is*," the alpha snarled. "Do you not remember that Uktena of the Waters is our totem?"

"Right," said Big Sis, "and even if he wasn't, we've got to do something fast." She waved her hand at the whispering, rustling sounds of the malevolent spirits farther up the mountain. "Unless the witch can call out for a whole bunch more glass stars to slow the Banes down."

Julia shook her head. Cries Havoc noticed for the first time that one of the enemy had torn her right ear partway off. "No," the Glass Walker said, "I'm as spent as the rest of you."

"Then I don't think we've got a lot of choice," said North Wind's Son. "Well, we *could* work our way around the edge of the lake and try to get past the Banes that way. But I think they'd catch us, and besides, we agreed we'd follow the glow wherever it led."

"All right," said Cries Havoc. He still mistrusted the luminous haze, but perhaps the pack would wind up going all the way across the lake and so evade the rest of the Banes. In any case, they couldn't stay where they were. "But we need to figure out exactly how we're going to do this. Can all of you swim?"

For a moment, no one responded. Then Storm-Eye grunted. Cries Havoc could see how it galled her to admit any sort of incapacity.

"Before New York, I had only swum in wolf form," the one-eyed Garou growled, "and I never put my head below the water. Still, I survived when the Wyrm-wolf threw me off the boat. All you do is hold your breath, paddle with your hands and kick, is that not so?"

"Basically," said Cries Havoc, "but wave if you have trouble. We're using the buddy system. You stick with Big Sis and me. North Wind's Son, Julia, you two look out for one another. We can stay on the surface until we reach the middle."

Big Sis said, "Sounds good." The others nodded.

"Then let's go," the Galliard said. The werewolves walked off a rocky overhang and jumped into the water.

Chilled by the winter just past, the lake was bitterly cold. As he breaststroked away from shore, keeping an eye on Big Sis and especially Storm-Eye all the while, Cries Havoc realized it was also far less tainted than the land beside it. Either the Wyrm hadn't tried so hard to spread fundamental corruption here, or else some power was resisting.

He also noticed something less encouraging. He could smell his blood and that of his companions in the water. Their open wounds were diffusing a vivid scent trail.

As if she could hear his thoughts, Big Sis lifted her head from the water. "Lucky we're not on my turf back in Florida. I don't guess we're going to attract any gators or sharks."

"No," Cries Havoc said. "But I wouldn't rule out Wyrm-spawn bred to live and kill in the water." It withered the grin on her face.

At his back, he heard a fresh contingent of abominations stumbling onto the shore. They set up a clamor when they beheld the werewolves cutting or, in Storm-Eye's case, floundering across the lake. Some threw missiles, but they all splashed down well short of their targets.

North Wind's Son turned and treaded water to gaze at his packmates. Despite the encumbrance of his spear, he had managed to keep up with everyone else. "This looks to be about the center," he said. "Shall we start diving?"

"If we're all ready," said Cries Havoc. He looked at Storm-Eye, whose hands were churning the water considerably faster than was necessary to keep her afloat.

The fur plastered to her face, she bared her fangs at his solicitude. "I'm fine."

"All right," he said. "Everyone, remember to stick with your buddies." He drew a deep breath and ducked under the surface. His packmates did the same.

For a moment, everything was black, and then his eyes began to adjust. The world was still murky, but at least he could make out Big Sis stroking and kicking along at his side. He pulled himself down a bit deeper, and then spotted the glow far below him. He appeared to be the only one who'd noticed it, and he wasn't surprised. The light shone more dimly than before, seemingly more dimly even than the obscuring properties of the water could explain.

He pointed the shining out to his friends, then signaled for them to surface.

"I thought we might as well take a fresh breath before we swim all the way down to it," he said.

Children of Gaia

"This lake is frickin' deep," said Big Sis. "Is it supposed to be this deep?"

"Let's review geology later," Julia said. "Against all probability, we seem to have pursued the light to its final destination. Now I'd like to make contact while I still have a drop or two of blood remaining in my veins."

"Yes," said Storm-Eye. "Come." She dived.

The other werewolves followed. About ten feet down, Cries Havoc's ears began to ache. He popped them, and then checked on Storm-Eye. She was grimacing and her eyes were wild, but she was dragging herself deeper. He waved to attract her attention, then pointed to his ears, held his nose and puffed his cheeks to show how to equalize the pressure. After a repetition, she got the idea.

They swam deeper. The glow started to look mottled, veins of white crisscrossing shadowy spots. Then a long, supple shape knifed out of the darkness.

Something knotted in Cries Havoc's chest. For a second, it almost felt as if, by imagining Banes infesting the lake, he had called them into being.

Like a wolf picking the weakling out of a herd, the spirit hurtled toward Storm-Eye, and she, who was virtually never taken by surprise on dry land, seemed so preoccupied with thrashing her way through the water that she didn't notice.

Cries Havoc wasted an instant pointing at the onrushing Bane before realizing that at that moment, Storm-Eye wasn't looking at him, either. He frantically kicked forward, brushed against her, felt her give a start and start to turn toward him, probably in irritation. A split second later, the Bane was upon them.

It was like a huge, diseased pike with a gaping bear trap of a mouth, human eyes and fringes of string warts flopping from its sides. Cries Havoc dodged its bite; grabbed hold of a writhing, slapping length of it and started to twist its head off.

Then he glimpsed another such creature streaking in on his flank. He turned, knowing the water was slowing him too much, and North Wind's Son rammed his spear through the Wyrm minion's gills.

Cries Havoc finished beheading the pike-thing he had in his hands, then looked around. The skirmish was over, but the Garou's problems were not. At least a dozen Banes were still circling the pack, and a new one glided out of the blackness to join them every ten or fifteen seconds. The Child of Gaia suspected that, employing the same strategy as their counterparts on the mountain, the Banes intended to amass overwhelming numerical superiority and then attack again.

Unless, of course, the werewolves drowned first. A Garou had greater lung capacity than either a human or a wolf, but Cries Havoc had burned air killing the pikes, and his lungs ached for a replenishing breath. He suspected that, with their wounds and their exhaustion, his friends would soon experience the same distress.

The packmates pushed deeper until the Child felt a tingling come over them, not the Wyrm's poison, but something sharp and clean. After a few more strokes, he saw why. The light the pack had chased so long had apparently localized itself in the center of a heap of large stones reposing on the

Children of Gaia

lakebed. The glow was leaking through the cracks among the rocks.

The stone mound was a caern, a Garou place of power, but the sight of it left Cries Havoc as hopeless as before. The aura of the monument had already touched and failed to restore him. Was he supposed to discover and enact some sort of healing rite in front of the pile? How was anyone supposed to accomplish such a thing submerged in a body of water teeming with Banes and fomori?

He looked up and around. The pack seemed to be floating inside an enormous black ball. If not for the glow escaping the caern, the wolves wouldn't be able to see. The next instant, the curved inner surface of the globe imploded as the thousands of Banes that had comprised it raced all at once at their prey.

Cries Havoc realized the significance of the caern, if it even had any, didn't matter. After all the pack's striving, this was the end. No five werewolves could defeat so many Banes, not without air.

Paddling slowly to keep herself in place, Big Sis studied the mound. She looked so intent that Cries Havoc suspected she didn't even realize the pike-things were coming. Maybe, of all the companions, she was the lucky one.

The Bone Gnawer extended her index finger and with the claw traced a twisting line through certain of the narrow fissures separating the stones. As soon as she finished, a section of the mound ceased to exist, the vacancy creating a roughly rectangular space like a doorway. The white light shining through made it impossible to discern what was on the other side, but at that point, Cries Havoc didn't care, and his packmates no doubt felt the same. They hauled themselves through as fast as they could. Going last, the storyteller entered inches ahead of the first flurry of Banes.

Chapter Nine

Cries Havoc could have sworn that, his head turned, he was looking backward continuously, but he missed the moment when the doorway closed on the horde of oncoming aquatic Banes and became just another section of rough, gray stone wall.

He realized he was still holding his breath. He blew it out and filled his chest with a fresh one.

"Not bad for a Philodox, huh?" Big Sis crowed, brandishing her knife. "Never hurts for a 'city wolf' like me to get to know some raccoon spirits. They can show you how to get in almost anywhere."

"Yes," said Storm-Eye, drops of bloody water pattering from her soaked fur onto the hard-packed earthen floor, "well done." Judging by her tone, the anxiety she had tried so hard to mask had dissolved as soon as she exited the lake. "Now be quiet. Look around. We must learn this place."

They could look around now that the white glare had dimmed to a faint, sourceless phosphorescence. Somehow, Cries Havoc's desperate vertical lunge through an open hole had taken him into a dry place that not only possessed air but was considerably bigger on the inside than the outside, like an Umbral subrealm. But they hadn't stepped sideways...had they? A pair of passageways diverged through the mound from the open space that was the werewolves' point of entry. The Child of Gaia could see no mortar between the fitted rocks, yet they obviously kept the lake water out. The Wyrm as well, for he felt not the slightest twinge of corruption. In fact, he smelled Garou...or something similar.

"It seems safe," said North Wind's Son. "Do we explore right away or take a break and try to keep our insides from falling out?"

"Inside the caern, you'll heal quickly," said a pleasant baritone voice. "Especially if you remain in Crinos form."

Startled, Cries Havoc jerked around, which sent sharp pains shooting throughout his torn and overtaxed limbs. In the entrance to the right-hand tunnel stood a figure who wore human shape, yet was the source of the almost-werewolf scent. Like North Wind's Son, the stranger was an Amerind. He was gray, gaunt and wrinkled, but fit looking, without any trace of a stoop. He wore only a deerskin loincloth and pictographs daubed in white and black on his skin. Cries Havoc couldn't imagine how the old man had come so close without any of the pack noticing him, unless he had just materialized out of the Umbra. But wouldn't they have noticed that, too?

"Are you the Record Keeper?" Storm-Eye asked.

The stranger smiled. "No."

"But he did send us to you," said North Wind's Son a shade uncertainly, wiping away the blood seeping down from a gash above his eye.

"Did he?" said the old man. "I have no idea. Perhaps it was he. Or a spirit. Or Gaia Herself. How could one tell for certain?"

"Okay," said Big Sis, in the voice of someone resolved to cut to the heart of things, "whatever. Are you the caern spirit?"

"If you like," said the stranger.

The Bone Gnawer pointed at Cries Havoc. "Our friend is messed up. Not just beat up like the rest of us. Sick on the inside. Can this place help him? Can *you* help him?"

"No."

Julia closed her eyes. "I knew it. But I didn't want it to be true."

"Don't you know the Litany?" the aged Amerind said, his tone gentle. "I may not tend the sickness of anoth—"

"This is the end time," said Storm-Eye, glaring, "and the Garou need Cries Havoc in the fight! A Stargazer seer proclaimed it!"

"You didn't let me finish. I cannot cure him, but by reaching this place, he has won a chance to cure himself." The stranger nodded to the storyteller. "Will you come with me?"

"I guess." Cries Havoc moved to accompany the old man down the passage. His packmates looked on dubiously but didn't object. How could they? Either the prize they sought was here, or it was nowhere.

Cries Havoc and the old man walked a few paces in silence. Eventually, despite his withered emotions, Cries Havoc fell prey to a certain impatience. "What is this place? I know it's a caern, but beyond that, what?"

"I told you, it was a place of healing. But even more than that, it was a haven for meditation. A place where many Theurges and Galliards searched for hidden truths."

They passed the opening of an intersecting tunnel, and another lay ahead. The submerged refuge was even larger than Cries Havoc had realized at first. A kind of labyrinth, in fact.

"When was this?" the werewolf asked.

"Some have said, not long after the second great ice receded."

"Why—"

The old man lifted his hand to cut off Cries Havoc. "We should speak of your sickness. Your time grows short."

Because the wounds in my mind and spirit are on the verge of killing me? the storyteller wondered. *I could believe it.*

"You might even welcome it," the old man said. "No more forcing yourself to take the next painful step when the truth is, you don't even care. It would be so much easier just to stop."

Cries Havoc blinked. "Are you reading my thoughts?"

The stranger shrugged. "I'm doing something that aids in understanding. I'm not going to try to explain it. You haven't time for that, either. Tell me of your illness."

"If you can look inside my head, don't you know already?"

"Whatever I know, I will learn more from hearing it in your own words."

"Okay." Strolling along at the caern keeper's side, the Garou tried to tell of that disastrous moment when his nemesis first pierced him with its fangs, and of all that had befallen him after—the coma, waking, discovering the loss of his Gifts and the blight inside his soul, following first the compass and then the light. It was storytelling of a sort, and his affliction did its best to strangle his efforts. Gradually, though, he stammered the explanation out in a graceless, disjointed, half-coherent mockery of a proper tale.

"I've even lost my emotions," he finished. "I've certainly lost my ability to hope. If not for my packmates, I would never have chased the shining. I didn't believe it could possibly do any good." He scowled. "Come to think of it, it hasn't yet, has it?"

"You still have a trace of your feelings," the Amerind with his grizzled braids replied, "otherwise you would already have dropped dead. It's just that you're deaf to their voices. Still, you're right, you're failing fast. Your grip on your essence is slipping. Be glad your friend North Wind's Son gave you a story to carry you this far."

"I don't know that it did, but I am grateful, I suppose." Cries Havoc stopped, took hold of the stranger's shoulder to halt him as well, and turned him around to face him. The werewolf did it fairly gently, yet even so, in Crinos form, he possessed a strength that no mere human frame, or the semblance of one, could resist.

"Now what do I do?" Cries Havoc said. "*Can* I heal myself? Tell me! You're the one who says my time is almost up, so let's have it."

"You must go back to go forward."

Cries Havoc narrowed his eyes. "Antonine said that, or something like it."

"Then, having heard it twice, you may believe it. You've lost portions of the story of your life, which is to say, your identity, and that's to blame for all your other miseries: the withering of your Gifts, the despair, everything. Recover what the winged Bane took from you and you'll regain all."

"That sounds reasonable, I guess. But how do I do it?"

"Take your hand from my shoulder and I'll show you."

"All right. Sorry." Cries Havoc let the painted man go.

They continued through the passages, the stranger leading the way and stepping more quickly now. "I assume a Galliard of your era knows the various Domains within the spirit world."

"Yeah."

"Including the Chimares."

"The lands of dream in the Near Umbra. Ghost worlds. The landscape and the creatures that live in it change from one visit to the next, sometimes one second to the next. You never know what you're going to find."

"That isn't necessarily true. Supposedly, by performing the proper rite, a Garou can go to one such place and relive moments from his past, either because it's a special Domain or because he's invested himself with a virtue that will make any dream world respond to him in that way. I don't know which. Were we wiser, perhaps we'd understand that *which* isn't a meaningful question."

"You're thinking that if I relive my past, I'll make new memories to take the place of the stolen ones."

"More or less."

"But you said *supposedly*."

"I myself have never journeyed to such a country. I've only heard it can be done. If so, here are the means." The stranger indicated them with a sweep of his arm, and the twist in Cries Havoc's breast tightened another turn. It seemed as if the world itself were laughing at him.

Beyond an arched opening was a chamber that, roundish with a domed ceiling, was almost like an igloo. Chiseled glyphs adorned the stones comprising the walls.

"When the ancient Garou discovered a secret during the course of a visit to the caern," the old man said, "they sometimes inscribed it here for the benefit of all." He pointed. "Those glyphs there are the ones you want."

"Didn't you understand what I told you?" Cries Havoc asked. "I'm not a Galliard anymore! Glyphs don't call out to me. I can't feel the life inside them. I can't tell how two signs hook together to change their meanings and say something completely different. It's all gone!"

"No," said the spirit, "not all. You've lost the instinct. The inspiration. But you still hold the knowledge your elders taught you. That will have to do."

"You don't know that I still remember the lore. Maybe the Bane bit a hole in that, too, or poisoned it somehow. Why don't you just tell me what the inscription says?"

"Because I don't know. Good hunting, son." The old man reached up, squeezed Cries Havoc's forearm, turned and walked away.

For a moment, the werewolf felt inclined to chase after his guide and demand some additional and more satisfactory answers, but he suspected it wouldn't do him any good. Instead he stalked into the igloolike chamber and sat down, legs crossed, in front of the glyphs alleged to hold the key to his redemption. As he lowered himself to the dirt floor, he noticed the bending barely hurt. His wounds were healing as quickly as the old man said they would. Cries Havoc tried to believe that that was something, anyway.

Chapter Ten

Once the worst of the pain ebbed away, Big Sis noticed that she was neither especially thirsty nor hungry. It was nice but weird. It must be part of the mojo of the rock pile, she thought, although she'd never seen a caern like this before. Although, come to think of it, she hadn't seen many, period. They weren't exactly a dime a dozen on Seventh Avenue in Tampa.

Anyway, this particular caern might be all super-powerful and sacred and the answer to everybody's prayers, but a girl could only hunker on a dirt floor in an empty space for so long. The boredom was killing her and she was pretty sure she was ready to kill for a Snickers bar. She needed to do something, and trying to act casual, she stood up.

North Wind's Son rumbled in his throat to attract her attention. When she looked at him, practically healed but still filthy and smelly with his own dried blood, she noticed again how cool that icicle pendant was. If she'd seen a human wearing it, she would have lifted it in a heartbeat.

"What?" she asked.

"What are you doing?" he replied.

"Going to look for a drink. I'm thirsty."

"You are not," Storm-Eye said. With the phosphorescence gleaming on it, her ruined eye looked a little creepy.

"Well, maybe not too much," Big Sis said. "But I figured I'd look around. Why not? You said we should explore."

"That was before our host appeared," the Red Talon said. "We will not prowl through his den without his permission."

"Don't you think we should see what's up with Cries Havoc?"

"It has only been a little while. Sit down. Stop behaving like a curious pup."

Julia looked up from her computer screen to grin at Big Sis. "Storm-Eye 1, Big Sis nil," she said. The Crinos form hid the Glass Walker's snooty English accent not a bit.

"Bite me," Big Sis growled. She made to flop back down again, then sensed someone at her back. She spun around. It was the old man. Speaking of creepy, how the hell did he keep sneaking up on everybody?

"I'm sorry your wait here has worn on you," he said. "I thought it best to talk with Cries Havoc privately. It gave me a better sense of his spirit."

Sitting, the other werewolves were almost as tall as the caern spirit.

"How is the Galliard?" Storm-Eye asked.

"He's seeking his path," the spirit said.

"How?" Julia closed her computer and put it away. Big Sis had noticed the fastidious Glass Walker trying to pick the clotted gore off her claws, but she hadn't gotten all of it.

"He is looking inside and outside himself," the spirit said.

"I may be a Theurge," said Julia, "a trader in mysteries myself, but I've never much cared for the sort of enlightened master who speaks only in vagaries and riddles. How about some concrete information for a change? It's not as if we find you all that enigmatic anyway. For example, I've determined what you are: an ancestor spirit. Correct?"

"If that is what you believe, you should show more respect." The stranger smiled. "But I don't blame you. You've walked through enough fire to frazzle anyone's nerves."

"Actually," said Big Sis, "Julia was already wound pretty tight when we hooked up." The Theurge glared at her. "But we all want to know what's going on. Throw us a bone, give us a tour or *something*."

"Let me tell you of the caern. It will help you understand where your own path leads."

Big Sis grinned at Julia. "See," the Bone Gnawer said, "you've just got to ask politely." On the trip down from Antonine's place in New York, traveling through the human world and actually sleeping indoors and paying for everything, the English Garou had periodically scolded her for what she saw as her lack of manners.

"Enough," Storm-Eye rapped. "You wished to hear, now listen."

"Thank you," said the caern spirit. "Ages ago, this place sat on dry land and was in its quiet way a bastion against the Wyrm. The wise came here to meditate, experiment and palaver, and together they discovered or devised much that served them well in the war. Clever strategies, tactics and alliances. Trails to newfound domains in the Umbra, where potent spiritual weapons could be obtained. The habits and weaknesses of many breeds of Banes. All manner of things, really."

Big Sis said, "I'm guessing that pissed the Wyrm off."

The caern spirit smiled sadly. "Indeed. For a long while, the Garou managed to keep the retreat a secret, but when the Banes finally found out about it, they didn't like it at all. They attacked.

"The first time the enemy came, the defenders of the mound won a glorious victory. And the second, and the third, and the tenth. But as you know, this world has no shortage of Wyrm-spawn, and the creatures would not relent. They laid siege to the site, so that pilgrims had to risk their lives merely to travel in or out, and the sept spread itself thin defending wayfarers and the sacred stones as well. One by one, the protectors laid down their lives for the caern, and the tribes throughout these mountains sent their bravest warriors to replace them.

"So matters stood for generations. Gradually, though, the Banes multiplied and tightened their grip on the lands adjacent to the blessed site. Few travelers dared to run that gauntlet, and fewer still survived it. Finally a time arrived when no one visited the caern, and the sept believed that no one could except at the head of an army."

"I agree," said North Wind's Son, "even though we did it."

"So the sept fended off the Banes and waited for an army to pour out of the trees. Surely it would come. The tribes beyond the ring of poisoned land, the tribes who had revered and supported the caern since the dawn of the time, would assemble such a force."

"But it didn't come," Julia sighed. Despite her usual too-cool-for-school kind of attitude, she seemed as caught up in the simple telling as any of the rest of them.

"No," said the old man, "never. Perhaps the Banes wiped out the neighboring tribes first, or some other threat destroyed them. Perhaps they had even forgotten the caern. Time can play tricks in a place where the two worlds fuse together."

"We didn't see any sign of other Garou on our way here," said North Wind's Son. "They are gone. I hope they didn't die. They may have departed to watch over a tribe of Native humans when the white man drove them west."

"Perhaps," the old man said. "Whatever was wrong, the sept fought alone and rebuffed the enemy time and time again. Yet each victory was likewise a defeat, because the waves of Bane surged at them like floodwaters scouring a mud bank, and every so often they washed one of the defenders away."

Big Sis felt a vague irrational pang of guilt, just as if it had been her personal responsibility to march to the aid of the sept hundreds of years before her birth. "Did the Banes kill them all?" she asked.

"No, not all, not the Banes. But in time, the few who remained realized help would never come. They were doomed, and the wise would seek out the caern no more, at least not in that age of the world. Yet even if the Garou must lose the use of the holy place, it seemed an ill thing that the servants of corruption should claim and defile it. So the sept, possessed of spirit-talkers and lorekeepers of its own, sought a way to seal the refuge, and eventually they found it."

Julia shook her head. "The rite cost them their lives, didn't it?"

"Yes," said the keeper. "They knew it would and paid the price willingly, perhaps even gladly, for surely by that time they were weary of their duty. They called up a powerful spirit of transformation, strengthened it further with their own vitality, and it changed the caern. Before that night, the stones themselves had in a physical sense been nothing more than the mound you saw when you were swimming around it. The sept had lived and the wise had done their pondering on the earth surrounding it. Somehow, the spirit took those hallowed spaces and threaded them through the caern in the form of passageways and chambers, with all the glyphs, record of the secrets the lorekeepers and spirit-talkers had discovered, now graven on the inside. Then it locked the knowledge in with a seal that no Wyrm creature could open nor even find. Only an especially clever Garou could find it." He gave Big Sis a nod.

"I guess it dropped the whole place in the lake for good measure," said North Wind's Son.

"Essentially," said the old man. "It lowered the ground and called the water out of it. Sometime after that, I woke here inside the mound."

"Because you're the shade of one of the last defenders of the sept," said Julia.

The caern spirit smiled crookedly. "You won't take your claws out of a thing until it tells you its name, will you? That's good. A Theurge should have a mind like that. But sometimes a thing is bigger or deeper than the best word anyone can find to call it."

Julia opened her jaws to say something back, but Storm-Eye cut her off. "Please go on, Grandfather. I take it there is more to your tale."

"Not much more," the old man replied, "except to say that it wasn't too long before I developed some awareness of what lies outside, and then I discovered that even after the change, the Banes hadn't gone away. They *still* felt a need to keep Garou away until they could find a way to break into the caern and destroy it. They even possessed and deformed certain fish, so they could approach the stones more easily."

Big Sis said, "Some people don't know when to quit."

"I wasn't surprised they remained," the spirit said. "I reckoned they sensed the same thing I did, the reason, perhaps, I was fated to linger here: whatever they may have believed, the sept hadn't truly sealed the caern merely to deny their foes the pleasure of its desecration. Someday, one last Garou would seek the pile on a matter of the greatest urgency."

"Cries Havoc," said North Wind's Son, the fetish spear dangling casually in his bloodstained hand.

"Evidently," the spirit replied.

"To consult the ancient glyphs," Julia said. "You might have said so plainly when I asked. As a matter of fact, you might have asked me to help."

"They were written by Galliards for Galliards."

"Indeed." Julia didn't sound convinced, but she let it go.

"Now at last the caern will perish," the old man said, "and I will take the path that has awaited me all these centuries. But if the site is to fulfill its purpose, you must take the place of its former servants and preserve it a little longer."

Big Sis cocked her head. "Say what?"

"You broke the seal," said Julia. "I'm not criticizing. It was necessary. But unfortunately, that was what kept all the corrupt spirits at bay."

"Unless I'm mistaken," the spirit said, "the Banes will try to break in right here where you entered. I need you to hold them back. I will be elsewhere, fighting in my own way. Let us hope that together, we can balk them long enough for your packmate to find his answer."

North Wind's Son looked around the stone chamber. Big Sis knew just what he was thinking: at least in the previous fight, they'd had room to maneuver. "Round two," he sighed.

"By the time Cries Havoc fixes himself," said Big Sis, "we're probably going to be up to our asses in Banes. Where's the back door out of here?"

"Your comrade seeks the way to a particular part of the Penumbra where he may heal himself. If he succeeds, you will presumably walk the path alongside him."

Presumably, thought Big Sis. *Great, nothing psyches a girl up like 'presumably.'*

"We will not fail you," Storm-Eye said. "Now that we have heard your tale, now that we know we were fated to come here since the morning of the world, we see the importance of our quest even more clearly than before."

Well, that was true enough. Big Sis did see it. She took a deep, steadying breath and told herself that maybe they were even fated to win. It could have been an inspiring mini–pep talk, if only she believed in fate.

"How long have we got till the party starts?" she asked.

The old man pointed. Water was seeping in between two of the stones.

Chapter Eleven

The Bane soared on its black, vulturine wings and contemplated the other corrupt spirits below. They were a sorry lot, and not just because they were of a cruder, stupider nature than their critic's quasi-avian breed. They were inept.

The flyer considered that, in contrast, it had proved itself remarkably deft. Back at the resort, it had worried that the Silver River werewolves would spot it as it pursued them through the mountains, but as it turned out, that had been a needless concern. By slipping sideways back and forth between the worlds and taking advantage of every bit of cover, the Bane had not only remained unobserved, it had occasionally managed to sneak close enough to extrude a spectral length of itself and take another nibble from one of the Garou's memories.

Indeed, when the white shining led them squarely into a veritable army of corrupt spirits, the winged Bane had almost regretted it. No more slow, subtle torture and no more snacks. But it had assumed the clash was actually for the best. The lesser Wyrm-spawn would put Cries Havoc and his pack out of the war in Serbia once and for all, and Jo'cllath'mattric's will would be done.

Unbelievably, the werewolves had cut their way through their foes. The flyer was fearless when fighting in the company of its own ferocious flock, more cautious otherwise, but it had risked discovery by swooping close and tearing a big bite out of Storm-Eye's mind, a wound that had frozen her in place and forced her comrades to stand fast around her. And *still* the guardians of the lake couldn't kill them.

Indeed, the winged Bane could only say one good thing about them. At least they were giving chase.

Three and four at a time, the spirits who had quite possibly infested this wood for millennia were jumping into the lake and doing their best to swim out to the center, joining the long, eel-like creatures who were already darting and circling out there. Some of the forest Banes managed to shapeshift into piscine forms. Many, cloaked in matter here in the physical world and so vulnerable to certain of its perils, tried to breathe while submerged, failed and drowned, but the deaths of their physical shells did nothing to deter any of the rest.

Happily, the vulturous Bane had no need to breathe, and its black-feathered wings would pull it through water almost as easily as air. That meant it could tag along with this motley force and catch up with its charge once more. As bound by Jo'cllath'mattric's command as the lesser spirits were by their own imperative, the flyer soared high in the moonlight, then dived. The water was cold, but not cold enough to bother it.

Chapter Twelve

North Wind's Son was seventeen. Usually, he felt older. He'd been through a lot since his First Change, and he thought it had made him grow up. The rest of the pack seemed to see something in him that made them think so, too. They never treated him like a pup.

At the moment, however, he did feel young, with a boy's uncertainty about what was to come. The Garou had beaten the Banes once. Now they had to fight them again, before they were completely healed and rested, and pinned down in this box of a room on top of it? To say it seemed unfair was like saying the Pacific seemed moist.

He didn't even understand how the coming battle was supposed to work. If the Banes broke through the stone wall, the water would pour in, and that would pretty much be the end of the Garou, wouldn't it?

Fretting, he'd fallen prey to a restless urge to prowl around. In contrast, Julia was sitting cross-legged, pecking and clicking away at her computer. Big Sis looked down at her and said, "I hope you're doing something witchy that'll kick the shit out of the Wyrm things."

"I'm afraid not," the Glass Walker said. "For the most part, I was simply wondering how a Galliard bereft of his Gifts can possibly be expected to decipher unfamiliar glyphs in only an hour or so."

"Go ahead," said Big Sis, "cheer me up."

Julia laughed. "Very funny. I like that. I trust you know I like you, too. All of you. I—"

"No farewells!" Storm-Eye snarled. "We defeated the Banes before and we will do it again. Cries Havoc will find his path. All will be well."

The English Garou inclined her head. "Yes, of course."

Suddenly water trickled from two new leaks between the rocks. North Wind's Son's fur bristled, stirred by a noxious electricity in the air. "They're here!" he shouted.

Contrary to his expectations, the wall didn't burst inward. Rather, three Banes simply materialized in the chamber and lunged.

The werewolves sprang to meet them. North Wind's Son rammed his spear through a pike-thing, which was crawling and rearing in a fair imitation of a snake. The corrupted fish thrashed in its death throes, and another Wyrm spirit, this one a pig-faced horror mincing on two dainty cloven hooves, appeared to take its place. The abomination lifted his machete for an overhand cut, and North Wind's Son yanked on the haft of his fetish to free it. As if with conscious spite, the expiring pike-creature somehow clenched around the lance and held it fast.

The Wendigo's first impulse was to pull again, but he realized the pig spirit would nail him with the machete if he tried. Instead, jostling Julia in the process, he sprang back and came on guard with the weapons Gaia had given him.

As he did so, water spattered atop his head and gurgled on all sides. He risked a fast glance about. A dozen more chinks in the walls and ceiling were leaking.

The pig-man danced forward, swinging his blade back and forth. North Wind's Son retreated a little farther—that was all he had in these tight quarters—meanwhile timing the cuts. The machete whizzed past one more time, and then, before the Bane could reverse it for a backhand cut, the werewolf stepped inside his reach, grabbed him, jerked him up off the floor and bit down on his head, piercing the rotten-tasting flesh and the rock-hard skull beneath.

Dropping his kill, North Wind's Son looked about. So far, his packmates were winning. Four more Banes lay mangled and inert on the floor. Storm-Eye disemboweled another, and that was the last of the first wave.

As if someone had turned a tap, some of the leaks stopped altogether, while others slowed the flow of water considerably. North Wind's Son had witnessed a good many marvels during his brief time as a Garou, but somehow, this current development so flouted common sense that he thought it the oddest thing he'd ever seen.

Julia spat out a mouthful of no-doubt vile Bane flesh and greenish pus. "Well," she said, "at least we now know the rules of the game."

"I feel so much better," Big Sis said.

North Wind's Son yanked his spear from the aquatic Bane's carcass, then felt the same unpleasant prickling in the air. An instant later, a second contingent of Wyrm-spawn popped into the artificial cave.

As the battle continued, the Wendigo verified that he and his packmates did indeed understand the parameters. Though the process occurred invisibly, somehow the presence of living abominations within the sacred caern created and exacerbated leaks. While the spirits were active, the water poured in. Once they were dead, it ebbed somewhat until the next bunch of enemies ghosted their way inside.

Unfortunately, understanding that didn't provide much in the way of practical help. It was like the caern spirit's story. The Banes died and died, but they were like water themselves, racing floodwater scouring away soil. The Silver River Pack couldn't slaughter them fast enough to stop more and more leaks from opening.

Indeed, as the minutes passed, each kill seemed more difficult than the last, even for an Ahroun, a warrior born. Water was falling everywhere and always seemed to splash in North Wind's Son's eyes at the most dangerous possible moment. Yet despite what ought to have been the torrent's cleansing properties, he was choking on the concentrated stink of the Banes. They were blinking in so fast that at any given moment, a dozen or more gibbered and shrieked within the chamber, filling the space with a pounding, echoing cacophony, jamming it so tightly that for the werewolves, dodging and displacing targets became virtually impossible. All they could do was stand in a line and lash out at whatever rushed in at them.

So that was what North Wind's Son did. In such close quarters, the length of his spear often made it impossible to bring the flint point to bear, in which case he let go of the haft to shred the foe with his claws. His exertions opened his half-healed wounds, and the Banes' talons and knives cut new ones, not mortal or crippling yet, but soon, he suspected, soon. His heart hammered, and the arteries in his neck throbbed. A bone-deep exhaustion numbed and weighted his limbs. He knew his packmates had to be in equally bad shape. It made sense to him that Storm-Eye was still clawing and snapping away—he figured the alpha would be the last to fall—but he was in awe of what must be the sheer iron determination that kept the pair the Red Talon called *city wolves* doing the same.

A Bane flung himself forward with pale, withered arms outstretched. Insanely, in the midst of all the streaming water, his hands crackled with halos of yellow flame. The fire gave off a stink like tires burning.

North Wind's Son thrust. With inhuman agility, the abomination stopped a fraction of an inch from the spear point, then backpedaled.

The Ahroun didn't like the look of the fire. He wanted to kill this particular Bane *now*, before it managed to grab and burn one of the werewolves. He knew he also had to hold the line—he didn't dare let any of the Wyrm-spawn get behind it—but for this instant, the assault had slackened. It looked like he could spring forward, spear the abomination with the torchlike hands and jump back before the Banes could take advantage of his being out of position.

If he weren't so tired, he might not have made the same decision. Might not have caught his foot on an obstruction that felt like the mangled carcass of a Bane someone had already killed. Might not have flailed desperately and failed to recover his balance.

As it was, he fell headlong and splashed down in the water on the floor. The liquid was cloudy with the gore and excretions of the Banes, and while he was focused on other things, had risen to at least a foot high.

Caught by surprise, he inhaled a choking mouthful of the putrid liquid and tried to scramble back up before he took in any more. Some clawed, some skeletal and some supple as a snake, some possessed of too few fingers and some too many, a score of hands gripped him and held him down.

North Wind's Son felt that he should be able to lift his face up out of the water anyway. He was a mighty protector of Gaia, wasn't he? But somehow, he couldn't achieve the necessary leverage. Around him, the nasty soup churned as other Banes scrambled forward to exploit the new gap in the pack's defenses.

That meant all the werewolves were going to die within the next few seconds. They hadn't held out nearly as long as the original sept. Strangling on the contaminated water, North Wind's Son guessed it wasn't all the fault of his crappy judgment, but it sure felt that way.

Then other racing feet splashed around him. Some of the hands pressing him down jerked away. With the last of his strength, he heaved himself up, tumbling other Banes off his back. A couple clung to him, scrabbling, pummeling, groping for a choke hold, until he flung them into the ranks of their fellows.

Coughing and retching, he looked around. Storm-Eye, Julia and Big Sis encircled him, slashing at Banes. Evidently, when he'd fallen, his packmates had charged forward and slaughtered some of the Banes who were trying to drown him, enough so that he could shake off the remainder.

They must have fought like the heroes of myth, like old Laughs-at-Pine-Cones himself, to reach him, and horribly, it wasn't going to matter. With the battle line dissolved, the Banes were scuttling and slithering along the walls of the cave, maneuvering to surround the werewolves. When they got that done, they wouldn't have much more trouble killing the Garou, and North Wind's Son could see no way to stop them. Other abominations were pressing him and his friends too hard.

Soaked in blood and water, Storm-Eye stood straight and tall. She still had her fangs bared, but she folded her arms and, turning her lupine head, raked the Banes with a stare of infinite contempt. A terrifying scarlet light seemed to burn in her good eye, while something even worse seethed in the ruined one.

In the cramped chamber, none of the abominations could miss her demeanor and expression. Over the course of a second or two, they ceased their hideous roaring and screeching, uncovering silence and the hiss of streaming water. The Banes shrank back. Four new ones popped into view, and they too fell under the spell.

"Reform the line," Storm-Eye murmured. "I do not think the fear will hold them very long."

"Since when can you do this?" asked Big Sis, scurrying to her side. "I mean the spirits teach that to some of us Philodox, sure, but only to the big wig lawgivers. Way outta my league and, I thought, yours."

"I have never done it," the Red Talon replied. "And, you are right, I should not be able to do it now. It is reserved for those wiser than me. Still, the thought came into my head to try."

"You're channeling the power of the caern," Julia said. "There was probably a wolf spirit who called this place home long ago. They can grant that Gift."

"Perhaps," Storm-Eye replied. "But not for much longer, so everyone *get in line!*"

The werewolves obeyed, and none too soon. Over the next few seconds, most of the Banes shook off their funk and charged.

North Wind's Son leveled his spear and summoned back the energizing Garou fury. It came, but it was a shadow of what it had been earlier in the fight, a brittle thing, nearly shattered by a surge of pain and fatigue. *Come on, Cries Havoc,* the Wendigo thought as he traded attacks with the next Bane, and the one after that, *read the damn thing!*

Chapter Thirteen

Cries Havoc had just about decided he was never going to figure out the glyphs. He tried to tell himself his doubts were merely a manifestation of the despair festering in his ruined spirit, but he was having trouble believing it, because the situation was fraught with plausible reasons for him to fail.

Somehow, the Bane back in Bosnia had swallowed his most precious ability, telling tales. And with it, the sensitivity needed to decipher these glyphs seemed to have vanished. Once, he could simply have glanced at the lines of chiseled glyphs and they would have all but burst into song for him, conveying the greater part of their significance in an instant. And if he'd needed to ferret out some more abstruse implication, he could have entered a trance where nothing existed but the subtle layers and interconnections of meaning in the symbols.

Now the inscription mocked him with its incomprehensibility. He examined a line, and his mind seemed to glance off it like a flat stone skipping across a pond. For an instant, he might glean a fragment of meaning from two or three of the glyphs, but then it evaporated out of his brain and left not a garbled word behind.

Unable to make any progress in his normal state of consciousness, he struggled and struggled until it became obvious that he was also now incapable of slipping into a lorekeeper's meditation. He lacked even the focus that a human scholar might have achieved. Time and again, his mind drifted from the task before it, and he caught himself brooding over how damaged and useless he was, or how impossible was his current problem, instead of actually working on it. Then he grimly resumed his concentration.

He became even more distracted when the water started coming in. No matter how he shifted around, he couldn't keep it from plopping or streaming onto his head, and even if he could, he still would have had the lower part of his body immersed in the icy flow. He doubted that even with all his faculties he could have deciphered the message under such miserable conditions.

The snarls and shrieks echoing down the tunnels were equally disruptive. He clenched and winced out at every particularly jarring cry or sudden swell in the volume. He told himself, *That's your pack out there, fighting, maybe dying, to give you your chance*, but that didn't help. It was just more unproductive thought to stick in his brain and lure him away from his chore.

Cries Havoc grappled with another line, or rather, with the first line, for what might be the hundredth time. For one bright, startling moment, it made sense to him, and then he realized the glyphs couldn't possibly say what he'd imagined. Not unless some ancient seer had anticipated a lyric from a Taj Mahal song the Child of Gaia had heard on the radio on the drive down from New York.

Perhaps the caern spirit was right. Perhaps Cries Havoc still did possess emotions, for right now, he had a sort of taut, hollow sensation in his head that made him wonder if he was going mad.

He did what seemed the only thing left to do. He contemplated the first symbol in the top line and that symbol alone, as youngsters did when first grappling with the alphabet. Maybe his crippled mind was at least capable of teasing the meaning out of one character at a time.

The glyphs beside and below the first one tugged at the edges of the storyteller's field of vision, trying to draw and fragment his attention. Wading through the water on the floor, he rose, walked to the inscription and covered the signs he wished to ignore with his hands and forearms.

Framed among his long, furry fingers, nicked and raw from the battle beside the lake, the remaining glyph looked like an arrowhead pointing upward. If that was what it was really supposed to be, it could mean *weapon*, *war*, *danger*, *anger* or simply indicate a direction. On the other hand, the glyph *also* resembled a stylized pine or fir. If that was what the carver had intended, it could signify *tree*, *forest* or *strength*.

If Cries Havoc's mind had been working properly, he would have known immediately and effortlessly which correspondence and meaning the ancient Galliard had intended. As it was, the Child of Gaia stared and stared until his eyes ached and blurred, and still he couldn't tell.

In the desolate heart of him, a jagged, unrecognizable shard, of muted panic or desperation, perhaps, twisted, snagged and gouged, insisting that he was doing everything wrong. He had to go back to looking at the entire inscription, for the first glyph, or any of them, would only define itself in the context of the whole.

Teeth bared, he shoved that traitor idea to the back of his mind with all the other babbling irrelevancies. He'd already tried examining the entire message, and it didn't work. Breaking it down was his only hope.

He stared some more, striving by the sheer intensity of his regard to make the meaning of the arrowhead/tree flip one way or the other. It didn't. After a time, water spilled from the rocks above the inscription and cascaded over it in a shimmering, whispering sheet. Startled, Cries Havoc gasped. For one lunatic moment, he was certain the liquid was going to wash away the carvings.

Still suspecting himself demented, he sniffed the glyph. The only smells were stone and lake water. He touched the carving, probing it, running his fingertip around the edges. Then his eyes widened.

A triangular notch indented one side of the vertical line comprising the foot of the glyph. Like a human suffering from a brain lesion, up until now, he hadn't been able to see the tiny detail, but he could feel it.

It told him the symbol represented a tree with a wound chopped in its trunk, and straining mightily, his mind declared that, altered thusly, the sign denoted *weakness* or *sickness*, the antithesis of strength.

If so, he had the first sign figured out. He wondered if he'd forget what he'd learned as soon as he switched to the second. Maybe, but he had to risk it, because the glyphs were no use unless he deciphered them all. He said, "Weakness, weakness, weakness," trying to fix the idea in his mind, then shifted the viewing frame he'd made of his hands.

The new sign was a spread pair of wings. It could signify *bird, flight*...or *the spirit*. Surely it was the latter.

Now, did he still remember the first glyph? Yes. *Weakness*. And did it make sense married to the second one? Again, yes, mending a *wounded spirit* was supposedly the point of the inscription. Somewhat encouraged, he moved on to the next sign.

It was slow going, but as he studied them with eyes and fingers alike, the glyphs grudgingly spoke to him. Sometimes the ideas occurred in what, to a human, might have seemed an incoherent, illogical sequence, but Cries Havoc understood Garou conventions of thought and discourse, and that was one thing the winged Bane hadn't ripped out of his brain.

As the caern keeper had promised, the inscription described a rite to carry a werewolf to a realm of dreams and memory where, if he wished, he could step back inside the early verses of his own story, his own past. Fortunately, the ceremony shouldn't be difficult to perform. It was mainly just a matter of saying a prayer.

That is, if Cries Havoc had translated every single glyph correctly, but really, how likely was that with his mind and talents in tatters?

He gave his head a shake. It was worse than useless to think like that. It was how the Wyrm wanted him to think. He wouldn't even worry about whether the rite would work or not. He would simply perform it as perfectly as he was able, as he would any such invocation, and see what happened.

Splashing up water, he danced through the ritual postures. Spoke the words. When the rite was done, nothing seemed to happen, and he thought he had indeed bungled it. Then something blasted through his body, staggering him. Had his soul been intact, he might have felt a flash of ecstasy. As it was, the blaze was simply a sensation, neither pleasant nor painful, but it charged him with a sort of vibrant power and the knowledge that the force could take him where he needed to go.

He howled to tell his packmates he was ready, then loped out of the chamber to find them. Elsewhere in the caern, something banged like a loud, sharp clap of thunder. The luminescence in the rock walls dimmed and died, smothering the passageway in darkness.

Chapter Fourteen

A Bane with horns made of rusty steel cable lowered his head and charged like a bull. Unable to dodge without opening a hole in the defensive line, Storm-Eye braced herself and caught hold of the spirit's "natural" weapons. Metal slivers pierced and abraded the insides of her hands, but she stopped the abomination dead in his tracks. She wrenched the horns in a half circle that broke their possessor's neck, and dropped him in the cold, filthy, ever-deepening water on the floor.

Then a howl reverberated up the passage at her back. Like any Garou, she could hear the sense in it, and despite her utter weariness, knew a thrill of satisfaction. Julia had been too pessimistic. Cries Havoc *had* deciphered the glyphs, and now he called for his packmates to join him.

The problem was that Storm-Eye couldn't really see any way to do that. The Banes were pressing too hard. If the werewolves turned to run, the spirits would pull them down in a heartbeat.

So spent was the Red Talon that, had she been alone, she might well have howled back to tell Cries Havoc to escape without her. But an alpha couldn't give up, not while she had a pack to look after, and so she shouted, "Backward! One step at a time! Keep the line!"

The werewolves started their retreat. The attempt enraged the Banes, and they attacked even more furiously. Then something crashed.

Storm-Eye looked toward the noise. Behind the Banes, several stones of the leaking wall had burst inward, making a sizable hole. Water roared in.

The torrent knocked down everyone, werewolf and spirit Bane. Perhaps because they weren't ready for it, even the pike-things tumbled about.

With a crunching roar, more of the breached wall collapsed. Meanwhile, the current shoved Storm-Eye along. She tried to get her feet under her, resist the pushing and stand, and a scabrous Bane slammed into her, robbing her of any semblance of balance and sending her splashing back down. She thought the creature had collided with her inadvertently as the cold, roaring water carried him, but he made the most of his opportunity. He skittered up her body with spiderish ability, clinging, mauling, biting with needle-pointed fangs.

Storm-Eye was glad she'd reflexively sucked in a breath as she fell. She didn't like having her face submerged—to say the least—but she knew she couldn't labor to lift it into the air and fight the Bane at the same time, and those murderous teeth had to take priority.

With some effort, she managed to hook her claws in the skinny, wriggling thing and thought, *Good, I'm in control, I'm coping with this*.

Then blackness swallowed her. The concentrated foulness of the Banes had finally smothered the benevolent power that for countless generations had shone from the sacred stones.

For a second, her mind tottered on the brink of an emotion she had never known: pure, mad panic. It was ludicrous, really. No Garou feared the dark, but

Children of Gaia

she'd nearly reached the end of her strength and courage, and with water clogging her nose and ears, the gloom seemed to blind her nearly as thoroughly as it would a human.

Once again, it was the thought of the pack that drew her back from the edge. She would not fail it.

She finished ripping the thrashing Bane apart, then floundered toward the air. The moment seemed to stretch out endlessly while all she touched was water. Perhaps she and the Bane had rolled about in the dark and she was swimming down or sideways instead of up. Or maybe the water pouring in had already filled the passage, and there wasn't any—

Her head broke the surface. As she gasped in a breath, and the current pushed her along, she sensed that her second conjecture was wrong, but not by all that much. She could feel the ceiling not too far above her head. The lake would finish drowning the tunnel, the caern and everyone still trapped in it soon enough.

She fumbled hold of a couple of the rocks comprising the passage wall. She didn't really know if it was the right thing to do, but her instincts prompted her to anchor herself somehow in the midst of streaming chaos.

Something else bumped against her. She slashed with one hand, tore flesh and winced when she realized that here amid the blackness, the body could just as easily be a packmate as a Bane. She groped for it as the current whisked it by, then slumped with relief. The thing whose flesh she had just torn didn't have fur.

Where were the other Garou, then? She heard Cries Havoc still howling somewhere deeper in the caern, his voice breaking as he strove to out-shout the endless clamor of the water. It was a good idea, and Storm-Eye did the same, letting out a somewhat gurgling howl.

"Here!" Big Sis called, coughing, from farther down the tunnel.

Storm-Eye didn't want to let go of the wall. But Big Sis and Cries Havoc were both downstream, and the alpha couldn't very well expect them to fight the current and come to her. She snarled the shameful trepidation out of her heart and pushed off, dumping herself back in the center of the flow.

At least this time she could paddle along with her head above water. She sensed another Bane splashing in with no extraordinary grace on her flank. She wrenched herself around, grabbed the thing, shoved it under the surface and wrung its neck until it stopped moving.

"Carlita!" she cried, then caught the Bone Gnawer's scent and North Wind's Son's as well. Her friends were just ahead and to the left. She reached out, and, groping, the Ahroun grasped her arm and pulled her to another perch on the wall.

"Are you all right?" Storm-Eye asked.

"Well, as all right as we were just before the dam broke," rasped North Wind's Son, just a shadow of humor manifest in his pain-ridden, dead-tired voice.

"A couple Banes pulled me under," babbled Big Sis. The same hysteria that Storm-Eye had barely quashed was obviously cutting through the younger Bone Gnawer's bravado. "I almost drowned before John got them off me. But now we don't know how to find Julia or Cries Havoc. I mean, he's howling—"

"Enough!" Storm-Eye snapped. "You are no coward, so calm yourself. We will find our packmates by scent and sound, and we will look after one another while we do it. Tell me you understand."

"Yeah," said Big Sis, her voice now only a little shaky. "Got it."

Suddenly the Garou smelled Banes all around them. The werewolves fought as best they could, blind, with water drumming maddeningly on their heads and likewise trying to slosh into their mouths and separate them. Eventually, the packmates tore their foes apart, but not before Storm-Eye acquired two new gashes, one on her forearm and one on her belly. They burned like fire for a few moments, then the frigid stream numbed them.

"Now we swim with the current," she said, "deeper into the caern."

Big Sis asked, "What if Julia's behind us?"

"We must stay together," Storm-Eye said, "and the only thing we know for certain is that Cries Havoc is calling us from somewhere up ahead."

"That sucks." The Bone Gnawer paused. "But, yeah, you're right."

"Then come." The werewolves let go of the wall.

As they swam on, they found other places where the water was gushing in. At one point, rocks dropped from the ceiling and missed the swimmers by a matter of inches. The entire caern was disintegrating.

The Banes found the werewolves periodically, if not quite as often as Storm-Eye had expected. She wondered if some of them had perished as a result of their own victory. It was paradoxical, considering that the Wyrm-spawn had survived their plunge to the bottom of the lake, but she had a hunch that some had drowned or been dashed against the stones when the water poured in.

Still, plenty remained, and the Garou perforce learned to fight them while floating along in the blackness and the surging, treacherous current that periodically sought to dash them against a wall. Storm-Eye got the impression that some of her attackers could see perfectly well in the dark, but the ones she had the most trouble with were the pike-things and the others adapted for existence in the water.

She was just finishing off another such threat, a creature like a festering mermaid with a head that was nothing but prehensile jaws, when Big Sis croaked, "My leg! Damn it!"

"What?" shouted North Wind's Son.

"I killed the thing that was after me," the Bone Gnawer said, "but it smashed my leg against the wall first. It's broken. A piece is sticking out of my skin."

"Can you still float?" Storm-Eye asked.

"Are you serious? Yeah, yeah, I guess. I'll try."

"You'll be all right," the alpha said. "We'll carry you if you need it. You just have to hang on."

"Sure," Big Sis gritted. "No problem."

The ordeal ground on until Storm-Eye felt she understood the human notion of hell. They didn't find Julia, although it was entirely possible that they'd obliviously paddled past her submerged corpse in the dark. At least Cries Havoc's howling kept leading them past the branching passages that might otherwise have taken them astray.

Until, abruptly, the calling stopped.

"This isn't happening," said Big Sis, sounding half-delirious with pain. "I didn't go through all this shit just so Cries Havoc could get croaked at the end."

"No, you did not," said Storm-Eye. "I do not know why the howling stopped, but the lorekeeper is still ahead somewhere, and we will find him."

After another moment, the Red Talon smelled a length of wet stone looming at the level of her head. She stretched out a hand and caught hold to keep herself from banging into it, then considered what it meant. At this point, the passage dipped, and for that reason the next section was already completely full of water.

"Maybe the water closing this space is what cut off the howling," said North Wind's Son.

"Perhaps," said Storm-Eye. "In any case, we must go on."

"Yeah," said Big Sis, "and hope we've got someplace to come up for air on the other side."

They dived without hesitation, Storm-Eye included, though she wished Carlita had kept that last remark to herself.

She kicked and stroked forward, then faltered in dismay. Though she could see nothing, she could feel and hear the water flowing on through two conduits. The passage branched, and she had no idea which fork to take.

A hand, Big Sis's by the size of it, tugged her toward the left. She passed the signal on to North Wind's Son, then took hold of the city wolf and somewhat clumsily helped her along in the direction she'd indicated.

They swam for a time, and then Big Sis pulled on her again, this time indicating they should ascend. It was fine with Storm-Eye. Her lungs were nearly empty. Perhaps air waited above her head, perhaps it didn't, but either way, she could kick and drag herself no farther.

She and the Bone Gnawer headed upward. Sensing their change in direction, North Wind's Son followed. Their heads broke the surface a few seconds later. They heard the constant gushing of incoming water and the splashing of falling stones, but no howling.

"It's the wrong way," groaned the warrior when he managed to catch his breath. "We have to go back."

"No!" said Big Sis. "Tampa street-kid, remember? Bone Gnawer judge in the making? I knows my way around in alleys."

"You're hurt," said John North Wind's Son, "and these tunnels aren't alleys."

"Close enough," Big Sis said.

"We trust you," said Storm-Eye. "Onward!"

"They swam forward, killed two more Banes, and then Cries Havoc began calling again.

"Told you, *Juanito*."

"Sorry," answered North Wind's Son.

Storm-Eye realized the passage was rising when her feet brushed the bottom. She gratefully *walked* on while the howling grew ever louder, and the stream sank to waist deep. Then she caught Cries Havoc's scent and saw a silvery glimmering. It was soft as moonlight, but after her immersion in total darkness, it made her squint.

Another turn and she discerned the source of the light was Cries Havoc himself. The body glowed as if his flesh were translucent and his bones phosphorescent. He had found a sort of ledge to perch on, and he bore fresh punctures and cuts attesting to the fact that somehow, some of the Banes had made their way around to where he had been waiting. The wounds shone more brightly than the rest of him.

"Sure," said Big Sis, catching hold of the stones beneath the shelf, "we fight our way through the whole stinking caern, and you sit your ass down and take it easy."

"I tried to get back to you," said Cries Havoc. "I knew the way the old man led me in, but I couldn't use it. At one point, the stones from the ceiling were falling like hail. They would have killed me for sure. After that, I thought that instead of all of us just blundering around in the dark, maybe I should call you, and I didn't know if I could swim, kill Banes, and howl at the same time. Where's Julia?"

The question wiped the grin off Big Sis's face. "We don't know. We lost her."

"No, you didn't," the Glass Walker said. Storm-Eye turned to see the Glass Walker hurrying up behind them.

"Thank God," said North Wind's Son.

"I was behind you the whole way," Julia said. "But whenever I got a chance to call out, you didn't hear me. It is quite noisy."

"How did you get through all the Banes by yourself?" Big Sis asked.

"Theurge techniques," said Julia. "Flickering back and forth between the worlds at the right moment and more than my share of luck, in other words. Cries Havoc, I surmise from the glow that you're ready to move on?"

"Yeah."

"Then get down in the water," Big Sis said, "I don't exactly feel like climbing up to you."

"Right." The storyteller jumped in. "Everybody, grab hold of me."

Storm-Eye moved to obey him, and then a pike-thing many times larger than the others they'd seen erupted from the water and opened its jaws to swallow her down. Bellowing, North Wind's Son rammed his spear into the spirit's misshapen head. Up until now, in the blackness and the confusion, the alpha hadn't realized that the Wendigo had managed to hold on to the fetish.

As the Wyrm-spawn thrashed and sank, North Wind's Son pulled the lance out of it. "Let's do it," he said.

They took hold of Cries Havoc, or he got hold of them, and then he shifted them across the Gauntlet. Abruptly, the frigid, relentlessly pushing water was gone, and they had solidity beneath their feet. They hastily shifted to gain their balance. Big Sis gasped and fell when her broken leg took her weight, but Storm-Eye and Julia caught her before she hit the ground.

Then the alpha looked around. Luna and the Red Star, harbinger of the Apocalypse, shone down on a memory, for in the spirit world, the caern retained the same form it had possessed in ancient times. It was a pile of stones on dry land, occupying the center of a forest glade, and around it were the marks of a

Children of Gaia

thriving Garou community, black, sunken places littered with ash and scraps of charred wood, tents, lean-tos, whittled poles lashed into racks for the scraping and drying of pelts, and smaller collections of glyph-carved stone on which one seer or another had recorded his discoveries, artifacts that in the material world had merged with the pile when it transformed. The carvings seemed strangely blurred, and Storm-Eye doubted the Banes had ever been able to make them out.

Now, however, time was catching up with the Penumbra's analogue of the sacred site. Individual stones shattered with sharp reports, and the central caern was crumbling. Stinking Banes swarmed everywhere, shrieking and gibbering in triumph, coming on guard when they noticed the werewolves, and more abominations were appearing by the moment, evidently pursuing the pack across the Gauntlet.

Storm-Eye felt like the victim of a cruel prank. Did Cries Havoc's newfound secret amount to nothing more than step sideways? Any Garou already knew how to accomplish that, and in this case, it wasn't enough to extricate the pack from the foes who were inexorably picking them apart. The Red Talon looked for a clear path out of the middle of them and wasn't at all surprised to find that none existed.

Then Big Sis said, "Check it out."

Storm-Eye turned. Still glowing, Cries Havoc held his arms raised in invocation. In response, a pathway, seemingly made of pearly light, appeared in the sky. It appeared to be a moon bridge, the same sort of magical trail certain Garou could create to link two caerns. The near end of it descended to the ground like a ramp.

"Come on!" said Cries Havoc. He and North Wind's Son scrambled onto the bridge. Still carrying Big Sis, Julia and Storm-Eye followed. Only a few feet behind charged the next wave of raging Wyrm-spawn.

The first time Storm-Eye had seen an arch of curdled light, she had wondered if it would be as smooth and thus slippery as it looked. Familiarity had taught her otherwise. Though not even the sharpest eye could see the grain, the surface of such a span felt rough enough that a Garou could even dash along it without danger of losing his footing.

The one Cries Havoc had conjured was no exception, but though it was no threat to her balance, her first stride upon it made the world stretch and blur in a disorienting fashion. Suddenly the babble of the pack's pursuers sounded faint and far away.

Curious, Storm-Eye glanced around and discovered that a single step had carried her and her friends far along the path and thus high above the disintegrating caern. Banes were racing up the bridge, but the span declined to help them along, and they were covering distance no more quickly than their legs alone could carry them.

"It's as if we're wearing seven-league boots," said Julia, making yet another reference Storm-Eye didn't recognize, "and if I'm not mistaken, the moon bridge has still another trick to play. Watch."

The first several yards of bridge abruptly vanished. Storm-Eye instinctively tensed, as if now that the span no longer rested its foot on the ground, it would topple. It didn't. It didn't inconvenience the Garou in any way. But their pursuers, who had still been traversing that initial stretch, plummeted when the support evaporated from beneath them.

Big Sis laughed. "Sweet."

"We should keep moving," said Cries Havoc. "I don't completely understand what I did. I don't know if the bridge will keep dissolving one length at a time or how long it might be before it disappears altogether."

"Very well," said Storm-Eye. "Forward."

They pressed on, each step eating up distance, smearing the world beyond the edges of the path in the same uncanny way. When she paused for a second and glanced down, the alpha sometimes saw what resembled an empty world. Many of the works of man—houses, freeways, factories, even whole cities—cast their shadows in the Penumbra, but rare was the actual human being who could do the same.

But of course that momentary impression was a lie. In reality, the Umbra teemed with life in the form of countless spirits, and between strides, she caught glimpses of a good many. The Weaver's spiders crawling in the Pattern Web. A magnificent buck, the essence of Deer, looking up at the moon bridge from the edge of a cliff. Glass elementals, manlike figures composed of glittering shards, picking pieces from one another's bodies to create a vast mosaic for some purpose that, of all the werewolves, only Julia might possibly understand. And far too many Banes, but to the lawgiver's relief, none who seemed capable of molesting the travelers on their mystic and elevated path.

Eventually Storm-Eye discerned that the bridge was bending downward. After a few more paces, it deposited the pack in a quiet field, seemingly untenanted save for grass and brush. A stream that smelled of iron ran through the center of it, and a thick wood lay beyond.

Chapter Fifteen

The luminous path through the sky disappeared. Julia helped Storm-Eye set Big Sis gently on the ground. Then, as if someone had thrown a switch, exhaustion crashed down on her, and she collapsed as much as sat down beside the Bone Gnawer.

Cries Havoc and North Wind's Son did the same. Storm-Eye managed to stay on her feet for one more moment, peering and sniffing in all directions, making sure the field really was safe, before she flopped down and sprawled on her back.

For a while, no one spoke. They just waited for their breathing and heartbeats to slow and savored the joy of remaining still. Gradually, as a bit of her strength trickled back, Julia realized how horribly thirsty she was. Evidently suffering from the same condition, Storm-Eye bestirred herself, limped to the creek, stooped and drank noisily.

When she returned, she gave her gashed, battered body a shake, flinging droplets of the lake water that still soaked her in all directions. "I have made what Julia calls an *executive decision*," she said, her voice hoarse. "No more swimming unless absolutely necessary."

The others stared for a moment. Then Julia said, "Did you just make a joke?"

"Of course," said the alpha. "Why are you so surprised?"

"Oh, I don't know," Julia said, trying to hide a smile. She dragged herself to her feet and trudged for the stream. It hurt. She'd already stiffened up considerably. She'd never experienced that before, not in Crinos form.

"I can't believe we all made it out of there," said North Wind's Son, feebly rubbing the gory point of his spear with a handful of grass. "It's amazing. When I can find the strength, I'm going to be really proud of us. Unless I bleed to death first."

"You will not," said Storm-Eye, sitting back down. "Nor will any of the rest of us. We each bear many wounds, but none grave enough to slay a Garou."

"We did kick ass," said Big Sis, "and it's a good thing. 'Cause as far as I could see, the old man didn't do shit to help us."

Cupping her hands and lifting them to her muzzle, Julia drank from the stream. To someone who'd lived her life in the city, the icy iron water tasted harsh and unpleasant, but that didn't stop her from gulping her fill.

Then she said, "Actually, that's unjust. The guardian spirit did help. The caern would have disintegrated far more quickly if he hadn't tried to hold it together. Even at the end, it didn't fall apart in a natural sort of way. If it had, we would have drowned long before we all found one another."

"Hm," Big Sis said. "Okay, I take it back. Do you think the guy made it out?"

"I believe so," the Glass Walker said. "I doubt the Banes could have done anything to stop him from embarking on that road he mentioned. Now, I'll fetch you some water, and when you've drunk your fill, we'll see about lining up the two ends of that broken tibia."

The lanky werewolf sighed. "I can't wait."

"What happens next?" asked North Wind's Son, turning to Cries Havoc. "Are you okay now?"

"No," said the storyteller, and indeed, Julia could still see the raw hollowness inside him. The only difference between now and earlier was that his bloody body no longer glowed. "But maybe I can be. The moon bridge brought us to the right place."

Cries Havoc crawled to the stream, slurped some water, then heaved himself to his feet. He swayed for a moment, and the Glass Walker lifted her hands to catch him, but then he found his balance.

"If I can be cured," he said, "the medicine's in those woods." He turned toward them.

"Rest," said Storm-Eye. "You have time. Recover your strength."

The lorekeeper glanced back. "I've got the strength for this. The rite gave it to me."

"Good," Big Sis said, "but wait a minute until my leg's fixed, and we'll all go with you."

Cries Havoc said, "Thanks. But I have to do the last part by myself, and I think I should get on with it." He walked on.

Julia knew he was right, but she also understood exactly how the Bone Gnawer felt. After all the pack had been through together, it seemed strange to let its most sorely damaged member, the one the rest had fought so hard to help, go on alone.

Perhaps Storm-Eye and North Wind's Son felt the same, for everyone watched in silence when Cries Havoc entered the trees. Then Big Sis said, "Yo, Princess Di, how about that drink?"

Chapter Sixteen

For a few paces, the wood seemed merely that, a stand of elm and maple. Here as in the material world, it was early spring, the air chilly and the trees showing only the subtlest signs of awakening life. Patches of rotten mulch, the remains of last autumn's fallen leaves, littered the ground.

Then everything changed. Cries Havoc had expected something to happen, but even so, the shift was so sudden and disorienting that it took him a second to sort out his impressions.

He rode clutched in a pair of powerful, furry arms, feeling the rhythm of a long, swift stride. A gibbous moon, his birth moon, hung overhead in air warmer than it had been a moment ago. He could smell his mother's scent, the milk in her breasts, and the Rocky Mountains spreading out all around him.

This isn't right, Cries Havoc thought. *I never remembered being a baby in my mother's arms. I didn't remember my mother at all.* But apparently that wasn't true. Somewhere deep inside him, he had remembered, until the Bane tore the knowledge out of him.

He also knew what night this was and what was happening. His elders had told him the story, insofar as they knew it. By mating with another werewolf and producing a freakish metis pup, his mother had broken sacred Garou law. Her pack would cherish and raise the baby, for that was the way of the Children of Gaia. But she would go into exile as soon as she recovered her strength.

Mother, however, refused to relinquish her son. She stole him and fled, and clasped in her embrace, he was fearless and content. Indeed, returned to this moment, Cries Havoc rediscovered a pure, astonishing bliss. It lasted until he noticed the white, four-legged beast silently pacing his mother as she raced down the mountainside.

The creature was beautiful, and Cries Havoc somehow knew it meant him no harm. The sight of it should have made the night even more wonderful. But he sensed the entity was a harbinger of change. Of loss. He tried to avoid its lustrous golden eye but met it anyway. The creature spoke without words, and he understood. Why not? Even the first time, as a baby and nothing more, he'd somehow understood.

Young Garou, this is not your path. You have a duty, a destiny, and this trail will not take you there. Still, I will not intervene unless you give me leave.

What newborn could possibly give a spirit such permission? And yet Cries Havoc knew he'd done it. Perhaps some buried wisdom from a past life had prompted him, or perhaps the entity's shining grace and majesty had awed him into acquiescence. In any case, his tiny heart already breaking for a reason he didn't quite yet comprehend, he'd answered, *Yes. Come. Do it.*

He sensed that he needed to do the same thing now to keep the tale of his life unfolding as it ought. If he diverted the dream into wishes, lies and might-have-beens, it couldn't cure him. Still, it was amazingly hard to give the invitation. Before, he had been dead inside. Now, he knew joy. How could he renounce it? The cure might fail. He might return to the same crippled, useless condition.

Yet he had to try. Otherwise, he would break faith with the friends who had risked all to find this place. So he forced the voiceless message out: *Yes. Come. Do it.*

Defining a silver arc that reminded Cries Havoc fleetingly of the moon bridge, the unicorn leaped into the fugitive mother's path. Unicorn, totem spirit of the Children of Gaia, embodied peace and harmony, but her emissary held her black, whorled horn poised in an unmistakably threatening manner.

Mother cried out and tried to dodge around the beast. With an effortless bound, the spirit blocked her, then lunged forward. The point of the slender horn stopped an inch in front of the werewolf's throat.

Her eyes wide, Mother floundered a step or two backward. With a dip of her head, the unicorn signaled that the werewolf should lay Cries Havoc on the ground.

Mother refused and continued to refuse through several more futile attempts at escape, until, with another sudden thrust, the unicorn proved her willingness to maim and likely even kill. The Garou stumbled, and the scent of her blood filled the air.

Weeping, she looked at Cries Havoc. Kissed him. Embraced him. He screamed, *No, no, I didn't understand! I take it back!* The unicorn ignored him.

Mother set him down gently and limped away, leaving a trail of bloody drops behind her, and then, impossibly, she was gone. After a moment, the unicorn departed as well, perhaps to shadow her and make sure she didn't double back.

The adult Cries Havoc thought, *Unicorn chose me from the beginning, and I never knew.* But the realization didn't comfort him. The feelings of his infant self were far more compelling, and he found himself overwhelmed by grief, guilt, loneliness, hunger and the cold. He shrieked and sobbed until daybreak, when the pack found him.

"Strong set of lungs in this one," a scarred old Ahroun said.

Chapter Seventeen

Beating its black-feathered wings, the Bane followed Cries Havoc into the wood. The very essence of forgetfulness, it found this dream-realm of memory utterly unpleasant, save for the fact that he seemed able to mask his presence. What was it, after all, other than the absence of memory? And so it remained invisible and immaterial, following the Galliard into the woods. Once it got far enough from its victim's comrades, then it would make itself known. Then it would attack.

The business with the caern had been a fiasco from start to finish. The local Banes were obviously even punier, stupider and in general more degenerate even than their European counterpart had first imagined. How else could a mere five Garou survive the worst the wretches could throw at them?

The winged Bane had done its best to help its fellows but, amid the chaos, hadn't been able to nip a piece out of any Garou's mind. Though the spirit had gotten lucky with Storm-Eye on the hillside above the lake, that stealthy attack actually worked better when the target hadn't already assumed a defensive attitude.

Fortunately, the vulturelike spirit *had* managed to follow the Garou over the moon bridge, and now that Cries Havoc had separated from his packmates, it would rend him as it had before, and this time finish the job. It had to. Now that the Child of Gaia had, against all probability, fought his way this close to his remedy, the time for wary sniping and nibbling had past.

The Bane reckoned that his prey had walked far enough. It put on solidity above the Garou's head, opened its fanged jaws and dived.

The world blurred in front of it. The spirit didn't connect with any tangible target and had to flap its wings frantically to keep itself from slamming ignominiously into the ground.

It soared higher, looked down and found everything altered. Day had given way to night. The terrain, which had been relatively level, now tilted in the form of another mountainside, this one somehow different from all the ones the Bane had traversed on the trek into the heart of the Appalachians. Certainly the trees were different, with a sudden preponderance of fragrant conifers.

A female Garou in Crinos form was running down the slope with a horned, furry baby—Cries Havoc, obviously—in her arms. Intermittently obscured by trees and brush, a unicorn bounded along beside her a few yards to her left. Evidently she hadn't noticed the spirit yet.

The winged spirit dived twice more, enough to demonstrate conclusively that it couldn't touch the baby, mother or horned messenger, and they could neither touch nor see it.

The Bane felt a sickening surge of rage and panic. It had waited a moment too long, and Cries Havoc had passed beyond its reach into conjured memory. Jo'cllath'mattric's wrath would be as terrible as it was inescapable.

But no. The spirit refused to believe its mission would end this way. Surely it would find a final opportunity to keep Cries Havoc and his pack from further meddling in its master's affairs. It just had to wait for the proper moment. It perched on a limb and stared fixedly down at the little drama playing out below, like a true vulture waiting for something to die.

"…and so Crookedclaw paid the price of the Spirit of the Valley and won a bountiful new home for his people. Their long years of wandering had reached an end."

The tale had likewise come to its conclusion, and the eleven-year-old Cries Havoc looked hopefully at his teacher. Seated atop a chuck of log the Garou used for a bench, slender, blue eyed, and sun bronzed in human form, dressed in an old plaid shirt with rolled sleeves, Song-of-the-Waterfall visibly recognized his desperation and sought to offer encouragement. "That wasn't bad at all," she said.

The boy's shoulders slumped. "That just means it wasn't good enough." Actually, now that he'd had a moment to think, he knew it wasn't. He'd enjoyed telling the story, had gotten caught up in it, but certainly hadn't felt any miraculous powers stirring within him.

Her agate pendant flashing in the sun, the pretty blonde Galliard rose and hugged him. With her in human shape and him in Crinos, the adult and boy were about the same height.

Song-of-the-Waterfall had been so kind. Cries Havoc had had a huge crush on her and struggled mightily to conceal it. Now, reliving this hour, his adult perspective dominating for a moment, he suspected that she'd known perfectly well.

"You'll get it," she said. Elsewhere among the lodges, an ax thunked into the wood it was chopping. The aroma of elk stew cooking over a fire tinged the air.

"Was it my diction?" Cries Havoc asked. "My cadence? My tone? My acting?" Song-of-the-Waterfall had taught him all those things and more, and he'd done his best to apply them in his performance.

"In and of themselves, they were all good," she said. "I guess the pieces just haven't quite fallen into place yet."

"What if they never do?"

"That's a silly thing to say. How can they not? You were born under the storyteller's moon."

"Yeah, but I was born a metis." He could almost feel the weight of the grotesque horns on his brow. "What if I'm a freak on the inside, too? What if the spirits won't teach me any Gifts?"

Song-of-the-Waterfall frowned. "Did someone put that idea in your head? I'll smack him the length of this camp and back again!"

"No," said Cries Havoc, "everyone treats me okay. But I know what I am. Maybe I'm wasting my time. Your time. Maybe I should just work on my hunting, fighting and fishing. I'm halfway good at those."

The teacher sighed. "I hate hearing you say that. But I can't choose your path for you. I certainly can't turn anyone into a bard if he doesn't want to work to become one."

Once again, the older Cries Havoc, his awareness fading in and out from one moment to the next, felt that what she'd said was true. It defied rationality, but in some sense, he *could* choose a different path within the dream and avoid the years of frustration and humiliation that still lay before him, and though it would be a mad, self-destructive thing to do, he felt

Children of Gaia

the temptation nonetheless, perhaps even more keenly than the first time.

"I don't' know," he said. "It's not that I don't like learning stories and the ancient secrets. I do. I just don't know if there's any point to it, not for me."

"I can only tell you these things," Song-of-the-Waterfall said. "First, in all our people's lore, I have *never* found mention of a Garou to whom the spirits didn't see fit to give of themselves.

"Second, the Children of Gaia are the teachers and peacemakers of the Garou. When walking the human world, we try to guide that teeming race to a better understanding of the world we share, so they'll break off their unwitting alliance with corruption. Among our own kind, we try to allay strife among the tribes and unite our people for the final struggle against the Wyrm. Such being the case, who needs eloquence more than we? It would be sad indeed if you have it in you to become a great orator, a fountainhead of inspiration for all fortunate enough to hear you, and never develop the capacity.

"Finally, I promise I'll never, ever stop trying to teach you."

Cries Havoc snorted. "Even when I'm old, lame and toothless?"

"Even then, it will be a glorious day when the stories finally speak to you."

He cocked his head. "They do speak to me. I mean, I understand them. They teach me things."

"Which means you understand them in the same way that any listener does. But I've taught you that stories are literally living spirits, the Garou's partners and benefactors. They suffer us to bind them into graven glyphs, words lovingly composed and committed to memory, pantomimes, games and dances so we may know and disseminate truth. Without them, I suspect, we could not live at all. Certainly we would lack any culture or capacity to defend Gaia against the Wyrm."

"Yeah," said the boy, "I remember."

"But what you don't *truly* understand, and what's difficult to explain, is that one day, you'll start telling a story and directly perceive it for the spirit it is. The two of you will enter into a communion. He'll guide you in your telling, infusing your reflection of his essence with power. You'll *fascinate* your audience, and you'll see that the spirits have already gifted you plentifully."

"I...I wish I was as sure as you."

Song-of-the-Waterfall took hold of his chin and turned his head to look him in the eye. "My friend, nothing is certain in this life. All we can do is choose, strive and hope. What do you choose?"

Perhaps it was once again the thought of his friends, or maybe this time, it was the bond that he and his teacher had shared, but somehow he mustered the strength to commit for a second time to the long work ahead. "I'll stick to it," he said. "I'll keep trying."

Chapter Nineteen

Something tapped Cries Havoc on his pointed ear. Startled, he turned his eye, and a second missile, a loop of braided leather, hit him on the nose. Troutcatcher, Hears-the-Quiet and Wally, who opted to use his human name even among his fellow Garou, laughed.

"It's called ring-toss," said Troutcatcher. He had a square head and wide, rounded shoulders, with a flabbiness around his middle that even life in the wild hadn't yet managed to trim away.

Cries Havoc belatedly understood that the other three teenagers had been trying to throw the leather rings over his horns, as if he were a toy for their amusement. The realization filled him with mingled shame and rage. He sprang to his feet. In Crinos guise, he towered over the other pups, who, homid breed, generally wore the shapes of their births while in camp.

But the other boys weren't intimidated. He hadn't really expected them to be, not when they could shift form in an instant and outnumbered him three to one. "Hey, Freaky, it's just a game," said Troutcatcher, all mock innocence. "We thought maybe you'd want to play."

"Well, I don't," said Cries Havoc. "Leave me alone."

"No problem," said Troutcatcher, "as soon as we get done." He tossed another ring, trying to snag one of the horns that was now a yard above his head.

Cries Havoc swatted the leather out of the air. "I told you to quit!"

"How are you gonna make us?" Troutcatcher replied. "Run crying to Song-of-the-Waterfall?"

"I bet he's going to fight all three of us," said Wally, fair and freckled, his skin perpetually pink and peeling because most of the time he chose not to shield it with fur. Troutcatcher was always the instigator, but once he started harassing Cries Havoc, the other two invariably joined in soon enough. "And get his ass beat. That's the retarded thing to do, isn't it, retard?"

Maybe it is, Cries Havoc thought, *but I guess I'm going to try it anyway. What choice do I have?*

An answer came. Perhaps it had been trying to emerge from the back of his mind for a long time. *I could just turn around and leave, leave the mountains, leave everything Garou. Why not? Could the human world be any worse?*

It was hard to remember that he'd actually been glad when their parents brought Troutcatcher, Hears-the-Quiet and Wally to the camp. The boys had just passed through their First Changes and so revealed their werewolf natures, and he'd thought it would be fun to have septmates his own age. And for a little while, it was. Since the newcomers were ignorant of nearly every aspect of Garou life, he'd taught them all he could, and they'd seemed to appreciate it.

Gradually, though, their attitude changed. Once they underwent a Rite of Passage and gained the Gifts from the spirits, becoming full cliath, the differences became all too clear: after years at the sept, Cries Havoc was still a cub, and they blamed that on his metis nature. The Children of Gaia believed they should accord a werewolf with tainted blood the same rights as any other, but simply by proclaiming such a tradition they likewise underscored the fact that a metis was a mistake, a creature of dubious worth in need of special dispensation.

The newcomers had surely assimilated the sad truth of Cries Havoc's condition, but he still wasn't sure why that had prompted them to turn on him so completely. Perhaps it had something to do with the fact that prior to the trio's discovery, the sept hadn't located any new offspring for a number of years and so was inclined to spoil them. Maybe Troutcatcher, Hears-the-Quiet and Wally carried their own inner stain, one acquired from the Wyrm-infected madness of human civilization. Or possibly groups of young males simply had a natural urge to appoint a pariah to bully.

Whatever the reason, in time, the newcomers came to torment Cries Havoc relentlessly, and unfortunately, he didn't feel he could complain to the elders, not even Song-of-the-Waterfall. Especially coming from the malformed spiritual cripple, a plea for intercession would seem a weak, cowardly, un-Garou act. But he didn't know what else to do, nor how much more abuse he could take.

But I do know what to do, the adult Cries Havoc thought. *What I did. The notion takes hold of me, and I just cut loose.*

Under the circumstances, it should have been easy, but it wasn't. The young part of him didn't know what would happen. It feared looking foolish and giving the other youths further cause for scorn, and indeed, though it was probably crazy, the old part shared that dread. After all, he'd entered these memories because he was a broken vestige of his former self. Why, then, should he assume that he could do what he'd done before?

But ultimately, he knew he had to try. He'd promised John North Wind's Son he wouldn't jump off the damn bridge, and giving up would amount to pretty much the same thing.

It was hard, but he stretched his lips into a grin, the one Song-of-the-Waterfall had taught him to wear for reciting a satire or playing a game of insults. His tormentors' eyes widened. He'd surprised them.

"Maybe I am a retard," Cries Havoc said. "I'm definitely a freak. But at least I'm not a fat pig with a fat gut hanging off me, and at least my bowels don't give me any trouble."

Troutcatcher scowled. "What are you talking about?"

"You know. Two nights ago, you snatched way more than your share of the duck meat, like usual. But this time, you paid for it. Everybody heard you trying to shit."

"You're crazy," said Troutcatcher, but Hears-the-Quiet and Wally smiled a little despite themselves. Because everyone *had* heard.

"It went on for *hours*," Cries Havoc said. He let out an imitative groan, and then it was as if he'd opened another pair of eyes to a gorgeous radiance, or lightning had flashed inside his skull and illuminated every shadowy corner of his mind.

This mockery he was about to attempt was a story of a sort, and suddenly he perceived the tale spirit at the heart of it as plainly as he saw the three youths standing before him. The bodiless but vibrant entity was his partner, his brother, ready to guide him in the telling and charge his every word and gesture with a captivating power.

Cries Havoc had always assumed that if the mantle of Galliard ever descended on him at all, it would happen as he related one of the great sagas or laments of his people. He had no idea why a vulgar impersonation of a septmate's constipation should at long last invest him with his birthright, nor would he ever understand. But he didn't care. Here at the beginning of his new life, all he wanted to do was express his newly exalted nature. He barely even cared about striking back at Troutcatcher anymore.

But he would, because that was the essence of the story that he and the tale spirit had to tell. He screwed up his face into an expression that, despite the handicap of his lupine features, was both suggestive of Troutcatcher's human ones and a mask of cramping anguish. Squatting, clenching, shifting back and forth, he commenced a series of anguished moans mixed with desperate, humiliating prayers for relief addressed to any Umbral being that might be listening.

Mesmerized by this first profligate expression of Cries Havoc's storytelling arts, Troutcatcher's companions had no choice but to find the demonstration hilarious. Smaller and younger-looking than his friends, a KA-BAR knife clipped to his belt, Hears-the-Quiet laughed so hard that tears streaked his grubby face.

Troutcatcher wasn't amused, but the magic in the storyteller's voice and gestures froze him in place, while more of the pack wandered up to watch the performance. Cries Havoc finished with the subject of obstructed intestines and moved on to the shrieking, pissing terror the stocky boy had experienced the first time he found himself in proximity to a grizzly.

Finally Troutcatcher shook off his paralysis. He shifted to wolfman form, snarled and lunged, but Cries Havoc in his moment of glory was invincible. He knocked his attacker cold with a single, almost casual sweep of his arm.

The horned werewolf stared at Hears-the-Quiet and Wally until they dropped their eyes, showing submission and silently giving a pledge to tease him no more. Then he went to find Song-of-the-Waterfall and tell her of his transformation. Full to bursting with his long-awaited role, feeling as if he were discovering and declaiming each story and verse for the first time, he kept on reciting as he marched through the camp. So potent was the telling that everyone who'd listened to his ridicule of Troutcatcher trailed along behind him, and other Garou hurried out of the lodges.

He was finally ready for his Rite of Passage. Finally able to be a full, adult Garou.

Chapter Twenty

Clad in wolf form, with only his horns to mark him as anything more, Cries Havoc stalked along the narrow ledge and drank in the night. This far from human habitation, the stars shone brightly, although Garou tradition maintained that before the human invention of electricity, they had blazed more brilliantly still, even in the remotest reaches of the wild. That, the storyteller supposed, was a glory he'd never see.

Still, the night was more than lovely enough to satisfy a Child of the End Time. Miles to the south, coyotes ripped, making their music. The breeze was cool and bracing and carried the appetizing scent of bighorn sheep. Had Cries Havoc not just come from a sumptuous feast, he might have gone hunting them, but with a full belly, it was more pleasant simply to laze about the heights and admire the view across the mountains.

Then he caught a different scent, and it stopped being pleasant at all.

His sept had invited three others from across the Rockies to a moot, a weeklong council and celebration. Like the rest of the Galliards, Cries Havoc had provided entertainment. It was his first time offering a story to strangers, and he was nervous, but the telling went splendidly.

Afterwards he was too excited to sleep and too preoccupied with his success to pay much heed to the rest of the festivities. He'd drifted away from camp to savor his triumph and clear his head.

And now he smelled the foul reek of Wyrm-spawn. Unless he was mistaken, of *many* Wyrm-spawn.

He peered down over the drop-off. His eyes widened in shock. A column, a veritable army of Wyrm-spawn, was skulking along at the base of the mountain, marching on the moot with a silence that could be the product only of some rite or Gift of the Wyrm. He didn't have the skill or the experience to tell which abomination was a fomor, a Black Spiral Dancer or a materialized Bane, but he was sure there were plenty of all three.

To say the least, the Garou gathering was unprepared to receive them. Some of the werewolves were drowsing from a surfeit of food and drink. Others were busy singing, dancing, playing games, courting or deliberating. No one expected to fight a battle tonight.

Cries Havoc had to warn them. He drew a deep breath, then hesitated.

If he revealed his presence, he would have to try to get down from his perch and away, because the enemy could scarcely fail to catch him if he stayed put. But unfortunately, the descent was difficult, dangerous even for a werewolf if he tried to take it quickly. He would have to try, however, because for much of its height, the mountain offered only a couple trails. Everywhere else was impassable. Which meant the twisted creatures would have a good chance of intercepting him even if he descended slowly, and a sure thing if he took his time.

The lorekeeper thought, *The camp has sentries. They'll give the alert.*

Children of Gaia

Yes, but they'd be giving it minutes before the abominations attacked. If he dared, Cries Havoc could warn everyone an *hour* in advance, and the extra time could make all the difference.

He forced himself to throw back his head and howled out a sharp-pitched warning to the entire sept.

The Wyrm-spawn heard and recognized the call for what it was. Some of them started up the scree at the foot of the mountain.

Knowing he was racing for his life, Cries Havoc spun and dashed back along the precarious shelf. Soil crumbled beneath his paws, and the grit fell over the edge.

***

Cries Havoc drank another plastic cup of water. It almost tasted like a different substance with all the chemicals the humans put in it, but he knew that wasn't the reason why, a minute later, his mouth was dry again.

"Nervous?" asked Song-of-the-Waterfall, who had a drearier name in this world of highways and high-rises. The paper oval stuck to her jacket lapel proclaimed it.

"Yes," he said, resisting an urge to tug his necktie looser. "Maybe I'm not ready. Maybe you should handle this."

A plump, frazzled-looking member of the League of Women Voters floundered through the curtain, perhaps to make sure the debaters hadn't ducked out, as Cries Havoc rather wished he could. She saw the two werewolves in Homid guise and the Wal-Mart spokesman, smiled, and said, "We're almost ready." Then she flailed back through the layers of heavy, hanging cloth.

"Relax," Song-of-the-Waterfall murmured, her voice pitched low enough that no dull-eared human would overhear. "You'll be fine. You're a storyteller and this is just another audience. If anything, they'll be less rancorous than the sept."

"That won't matter if my opponent completely discredits me. What if the business people figured out I'm not a real biology professor?"

"They have no reason to doubt you, and even if they checked, Malcolm built you a paper life that will stand up to almost any scrutiny. They fabricated everything from your birth certificate to your last credit-card purchase."

Malcolm was Kinfolk, a human relation of the Children of Gaia. The change had never come over him, or any of his cousins that generation, but he made his own contribution to the struggle to save the world. Dealing with the bureaucracy of human life was his specialty; the sept had realized long ago that when dealing with humans, few words were as terrifying as "tax attorney."

"If you say so," Cries Havoc said.

"Brighten up! You can do this. You were born to it, and it may be the most important thing any Garou can do to oppose the Wyrm. Listen, Mr. Caulder is announcing you."

The younger werewolf turned, and his horned shadow glided along the curtain. He froze, abruptly, crazily certain that if he stepped through, all the people in the rows of tightly packed, weirdly identical seats would see the deformity, too.

He realized it was nonsense. Hears-the-Quiet, who'd matured into a Theurge to be reckoned with, had called on a moth spirit to veil the horns from human sight.

Or had he? He loved to play pranks on Cries Havoc, didn't he? What if he'd arranged for the mask to fall at the worst possible moment?

The storyteller shook his head. He was just apprehensive about addressing his first human audience, about all the sept depending on his eloquence, and it was making him fret over nonexistent concerns. He'd mended his quarrel with Hears-the-Quiet long ago, and even if he hadn't, his septmate wouldn't dare sabotage a mission of genuine importance. The evening would go all right. Cries Havoc *remembered* it going all right.

The moderator finished listing the storyteller's bogus credentials. The corporate spokesman, who smelled of coffee and whose chestnut hair looked like a single sculpted piece of leather, gave the metis a surprisingly friendly smile. Then the two of them walked out onto the stage of the high school auditorium, where they would argue the wisdom of cutting down a stand of ancient trees to erect something called a *warehouse store*.

***

"It's an honor to be chosen," said Song-of-the-Waterfall.

"I know." Cries Havoc didn't sound convinced.

"It *is*. It means the pack elders think you're the most sensible of all our youths, the one most likely to reflect credit on us."

"I appreciate it. I just wonder what they think about metis at the Sept of the Dawn." *And if I'll ever see you again, or anyone else from our sept.*

"Dawntreader's people are Children of Gaia no less than we. They will treat you like one of their own."

"I guess, but I've barely been outside of Colorado. This is the Ukraine we're talking about."

She sighed. "I truly believe this plan of fostering the young between septs and even tribes is important. It will unite us all to stand against the Wyrm. But no one will force you to go if you can't stand the thought of it."

She'd offered a reprieve, and he wanted to take it. The young half of him feared the future. The old half *knew* that at times, life would be hard at the Sept of the Dawn, and harder still when he moved on to the Sept of the Anvil-Klaiven and had to fight for an honorable place among the harsh Get of Fenris.

He did his best to swallow his reluctance. "No, it's all right. I'll go. Maybe I'll pick up some new stories."

***

And so it went. Cries Havoc relived one incident after the next. Most involved a choice he'd made, and no matter how vehemently he insisted to himself that it would be madness to deviate from the path he'd walked before, still, every fear, doubt and pain whispered to him, enticing him to take an easier way. Somehow he resisted.

Chapter Twenty-One

Hunkered in its tree, talons clutching the limb beneath it and tail wrapped around another, the vulture-thing watched its victim's life replaying. The highlights, anyway.

The winged Bane was glad the dream was proceeding so rapidly. In another minute or two, the parade of memories would reach its conclusion and then presumably restore Cries Havoc to the same frame of reference as his nemesis. At that moment, it wouldn't matter if the bard had healed or not, because the spirit would strike him down immediately.

Or so the Bane thought, until it heard rustling in the foliage and the she-wolf Storm-Eye's blunt, commanding voice. Startled, the vulture-thing wrenched itself around on its perch to see how the rest of the Silver River Pack had crept so close without it noticing.

Then the Bane felt a pang of annoyance at its own confusion. Storm-Eye and the others hadn't actually entered the wood. Instead, commencing a new phase, Cries Havoc's dream had created phantoms in their images.

The shadow show had cast up another apparition as well. When the vulture saw it, it discerned exactly what was about to transpire. The realization inspired a clever notion, a ploy to help the stalker take its prey by complete surprise.

Chapter Twenty-Two

The last choice was the most difficult of all. Knowing what was coming, Cries Havoc could run away from it. Or he could stand and endure indescribable agony.

The Silver River Pack had journeyed deep into the Wyrm's territory when the Child of Gaia caught sight of a strange sort of Bane. It had no real body connecting its two black-feathered wings, just a pair of fearsome jaws, with long fangs that made them resemble a giant staple-remover, clawed raptor feet and a lashing whip of a tail. Though Cries Havoc had never encountered such an abomination before, he knew a little about its breed from his studies. He started to share the information with his comrades.

Then suddenly, somehow, the abomination was right on top of him. It caught the werewolf in its fangs and savaged him. He could feel the spikelike teeth tearing away pieces of his flesh and soul. The pain was unbearable, and he blacked out. When he came to, the Bane was diving for a second attack.

Cries Havoc had resolved to live the dream as he had lived his life, to accept every adversity he had known before. He stood still and waited for the Lore Bane—he knew its name again—to seize him.

Then he noticed that, even though they certainly hadn't deserted him the first time around, his packmates had disappeared. The landscape no longer looked like a blighted Serbian city, but rather the Umbral wood where his visions had commenced. Moreover, a newly recovered memory told him that during their first encounter, the vulture-thing had flown at him only once.

This, then, was no longer a dream. It was really happening, and the spirit was nearly upon him.

Cries Havoc frantically flung himself down and to the side. The talons barely missed him. The flexible bludgeon of a tail clipped him, but not squarely enough to do much damage.

The Lore Bane hurtled past and soared upward, no doubt gaining altitude for another pass. Meanwhile, Cries Havoc took stock of himself. Was he healed?

He couldn't tell. Before, he had been empty. Now, he was full but felt an ambiguity, as if his ordeal might not have stuffed all his spiritual bones and viscera back in the right places. Certainly his Gifts still seemed out of reach. He snarled in frustration.

The vulture-thing plunged down at him, this time with a cunning zigzag in its trajectory that made its prey dodge in the wrong direction. Cries Havoc corrected, but not quickly enough, for now that he'd returned to conventional reality, his injuries from the previous battles slowed him. A talon opened a gash in his shoulder. He lashed out with a riposte, which didn't land. The abomination climbed.

Cries Havoc realized that if he couldn't employ the full range of his Garou abilities, he was unquestionably going to die. He thought of calling to his packmates for succor, but his instincts forbade it. For good or ill, this was *his* fight.

He did use his voice, though, in one last attempt to unlock his powers. He tried to tell the story that John North Wind's Son had shared atop the bridge.

"In the sweet morning of the world, when Luna's face was as clear as a sheet of freshly fallen snow, and malice, rare as a fish in a desert…"

The vulture-thing dived. Somehow Cries Havoc evaded without the effort throwing off his tone or rhythm.

"Bright of eye, sharp of tooth and fleet of foot, Laughs-at-Pines-Cones walked…"

And the Child's powers roared up inside him like a geyser. His bardic talents. Gifts from spirits gained during his years in the Rockies and in the Ukraine. The rage, a fire to burn soreness and fatigue away. Everything was there.

Certainly his passions were. In other circumstances, he would likely have collapsed weeping with joy at his restoration. But he had a Lore Bane to kill. Fortunately, that too would bring him pleasure.

Chapter Twenty-Three

The Lore Bane dived. Exalted by a fury that, paradoxically, did nothing to diminish his clarity of thought, Cries Havoc filled his lungs and shouted. His bellow seemed percussive as a thunderclap and ended with a sharp snarl. *I am your end*, the call said to the Lore Bane in a way no human speech could.

The vulture-thing lurched and flailed its wings spastically. It looked like it would fall out of the air, and the storyteller grinned. Then his foe snapped its black-feathered appendages, regained the proper attitude for controlled flight and hurtled at him.

The ploy caught Cries Havoc by surprise, but the rage made him strong and quick as he had ever been in his life, and he still managed to spin out of the Lore Bane's path, meanwhile swinging his arm in a horizontal arc. His hand slammed into the abomination's tail, and his claws plunged into its rubbery flesh.

He tried to hold on, but with a frantic jerk of the member, the Lore Bane pulled free and fell on the ground before him. He lunged, and the Wyrm-spawn pivoted. One of its wings slapped him in the face. Though it didn't injure him, it startled and balked him for the instant the creature needed to heave itself back into the air.

Drops of steaming black ichor fell from the punctured tail. Cries Havoc laughed, partially to goad the Bane into doing something stupid but with honest pleasure as well.

Not as easy, is it, he thought, *when I'm fully myself, and you haven't taken me by surprise*.

He beckoned to his adversary, then spread his arms wide, exposing his torso in invitation. More important, he uttered a series of yips and yelps that, even if a listener were ignorant of the Garou tongue, conveyed a scathing, maddening derision.

The Lore Bane dived. If Cries Havoc had succeeded in driving it crazy with anger, it should be coming in hard and straight, without any tricks or deceptive maneuvering. The werewolf stood in place until the spirit was almost upon him. At the last possible moment, he sidestepped and grabbed one of the wings.

The Wyrm-spawn's momentum nearly yanked him over, but throwing his weight against it, he managed to keep his feet. This time, the Lore Bane crashed down hard.

Cries Havoc tore and twisted the spirit's pinion. He hoped that if he disabled it and kept the Bane on the ground, he could finish it.

Feathers flew, flesh tore and dark, scalding ichor splashed. He was sure the bones in the wing were starting to give way. Then the tip of the Lore Bane's tail lashed at his knee.

He sensed the attack coming and jerked his leg back out of harm's way. The frantic evasion must have loosened his grip, however, because the Lore Bane wrenched free, leaving handfuls of its meat and gore behind.

Cries Havoc dropped them and grabbed for a new hold. The tail whipped at him, this time cracking him painfully across the knuckles of his right hand. Wings beating, the Bane hopped around and bit at him.

The Galliard twisted aside and seemingly escaped grievous injury. The point of one of the abomination's lower fangs merely grazed his thigh. He struck, clawed away a gob of flesh at the top of the Lore Bane's mouth and started to follow up.

Pain broke through his energizing rage and locked up his muscles. The fang had barely cut him, but it was a fresh wound to his spirit as well as his body, and it *hurt!* Shadow drowned the wood as he started to pass out, the same as he had the first time. He roared, seeking the fury once more, and it surged up and masked the agony.

Believing him incapacitated, the Lore Bane had spread its jaws wide to gulp him in. He deterred it with a slash of his claws, inflicting another wound above the mouth. Alas, he hadn't quite recovered his balance from the spasm, and before he could strike another blow, the Wyrm-spawn took to the air with a frantic flailing.

Cries Havoc was a little disappointed that it could still fly, albeit now in a floundering, lurching, unbalanced kind of way. Hoping it wouldn't use its wings to flee the battle, he resumed taunting it.

Please come back down. I have more tricks to show you.

Chapter Twenty-Four

Somewhere among the trees, a Garou roared. The sound was sudden and preternaturally frightening. Startled, Julia nearly dropped her handheld computer.

"Was that Cries Havoc?" asked North Wind's Son.

"The cry had power in it," the English werewolf said. "It may well have been the voice of a Galliard."

"Does that mean he's okay?" asked Big Sis, her fang dagger, still spattered brown with dried gore, lying beside her on the grass.

Be quiet, Storm-Eye yipped in wolf-tongue. *Keep listening.*

When they did, they heard thumping, lashing and scraping noises that sounded like a duel or battle. The breeze carried them the scent of fresh werewolf blood and a hot stink that might be the life essence of a Bane. An abrasive yelping commenced.

"Cries Havoc's in a fight." John North Wind's Son's icicle pendant glinted in the Umbral light as he assumed his towering Crinos form. "Do we go help him?"

Julia closed her computer case. "He said he needed to complete his cure unassisted—"

"Who cares what he said?" snapped Big Sis. "He's like, brain damaged, right? That's why we're here."

"Let me finish!" Julia took a moment to suppress a sudden urge to lash out at the infuriating Bone Gnawer. "I was attempting to say that while he wanted to be alone, this doesn't feel like a healing rite or a vision quest to me. I sense a genuine combat. I think we should find him."

"Then we will," said Storm-Eye, now using the Garou tongue. "Carlita, how is your leg?"

"Much better." Big Sis, who had stayed in wolf-woman form, pointed down at her leg, which had a nasty scar but seemed otherwise to be healed. Gaia's gift of healing was a great one indeed. "Think this'll score me a special place in Cries-for-Mama's stories?"

Storm-Eye didn't bother answering. "Come, then."

Chapter Twenty-Five

From its vantage point flying above the trees, the Lore Bane abruptly spotted the other four werewolves loping through the wood. This was it, then. The creature knew it couldn't fight them all. If it couldn't kill Cries Havoc within the next minute or so, it would never kill him at all.

Unfortunately, at the moment, the storyteller was winning the fight. The vulture-thing was grievously wounded. Its strength was failing, and it was grueling labor simply to stay aloft. The mangled wing throbbed with every beat. And here in this Umbral subrealm, this werewolf could actually destroy it outright rather than simply shattering a physical shell.

Even more debilitating than the pain was the sound of Cries Havoc's voice. The taunting jabbed inside the spirit's mind and made it too angry to think.

It struggled to ignore the yelping. It had to come up with a plan quickly, a way to slaughter the Child of Gaia even at the cost of its own existence. It feared its lord too profoundly to contemplate any other course, for surely Jo'cllath'mattric could find and punish it anywhere in any world, in any condition of life or death.

No matter how it tried, the Lore Bane could think only of one stratagem. It was less than delighted with the idea, because it would further dilute its already ebbing might, and because it had only a remote chance of success. It was tremendously difficult to damage a werewolf's spirit with a ghostly tendril when the beastman was already on his guard. Yet the Lore Bane had to try something, and so it frayed the outer surfaces of its body into long, invisible, insubstantial threads. Then it dived at its foe.

As before, Cries Havoc didn't shift into any sort of obvious fighting stance. He just stood casually, looking incapable of protecting himself against a swift attack.

The Lore Bane had learned just how misleading that appearance was. This time, however, it reckoned it had outsmarted the Garou. No matter what trick Cries Havoc had in mind, he couldn't hurt the Wyrm spirit if it didn't swoop down low enough for him to reach, and it had no intention of doing so. Not yet.

The winged Bane started to arrange its spectral tentacles for a sweep along the ground. Cries Havoc left off yipping, swung his arm back, then lashed it forward.

It seemed a pointless action until the Lore Bane noticed the stone hurtling through the air, and then it was astounded. The werewolf's hands had been empty. The vulture-thing had perceived the fact clearly. Where, then, had the rock come from? Damn the nature spirits who taught these beastmen their Gifts!

The Lore Bane tried to dodge, but it had spotted the missile too late. Impelled by a Garou's strength, the stone hit harder than the spirit would have believed possible. The shock paralyzed it, and it plummeted.

On the way down, however, the Bane had one piece of extraordinary luck. It felt the end of one of its flailing, intangible arms tear into Cries Havoc's soul like a fishhook.

Then the Lore Bane crashed into the ground. The universe seemed to skip somehow, and it realized it had passed out and roused. Its body was crumpled and shattered. It would never fly again nor, most likely, survive the next few minutes.

Casting about with its eyeless senses, it discerned Cries Havoc lying motionless save for the rise and fall of his chest. The Bane had to reach him before his packmates arrived on the scene.

Every move a torture, the Lore Bane dragged itself across the ground to its prey. It clambered on top of him, pinning his limbs with its broken legs and tail. They were still good for that much, anyway. Then it opened its jaws to plunge its fangs into his head,

The werewolf's eyes flew open. *Just a second too late*, the Wyrm spirit gloated. *You're helpless now*.

Cries Havoc dipped his head and brought it up. The Lore Bane's jaws snapped shut over his head, but caught on his hard ram horns. Unable, or unwilling, to release its surprisingly hard-shelled prey, the Bane was momentarily paralyzed.

Cries Havoc plunged his clawed hand into the thing with all his might.

Chapter Twenty-Six

Cries Havoc sensed that he had struck a mortal blow, but he wasn't prepared for what happened next. The Lore Bane exploded.

He flinched from the blast, but nothing struck him. Nothing tangible, anyway. At the moment of dissolution, the abomination's substance changed. One portion, a foulness, simply dissolved. The rest turned into tale spirits.

Exulting, the ghostly entities swooped and darted about. Several flashed into Cries Havoc's head. His own stories and memories returned to him in their entirety, while new tales revealed themselves in a silent, ecstatic cacophony. Many, their living embodiments proclaimed, had not been heard for generations.

Then it was over. The spirits vanished from his ken until such time as he would tell their stories.

The revelations left him feeling blissfully dazed. He shook his head and looked around.

His packmates were standing just a few yards away. They looked drunk, too. He realized there'd been too many tale spirits flying around for anyone, even a Galliard, to encounter all at once. The extra ones had struck sparks in the minds of his friends.

"Mother Eldridge and the rest of 'em back in Tampa ain't ever gonna believe some of these stories!" Grinning wildly, Carlita walked toward Cries Havoc. "You gonna make me look like prime alpha material back home, *amigo*."

Walking just behind the Bone Gnawer, Julia sighed. "Thank goodness you grasp the greater implications."

Big Sis blinked. "Was that a slam?"

Storm-Eye said, "Cries Havoc. You have recovered yourself?"

"Yes," the storyteller said, "thanks to my pack. Laughs-at-Pine-Cones had the river, the earth and the forest to heal him, and I had you."

"You're welcome," said North Wind's Son. "Now, what just happened? Was that the same Bane that tore you up in Serbia?"

"Yes. It followed us all this way, apparently to make sure I'd never get better."

The Wendigo winced. "I'm supposed to be the Ahroun, the warrior, the sentry, and I never spotted it."

"I'm the Theurge," said Julia, "the expert on spirits, and I never did either. It was attacking us in some subtle way, wasn't it, stealing one bit of memory at a time? That's why our minds kept freezing and glitching."

Cries Havoc nodded. "I wasn't contagious after all."

"No one ever thought you were," said Storm-Eye. "What happened when the Bane died? My stolen memories came back to me, but I have new things in my head as well, legends no Galliard ever taught me."

"The vulture-thing was a Lore Bane." The fresh slice in Cries Havoc's shoulder gave him a twinge, and he shrugged the pain away. "I'd heard of them, heard they consumed stories somehow, but I didn't know just how literally true it was. I still don't entirely

Children of Gaia

understand how it works, but the abomination had tale spirits trapped inside it. Maybe it was leeching strength from them. When I killed it, I set them free, and they shared themselves with us."

John North Wind's Son narrowed his eyes. "We Garou have lost a lot of secrets, things we need to beat the Wyrm. And there are more Lore Banes."

"With who knows what information pent up inside them," Julia said. "It may be possible to recover every piece of data, every *weapon* we've forgotten."

"This is big," said Big Sis.

Julia smiled. "To say the least."

"Then is this it?" Big Sis asked. "The reason Antonine said there had to be a third pack, the white light led us into the mountains, and the old caern was waiting for us? Have we done what we're supposed to do? After we tell the other Garou what we found out, can we kick back?"

Storm-Eye smiled one of her infrequent smiles. "The war is not over, and my instinct tells me the Silver River Pack has only begun its work."

Cries Havoc looked as his companions and felt all the love he had been unable to find on his long trek toward redemption. "That's all right with me."

About the Author

Richard Lee Byers holds an M.A. in Psychology. He worked in an emergency psychiatric facility for over a decade, then left the mental health field to become a writer. He is the author of more than fifteen novels, including *The Shattered Mask*, *Soul Killer*, *The Vampire's Apprentice*, *Dead Time*, *Dark Fortune*, and, in the World of Darkness, **On a Darkling Plain, Caravan of Shadows, Netherworld,** and **Dark Kingdoms.** His short fiction appears in numerous anthologies. A resident of the Tampa Bay area, a setting for much of his horror fiction, he spends much of his free time fencing and is a frequent guest at Florida SF conventions.

TRIBE NOVEL:

Uktena

STEFAN PETRUCHA

author:	stefan petrucha
cover artist:	steve prescott
series editors:	eric griffin
	john h. steele
	stewart wieck
copyeditor:	jeanée ledoux
graphic designer:	aaron voss
art director:	richard thomas

More information and previews available at
white–wolf.com/clannovels

ISBN 1-58846-812-7
First Edition: March 2002
Printed in Canada.

White Wolf Publishing
735 Park North Boulevard, Suite 128
Clarkston, GA 30021
www.white-wolf.com/fiction

Acknowledgments

A very special thanks to Eric Griffin, who provided not only much guidance and encouragement, but also the idea for the finale. Thanks also to Ethan Skemp, John H. Steele, Carl Bowen and, of course, Stewart Wieck, for the opportunity to once more put forth my words before an unwary public.

TRIBE NOVEL:

Uktena

STEFAN PETRUCHA

Chapter One

My shame is as big as the earth.
—Motavato (Black Kettle) of the Southern
Cheyennes

"…'twas a full seconds five before the vile fomor
realized the feet he now faced were his own. Though
he was dying himself from a score of pulpy, infected
wounds, the final swipe of brave Clackton's klaive
had completely severed the head of Gaia's enemy,
allowing the creature a glimpse of its own twisted body
before its tainted consciousness faded from
existence…forever!"

A pause. Some silence. And then.

With no immediate word coming from Claws,
Amy Hundred-Voices tried to go back to sewing her
Kente cloth. The purple, black and white design she
was working into the fabric was named "Mother Hen,"
or in the language of the African Asante tribe,
"*Akokobaatan*." Translated, it meant, "when the hen
steps on the feet of her chicks, she does not mean to
kill them." She began working on it over a year ago
and intended the blanket to symbolize motherhood,
tenderness, parental care and discipline, concepts she
once thought appropriate for an Uktena songkeeper—
giving birth to song, caring for secrets so they should
not wander off into the wrong hands. Now she was
thinking mostly about the children she'd felt she
stepped on. As she sewed, she paused repeatedly to
look up at Claws, waiting for him to venture some
comment on her tale. Chottle, her third packmate,

was equally silent, but that was to be expected given that the sad metis could hardly speak at all.

"That was…a lousy story," Claws with Teeth finally said. Then he wedged the tip of his tongue twixt gum and incisor in an effort to dislodge a piece of raw rabbit. The rebuke pinched a nerve in the teller, but the feeling, rather than fanning into rage, shriveled into an embarrassed pang. Hoping to find some balm for her pride in the wide Nebraskan night sky, she looked up, only to see a wrinkled cloud above the waxing half-moon, giving Luna the look of a wry, disappointed eye. Even the moon disapproved.

So, without the posturing and deep offense most songkeepers offer, she made a gruff shrug with her human shoulders and admitted in a near mumble, "Yeah, it was."

Seven years since her First Change, six as an active songkeeper for the Uktena and five years of hard study under masters both human and Garou. She'd even earned a bachelor's degree in Native American Mythic Traditions from the University of New Mexico, and a Master's in Occidental Culture, both under the careful guidance of the renowned Professor Randolph Stinton. But her stories still sucked. Her tellings had gotten even worse since their return from the disaster in Alaska. Sometimes it seemed the only thing she could do for the Garou was occasionally hit something with an arrow launched from her fetish bow, and even that was more practice than natural talent.

With a sigh, she pulled her calves into a half-lotus and asked her packmate, while trying to seem nonchalant, "Any idea why it was a lousy story?"

Still poking and clicking with tongue and teeth, the young warrior rolled up onto all fours. "Well...what the hell is 'a full seconds five?'"

"It was a reference to *The Tempest*, you know? 'Full fathoms five thy father lies?'"

Claws covered his head with his hands and pushed his palms back across his thick, furry scalp. "Please! Let's either kill something else or find a place to sleep," he said. Then he added, jokingly, "You sure about your auspice? Maybe you're just not supposed to be a songkeeper."

Amy forced herself to rear up at that: "Yes, I'm sure! At least I've got the keeping part down."

"Yeah, but if you keep things too long, sometimes they go bad," Claws observed. Before he could complete a chuckle, Amy leapt on him, rolling the muscular twenty-year-old into the tall, dry stalks of the wheat field where they had stopped to rest. When he came to a stop, the flaps of his torn denim jacket piled under the small of his back, she had her knees in his chest and her thumbs firmly planted on his throat.

"*Non ogni giorno è festa*," Amy said, pushing her thumbs down just enough to show she meant business. When he looked more confused than cowed by her use of Italian, she added, "Not every day is a holiday, little man."

"Easy! Just wanted to make sure you were still alive in there. You've been in a dark place since you found that stupid hunk of bone and leather in Alaska," Claws spat.

"There's been lots to brood about," Amy said. She gave him a little bow and let him rise.

"It's not your fault the Wendigo of Greyrock Sept died, Amy. We're Garou, we live, we fight, we die. Okay, and sometimes we look for ancient cities, but if we hadn't been on your quest for the Great Shopping Mall of the Hutsa-whatsis, we just would have died with them," he said.

Once on his feet, Claws morphed into the wolfman Crinos form, in which his fur was mostly black, with a few streaks of white along his powerful arms and legs. In part he wanted to impress Amy with his size, lest she entertain any notion that she was a real match for him, but mostly, he wanted to alter the size of his mouth and better clean his teeth. With a final nudge, the rabbit came loose and he sucked the tiny piece of meat onto his tongue. The edges of his half-snout rolled into a satisfied grin as he swallowed the offending morsel with a gulp.

"*Got it!*" he beamed, as if felling a foe.

Amy shook her head, marveling that the death of an entire Wendigo sept hadn't left more of a mark on his mood. He wasn't stupid, or unfeeling. On occasion, he even said things that hinted at wisdom. But those comments were so few and far between, it was easy for her to dismiss them as the lucky gems of a wandering mind. She may sometimes call him "Chews with Hands," and mean it in the worst possible way, but even now she admired his comfort with himself. She wondered how quickly that comfort would vanish if she told him the whole story.

Licking his chops, Claws nodded toward a tall stone outcropping a half mile northwest. It looked odd amidst all the flatness but would provide a good view of their surroundings. "Camp for the day? If you think Chottle can manage the climb." He spoke in the strange half-growled, half-spoken High Tongue of werewolves, which Amy had taught him and insisted he use when not in human form, for practice.

Amy nodded her oval head, wiped her own black hair back from her forehead and stood. Her dark eyes, Asian in shape but African in color, made a final scan of the low, flat area in which they'd enjoyed their minor meal. To the northwest were some paltry woods and a glimpse of the river they followed. Beyond that was the hilly area where they did most of their traveling. With scant pickings, the scent of rabbit had brought them out from the tree cover. Here, the long, deep, cultivated fields of grain, little more than blue and white lines in the moonlight, made the hunt quick and easy—but they were also a great impediment to Amy's secondary purpose: finding traces of the ancients. If there were signs of old trails, campsites or burial mounds anywhere nearby, she wasn't seeing them. Even a quick peek into the Umbra, where the spirits of all things became visible, revealed only the ghosts of a few settlers' homes, little more than two hundred years old.

Satisfied that there wasn't anything to miss, she packed her sewing into her handmade rucksack, turned back to the outcropping and shifted to Lupus, the wolf form, to speed the journey. With Claws and Chottle on either side, the standard formation, the pack reached the base in a few minutes.

As she clambered up the side of the stone, Amy kept looking back to check on Chottle's progress. Though born in Alaska, here in the flatter, less turbulent terrain, his ground speed was practically acceptable, and he could even hunt with some success. Still, he had terrific difficulty climbing, and now on the outcropping, his awkward form had gotten itself wedged between a crevice and a foothold. Having no idea how to free himself, he repeated the same sad movement over and over again, with the same result.

As the Wendigo of Greyrock told it, his mother screamed louder upon first seeing him than she had during the terrible birth. The pitiful thing, so deformed it could hardly be called he or she, spent years passed from Wendigo pack to pack in the hope that time would bring it some stability, or that Gaia or a great spirit would reveal some purpose for him, or that he would die of his own accord. Eventually, he'd been left at the Greyrock Sept, where his help with the simpler chores often complicated things. In the days before their own destruction, there was still talk among the warriors that he should be exposed to the elements and left to die. Even so, Amy had been quite surprised to learn that they hadn't even named him. Though he slowed them down and made them look even more suspicious, she insisted he remain with them.

She didn't know what he thought or felt, or if he even did either exactly, but from the start she felt a connection, if only because his physicality, especially now, stuck in the middle of a simple climb, seemed to echo the shape of her sadness: Can't go forward. Can't go back. Can't stay. Pinned in an untenable present, trapped by an unfathomable past, headed for a bleak future.

In perhaps a mere imitation of optimism, she tried to convince herself that if she could somehow reach him, offer proper care and guidance, the sole survivor of Greyrock might one day take part in his auspice as a Ragabash trickster and become more than he seemed. But other than her desire, and her failed efforts, there'd been no indications this might ever be the case.

While Amy nudged Chottle along, Claws leapt up onto the top of the rock and shifted from Lupus to Glabro. Except in times of battle, the Neanderthalic near-man was his favorite of the forms. He enjoyed the extra body weight and even the raspy quality his voice had when he spoke English. Claws always thought his Homid voice, naturally a tenor, was too high pitched for a proper Garou warrior. He caught a glimpse of the Loup River, which they'd be following toward the sept, just to the north. Sniffing the air, he turned northeast, toward a dim haze on the horizon.

"Fullerton rises early. It must be 5 A.M. Anyway, we're still maybe a hundred miles from the Sept of the Hungry Flower. A half day if we take it slowly, but like it or not, Amy, soon we'll be there."

The last to reach the outcropping, Chottle pressed his head into the dirt and rubbed what must have been his forehead against the ground, as if scratching an itch.

"There…there…there," he repeated in perfect imitation of Claws' pitch and tone. He would often latch onto the last syllable of a sentence and repeat it, as if he were a broken recorder with only a few seconds of memory.

Suddenly, Chottle moaned a bit and quivered. The flesh of his form pulsed and puffed. Amy, now Homid, lay her quiver of arrows, her fetish bow and her handmade rucksack on the ground and frowned, puzzled.

"He's changed," she finally decided.

"Did he? Are you sure?"

"Yeah. Look. There's at least another foot of him."

"Maybe. But what do you think he is?"

"Depends. What do you think he *was*?"

For most Garou, during the change there was a specific moment when the center of balance shifted. How one managed that shift in balance said a lot about what one was. Many Uktena warriors, like Claws, tended to fall forward with a lusty, threatening thud. Shamans moved with the change, trying to conceal the shift in balance altogether, so the change itself became the focal point to an observer. Amy tried to make it more of a dance, though she hadn't noticed many other songkeepers doing so.

But for Chottle, it was more like a plate of Jell-O had shifted from left to right. It was difficult, to say the least, to determine exactly which form Chottle had assumed, since there often seemed to be no discernible difference.

"Hispo?" Claws ventured.

"No. Too much skin," Amy said, twisting her head to the side. "Crinos?"

Claws stepped closer, "Maybe. Is that an ear or just some fur?"

Amy leaned down for a closer look. Though the top of her knee brushed the spot and her nose was less than an inch from it, she still couldn't tell if it was cartilage or hair.

"Poor Chottle," Amy whispered. "No one can even tell what shape you're in."

"Urine...urine...urine," Chottle said. Claws picked his head up and gave Amy a half grin.

"He making fun of you?"

"I hope so. At least it would be a sign of life." Turning to Claws, she said, "I know why he's here. He doesn't have much of a choice. But why do you stay with me, Claws?"

He thought about it for a moment, then answered, "I like the way you move when you hunt."

By the time they settled in, a band of deep, rich red at the horizon was eating away at the lower stars. Though there were no fingers to it to be seen, she wistfully intoned, "*Rhododaktulos eos.*" The Greeks had no equal in speaking of the rosy-fingered dawn.

Her companions didn't hear, but even if they had, it would have been Greek to them. Claws was already asleep. Chottle was doing whatever it was Chottle did.

To fend off an increasingly familiar gloom, Amy tried to hum a song, but she wasn't very good at that either. Unable to continue sewing, she played absently with the alternating Nordic runestones, I-Ching coins and Tarot symbols that comprised her homemade necklace, but as she rubbed the metal and ivory pieces between thumb and forefinger, she found them pretentious. Intended as a symbol of her diversity, they seemed more an indication of her lack of focus. Without some physical focal point, Amy's mind raced, grinding dry thoughts that burned and chafed.

Though she was loath to admit it, finding signs of the ancients wasn't why she was here. She was here because she'd been called to task. She was here because others were worried about her, suspicious. She was here because the Wendigo likely sought her death. It all seemed as hopeless as the land she was in. Looking over the fields, the distant farm buildings, the vast stretches of utter flatness, she knew in her heart that any war to restore this place to the Mother, to Gaia, was long over, and wondered if her own fate had already been similarly sealed.

She should be in South America, among the rain forests, where the real battle was being lost. Professor Stinton was there, driven by his desire to do some good and studying Mayan ruins in his spare time. And he, a mere human, not even Kinfolk, knew nothing of the Garou, the supposed protectors of the Wyld. Claws talked of going, but he had feelings for Amy, as well as a bit of a lazy streak. Instead they were here, in what even she thought of as occupied territory or, worse still, some minor variation on Vichy, France.

Can't go forward. Can't go back. Can't stay.

In Washington State, where they rested in the shadow of Mt. Ranier, licking their wounds, a few weeks after their return from Alaska, a terribly formal messenger approached their camp, bloated with ritual and circus. His head in Crinos, his body human, he took twenty minutes to say what could have been conveyed in a single short, declarative sentence: Amy Hundred-Voices was requested to appear, at her earliest convenience, before Johnny

Sees the Wind, an Uktena elder, at the Nebraskan Sept of the Hungry Flower. The reason: to discuss a matter pertaining to her future and the future of her tribe. As a capper, the messenger insisted on rattling off everyone's lineage, then doing a little dance about how he defeated a fomor and ate a rabbit before he found them.

Refusal would have been suicide, she knew. Her instability, mood swings and complete inability to tell a decent story were well known among the Uktena, and all had increased threefold since Alaska—and, far worse still, she had not yet told anyone the story of what had happened there. She hadn't refused as much as avoided it with an incredible lack of grace. Word about that traveled faster and wider than any story she'd ever told. In some corners it even beat out news about the recent events in Europe. As a result, as far as anyone knew, she and Claws had murdered them all in their sleep. Ever since, they felt watched and followed. The invitation was the Uktena way of reaching out to her.

At best, they likely feared she was headed straight for Harano, the deep, black depression that took as many Garou as did the war. At worst, that she'd been tainted by the Wyrm. Of course, the Uktena would do all they could to prevent losing another one of their number to depression. And now someone, somewhere, had planned what amounted to an intervention.

Nebraska was far past the fringes of Uktena stomping grounds. Because of its remote, utterly undesirable location, the Sept of the Hungry Flower was considered highly secure and rumored to be near a hidden cache containing artifacts of incredible power. The sept leader, Johnny Sees the Wind, though highly respected, was also considered in some quarters utterly mad, a result of his increasingly lengthy sojourns into the mystic realms of the Deep Umbra.

Reaching the sept quickly would have been no problem—simply taking a moon bridge would have been rapid and painless. Yet, when they arrived in San Francisco, Amy insisted on making the bulk of the journey by foot. And Claws, Gaia bless him, though clearly pressed by her erratic behavior himself, didn't balk. He knew she just wanted some time and he was always game for camping out. Of course, that was before he saw how boring the terrain of Nebraska really was.

But she needed a better reason than that to explain the delay to Johnny Sees the Wind. Fortunately, she had one, one involving the Anasazi, a subject of particular importance to the Uktena. The lost human tribe was more properly called the Hisatsinom, as they were named by their Hopi descendants. The popular name, Anasazi, meant "Ancient Enemy" in the Navajo tongue. Believing no tribe would call itself an enemy, Amy was loath to use it.

Eleven hundred years ago, the Hisatsinom founded a great civilization in the Pure Lands. They built incredible stone cities, highways that connected an intricate web of trade routes and more, all in perfect harmony with the Wyld. By the turn of the first millennium, dating by European standards, they'd built the largest apartment building in the world, unrivaled until a bigger one was built in New York City in 1882. Then, around AD 1130, a great diaspora began, during which, in fifty years, the Hisatsinom cities were simply abandoned. The tribe didn't vanish; it went back to its nomadic roots, eventually emerging as other tribes, including the Hopi and the Pueblos. Tales of their great wanderings were preserved in the folklore of those tribes.

Evidence of their wandering could be found throughout the Uktena's base, known as the Four Corners, which included Utah, Colorado, Arizona and New Mexico. A few years ago, Professor Stinton had shared his theory with Amy that they'd made it much farther north, not only to Nebraska in the west, but ever farther, to Alaska. Bolstering his belief were the centuries old travelers' stories of "phantom cities." Though some accounts dismissed them as mirages, or even reflections of far-off European towns, the descriptions sounded an awful lot like the canyon cities of the Hisatsinom. Girlishly believing she'd found her *raison d'être*, Amy latched onto her mentor's idle theory as if it were fact.

Though she doubted the human anthropologist could have guessed that the nomads were in close contact with their Garou protectors, Amy knew they were. That's what made the tribe's wanderings crucial to the Uktena. Those Garou that guarded the Hisatsinom were in charge of some of the infamous forgotten Banes the Uktena had somehow lost track of in the mists of history. The shameful fact was concealed from the other tribes, with good reason. These ancient Wyrm-spirits were time bombs waiting to go off—and an Uktena responsibility.

With such a strong rationale behind her, she was easily able to delay her appearance before Sees the Wind. It would have been even better if she'd arrived with some artifact as a gift for the elder. Parrot bones in particular would have been a prize, and probably a powerful fetish as well. They weren't native to the area, and the Hisatsinom were fond of being buried with the colorful creatures. Stinton had given her a small resin replica of one, carved with Hisatsinom runes, but she'd lost that, along with much else, in Alaska.

Though it had shielded her for a time from Sees the Wind, the mesh of lore and theory was ill equipped to block the self-hatred with which she flailed herself daily. Why couldn't she tell them? Why couldn't she even tell Claws the part he didn't know? Because all she had to show for it was some stupid ball? Because the death of that sept had been her fault? Because they had all died for the sake of her silly dream? History swallowed so many things whole, she wondered if it could also swallow her alive.

Before her life had acquired the vague texture of nightmare, there was a time (or was it something she just imagined?) when she could actually find the stillness at the center of her being and ask it a question or two. A voice, sounding oh so wise and oh so soothing, would sometimes answer in the most plain, unambiguous terms. Oh, the answers were never given in a way she expected, but always in a fashion that seemed to take her most pained, heartfelt question and make it seem trite. And with that voice came a sense of comfort that carried in it a call to action. But when was the last time she'd heard that voice? Or had she ever heard it at all?

Amy looked up and tried to feel the Great Mother, Gaia, somewhere in the air or in herself. She could not. She tried to feel something other than guilt or inadequacy. She could not. Helpless to halt her own diaspora, in an unspoken prayer, she asked the blackness between the fading stars, "Now will my whole life ache?"

Though she didn't hear it, Chottle, in repetition of words she had not spoken aloud, muttered quietly, "Ache...ache...ache..."

***

The Psychomachia pressed its sharp, bony fingers into his back, but Arkady did not hesitate. Arkady did not fear. He forced his elbows back into the thing's mesomorphic frame, cracking the exoskeleton. It staggered back, not understanding what could be so powerful. Arkady turned and with a single blow from his sword cut it in two.

He was always more than other Garou, but walking the Silver Spiral made him feel more alive, more aware than did even his greatest battles. It seemed there was no longer room in him for doubt or weakness. He now knew in his blood that this wheel-within-a-wheel would take him safe, whole and sane to Malfeas, the heart of the Wyrm. There, he would face the core of the blight that beset the Tellurian itself.

Was this dizzying change a gift of the Spiral or just a natural unfolding of his spirit into its destiny, what Teardrop might have called its dharma? The whys and wherefores didn't matter, not as long as he could see and follow the silver threads that danced along, but never lost themselves among, the pitch black blotches that formed the bulk of the vile road.

As his feet propelled him from one shiny patch to the next, Arkady knew the instant one of his paws touched ground exactly how many pebbles his skin came in contact with—their size, their shape, their texture. The hairs on his coat felt each gust of wind that hit him so clearly he knew its direction, dimensions and origin intimately.

All the while, his eyes sifted purposefully between Umbra and Gaia, differentiating, cataloging and, when necessary, dispatching destruction. From the moment he stepped on the opened Spiral, Arkady's being had become a machine at war, as if all on his own, he was set to heal the rift between body and spirit.

Pattern spiders scattered as he came. A pack of Scrags rose against him. Slide. Duck. Dive. Turn. Slice. And they were undone. Another Psychomachia? He dispatched it with a growl. But there was a long road down to the pitted Heart of Darkness he would dare claim as a prize, and the Spiral had many signposts.

By the end, even Arkady, in this, his most perfect form, might need help.

Chapter Two

Language—human language—after all, is but little better than the croak and cackle of fowls, and other utterances of brute nature—sometimes not so adequate.

—Nathaniel Hawthorne, *American Notebooks*, 1850

Unable to sleep, a few hours before sunset and the start of her final night of travel, Amy watched a fat, gray hedgehog amble about in a small, roundish clearing no more than fifty yards from the outcropping. It was sniffing, nose down, poking for stray bits of fallen grain or bugs. When the wind shifted, a whiff of predator made its way to the hedgehog's nose. Brown-gray nostrils flared—small lungs sucked sharply in. *Sniff!* Innately recognizing the scent of wolf, the golf-ball sized brain signaled danger to the whole of its foot-long nervous system. Little feet pumping, chubby skin warbling beneath gray fur, it dived toward the safety of the river. In moments, with a flurry of grass stalks and a small ripple in the water, it was gone. Amy wished she could join it but, despite her own best instincts, still couldn't figure out how to run from herself.

Though not particularly cold, she pulled her unfinished Kente cloth around her shoulders. Having failed at finding parrot bones to offer Johnny Sees the Wind, both as gift and proof of her worth, she needed something else to present. Realizing that no sleep was forthcoming, Amy sat up and quietly rifled through the fetishes carefully collected in her rucksack. The large rucksack itself was covered with emblems, signs and symbols that ranged from an Egyptian ankh to a stop sign. Among her prizes was a harmony flute, a spirit whistle and sanctuary chimes—all items of considerable power, all musical. Odd, since she didn't have a musical bone in her body. Ah, there it was. Jutting from careful cloth wrapping were two of the five pieces of what could only be a grand klaive. She'd found it in New Mexico, not far from the Pyramid of the Sun. But who made it, or to whom it once belonged, she had no idea. It would be a worthy gift for the sept, and should it turn out to have a particularly strong spirit behind it, it was probably safer there than traveling with her. The two-piece blade itself, doubtless cracked in battle, was a bit in need of polishing, so she reached into the sack to pull it out.

As she folded the edge of the rucksack to better reach the klaive pieces, the hideous ball she'd found in Alaska rolled out and, before she could catch it, hit the ground with a *gonk*. At first she feared it was damaged, but it seemed as oddly unharmed as it had been when Claws found her with it. Oddly was the operative word—she was clueless as to what it was, but just seeing it again made her remember how her sadness had started.

A thing of carved bone tied with strips of leather, it was a rough sphere less than a foot in diameter. The bones, each covered in an intricate series of glyphs, formed an interlocked series, half tied to the left, half to the right—almost like two sets of ribs half-turned and fitted together with such great precision that the edge of a piece of paper could not be forced between them. The bones formed a complete ball, and though it seemed the leather strips were somehow holding the thing together, Amy wasn't quite sure how. She was certain only of one thing: it wasn't Wyrm-tainted. Spirit servants of the great Uktena totem itself had long since taught her to sense both the flow of magical ritual and the power of the Wyrm itself. The energy she sensed from this thing was very quiet, but deep and definitely not of the Wyrm.

A sniff of the aged leather recalled the smell of the burnt corpses at the Wendigo sept. Amy put it down and turned to trying to polish the klaive pieces. But, alone and awake, without much else to do, she invariably turned back to the ball. There might be something to it, and if there was, it could be Greyrock's legacy, but she didn't want to raise her hopes. Its aura was barely iridescent, until she meditated on it and tried to lose herself in the sensation. All at once, it seemed to suck her spirit along deeper and deeper, until a sudden wash of vertigo pulled her back from the meditation. Recovering from the abrupt psychic tug, she wasn't sure if it was the sphere or if exhaustion had made her briefly fall asleep.

As for the carvings, three to five glyphs on each bony finger, they could be Hisatsinom runes, or druidic or not even writing at all, simply some designs. Holding it now, her memories of finding it returned, and she realized, with a gasp, that her real bout with melancholia began not at the moment the Greyrock Sept died, or the moment she learned of her culpability, or even the moment she first touched the ball, but at the precise moment she first let it go.

Curiosity surging like adrenaline, Amy wanted to take it apart but was terrified she would break it. Ultimately the obsessive inquisitiveness that lifted and cursed all her tribe got the better of her, and she began to think about how best to disassemble the relic. Delicately, she ran her finger along the writing on one of the bones, letting her long nails dip down along one of the slight depressions that ran between them. All at once, the bone lifted, just a bit. Amy gasped, afraid to move. As gently as she could, she pulled her finger away. The bone slipped back into place and gave off a single, beautiful tone:

dooooooon

It was like an evening bird's song, bridging the moments between day and night. More than that, it was like the sound of something that didn't belong in the world at all, like the laughter of a dragon. It was a sound more of spirit than substance. Music.

It was an instrument! Why hadn't she realized that before? The bones acted as keys, each resonating at a different pitch, wrapped around what must be some sort of sounding board. And what a sound it made! Gingerly, in deference to what she imagined must be its great age, she plucked the same bone again.

dooooooon

Though Claws only muttered something in his sleep and Chottle seemed more like a rock in the darkness than a living thing, the sound filled Amy with alternating feelings of such comfort and stimulation that she swooned and nearly fell over backward. She didn't realize it, but she was smiling, broadly and deeply.

"Whoa!" she half-whispered, then clapped her hand over her mouth to stifle a giggle. Wide eyed, like a child, she flicked three of the bones in quick succession.

wooon diiiin deeen

Each new sound overlapped the last, until a final, resonant tone was produced that hit Amy's nervous system like heroin and sent her reeling into all the long-forgotten corners of her mind. The dirt, the sky, the distant shadowy hills shimmered, and nameless colors began to paint the low, flat plains. The grain of the rock upon which the group camped spoke warmly of the nebulae in which it was formed.

It took Amy a moment to recognize that the sensation had driven her into the Umbra. Here, the spirit-self of every physical object dwelled. Full of delight, she turned to look at the spirit of the sphere. And there it was, polychromic, pulsing, changing shape from one moment to the next: first it was a three-headed serpent in ice, then a flying toad, then the universe in the mouth of a child, a trickster, a shaman, the Wyrm when it was whole, the seed in a cherry an old master eats before dying. Faster than the words came to Amy's mind to describe it, the spirit of the sphere changed shape in a grand, mad dance. Perhaps to give her a chance to catch up, it slowed and stopped.

ta-roo ta-rill ta-raah, it sang, fluttering before her, in this moment a great fiery roadrunner.

In the sounds it was making, in the song that it sang, she could hear, quite clearly, all the scattered voices that filled her own head—the tribal lore of the Uktena; the clicking tongue of the Inuit; the charms of the Santeria; the twenty languages she spoke fluently; the tales of all the tribes of the Garou she had heard, of their revered leaders, their battles, their triumphs, their deaths; the countless over-worded histories of men; the deep, simple myths of Gaia. Every collection of word, sound and picture Amy's mind had ever arranged into a semblance of sense and story was in this creature's trilling song—even the inner voice of wisdom whose comfort Amy had missed all these years.

It was an epiphany. All things were linked. Here, in this moment, she could see and sense how even her own psyche was just an aspect of the dancing war between form, balance and drive, between Weaver, Wyrm and Wyld. And every voice, everything she had seen and tried to catalog for the good of her tribe and the growth of her soul, here seemed to be in its rightful place.

In a few moments, the flaming bird began to fade, along with the sound it had made. Exhausted, tickled to numbness, Amy was once more back in the physical world, as if coming down from some hallucinogenic high. More sober sounds reached her ears: Claws' snore, Chottle's rasp and the pale sounds of real evening birds. She stared, transfixed, at the thing of carved bone and tanned flesh in her hands. As the memory of its tones faded, a terrible loneliness came upon her. The sensation of oneness was gone now, too. The voice she missed so dearly for so long was once again trapped in a part of herself she couldn't reach.

The puzzle pieces of her mind tumbled back into a more familiar shape. Cold, rational thoughts bubbled up to reclaim her consciousness: Was it a drug? An illusion? Was any of it even real? Perhaps, despite her conviction, there was Wyrm-taint to it.

Carefully, and a bit afraid, she wrapped it in the cloth meant for the Grand Klaive, then returned everything to her rucksack. With the sphere out of sight, the memory of its gifts were chewed, cataloged and contained. With no answer forthcoming for the questions that blazed in her mind, or the hollow throbbing in her chest, she thought about the significance of the sphere until exhausted, then rolled over and surrendered to more animal dreams.

***

The silver hot-dog van along the highway was just about to pack it in for the day. There hadn't been any customers for hours, and Jeremy, the sole proprietor, wanted to go home. He flipped off the recorded chimes. A holdover from the van's past life as an ice-cream truck, they still served as a lure for children. Today, however, along with the shiny surface of the vehicle, they'd caught the attention of something else.

As he lowered the window, he thought he saw something moving in the distance, off the road, toward the truck. It was too small for a car. A dirt bike? Maybe, but the way it was moving was all wrong. Jeremy had no idea his vehicle had become a signpost on Arkady's Silver Spiral.

Back right, front left, front right, back left, the four paws drummed, pushing the terrain beneath Arkady in a steady, staccato beat. Were it not for the organic fluidity of the muscles, cartilage and bone that enacted Arkady's will, his precise, deliberate pace could have been called mechanical.

As he leapt at the truck, the human within it fled. Once inside the guts of the great beast, Arkady tore at its innards, destroying the small kitchen. Silver, silver. The silver had offended him, confused him, reminded him of the crown he once wore. But why the sounds? The creaky song? At any rate, another signpost had been completed. It was time to find the next.

Banes and other horrors rose with such increasing regularity that even the newly resplendent Arkady grew tired and began to fear he might become incautious. Physically, he had to keep moving. This was not a path one could go back on. To keep his concentration, he kept his mind moving, too, rolling over old verbal saws, human and Garou, as he might prod a felled foe to see if its spirit remained.

Any path worth walking is not an easy one.

I have taken the road less traveled and that made all the difference.

It was more mantra than rumination, and within, he heard more cadence than meaning. The familiarity allowed him to concentrate that much more on sensing the trail ahead. Thinking, like so many things, was simply a trick. He smelled the reds and blues, saw the pungent odors and tasted ethereal wind.

Then all at once, he stopped, responding to something unseen. A nearby pattern spider paused as well, just for a moment, before returning to the intricate order it was weaving, thinking nothing of what it had heard.

Arkady, however, thought a great deal of it.

It was a sound, a very unusual sound—to the west.

Chapter Three

One impulse from a vernal wood
May teach you more of man,
Of moral evil and of good,
Than all the sages can.
—William Wordsworth, *The Tables Turned*

As the thicker blues and blacks wrenched free of the day's tyranny, and a few stars could once more be discerned, Chottle made a pained rasping noise that indicated he was about to awake. The phlegmy gasp lay somewhere between a gag and a normal waking breath. Not unlike a cub's panicked cry, it seemed geared by evolution to rake the Garou nervous system. Agitated, Claws bolted up and turned to Chottle to shake him, but he couldn't decide which part to shake. As Amy roused, she wasn't annoyed at all. In fact, she felt light and energetic, as if she'd slept the whole night instead of little more than sixty minutes. As she sat up and stretched, a grouchy Claws noticed her brighter mood.

"Pleasant dreams?" he asked, suspicious.

"Don't remember," she said with a smile.

"Really? I do. I was in a death struggle with a Bane. It had torn my right arm clean off, but my left had found its way into its mouth, and I was reaching down into its gullet to squeeze its innards," Claws recalled wistfully. "In its death throes, I think it made the same sound Chottle does upon waking."

Ignoring him, she pivoted her head in a slow, deliberate semicircle. At once she stopped. Her eyes had fallen on the vestiges of a thin trail.

"Don't tell me you've actually got something?" Claws asked with vague excitement.

Amy shook her head. "Some prehistoric migration trails. This whole area was covered with rhinos, three-toed horses, camels and a bunch of others a few hundred thousand years ago. Volcanic activity buried most of them. I think that's just a path they took north during mating season."

"Just like you, eh?" Claws said, immediately thinking better of it.

Amy glared at him.

"What do you mean, 'like me?'"

"Uh…nothing," Claws said. "Did I tell you about my dream?"

Amy grabbed his face between her hands and twisted it toward her.

"Whoa-whoa-whoa! Am I traveling north to mate? Is that what this is all about? What do you know about this meeting with Johnny Sees the Wind?"

Claws sighed, hemmed and hawed.

"Well…you know, it's been, well, sort of suggested that, after the whole Alaska thing, that perhaps having a cub might provide you with some grounding,…" he began.

"That brain-rotted old apple has spent too much time in the Umbra if he thinks whelping will cheer me up! Is he nuts? Haven't any of the Garou ever heard of postpartum depression? I don't believe it! Why on earth would I bring a new life into a world I'm not even sure *I* want to be in?"

"Yeah, well. That's the problem. Try to calm down, Amy."

"He probably figures that even if they lose *me* to Harano, at least they'll get another tribe member out of the deal…"

"I hear the potential mate has some very impressive lineage…"

"Agghhh!" Amy shouted. "Don't talk to me!" She paced the tiny rock, nearly kicking Claws and Chottle over the edge in the process. Out of nowhere, a shiver ran through her body. Some saliva dripped from her teeth.

She smacked her lips and said, "I'm hungry."

"Gree…gree…gree," Chottle repeated. Claws was happy for the change in subject.

"Hm. Won't be much game in this damnable grass, unless you want more rabbit?" Claws said. Nebraska had more varieties of grass than any other state in the union, and over the last few weeks, the small pack had become intimate with each.

"Nah. Not again. Something bigger," Amy answered. Shifting to Hispo, the dire wolf form, she stuck her snout in the air and sampled the cool night air. Save for her white left forepaw and a small white splotch that covered an area from the base of her throat to her chest, her coat was entirely black. After a moment of tasting the different spores and scents the wind carried, she reported in the High Tongue, "Thirty yards, due west, just into the woods. Deer. Two. Maybe three. One's definitely a buck. If the wind stays with us, they won't catch our scent until it's too late."

By the time the impressed Claws said "Shall we?" Amy had leapt off the outcropping. As the highlights of her black fur glowed in flashes beneath Luna's rising light, her racing body made a serpentlike wake in the field. The image brought to Claws' mind Uktena himself, the great serpent and totem of the whole tribe, riding along the earth. Chottle rolled off the rock with a lurch and hit the ground, hard. He made a sound that approximated a howl, changed into one form or another, then loped off after Amy. Claws watched as Chottle's blotchy ripple began to gain on Amy's. He realized she'd slowed up for the metis. As it occurred to him that even Chottle might beat him to the prey, Claws dove into the grass and made for the wood, shifting to Hispo himself along the way.

Claws watched the line of trees rise and fall as he bounded along the ground. He couldn't see either Amy or Chottle, but he could sense them easily enough. If he hadn't been so worried about her recently, he might have been embarrassed that Amy had found prey, not he. But now he was catching the scent as well. One of the deer was definitely big. Maybe it would even put up a fight. He slowed as he neared the edge of the woods and the prey came into view. The three fed on some ivy. A pregnant doe and male fawn were of little interest, but with them was a ten-point buck the sight of which filled Claws' mouth with saliva. Amy and Chottle were already crouching in wait when he caught up. They were upwind and well within striking range. None of the deer seemed any the wiser.

"Easy kill," Claws whispered in the High Tongue.

"Hmm. In that case," Amy said, "why don't we try to get Chottle to flush them out?"

"Chottle? Don't be silly. You can't even tell him where to piss. How can you talk strategy with him?"

"Pack hunting is innate. I just have to get the idea across. Instinct should take it from there," Amy said.

"And when did you get so confident?"

Amy thought about it a moment, then shrugged, "In a dream."

"Okay, but make it quick," Claws said.

Amy sidled up next to Chottle and stared deep into his mirrorlike eyes. Having no idea whether anything was looking back at her, she shifted her gaze to the position behind a large tree that she wanted the metis to take.

"Go," she whispered.

"Go…go…go," Chottle repeated. But he didn't move.

"No," Amy said.

"No…no…no…"

"Forget it, Amy. There's no telling how long the wind will stay with us," Claws said.

"Give me a minute. He can do this."

She stared into his eyes again, so dead, so reflective she could use them to sidestep into the Umbra. Slowly, deliberately, she shifted her head once more to the tree.

"Go…go," Chottle whispered. Then, he shambled off in the right direction. Claws suppressed a laugh.

"You did it!"

After a few tense moments, Chottle quietly made his way to the hiding spot Amy picked out for him, behind a thick oak no more than three yards from their prey. He even quieted his breath, so the deer still suspected nothing.

"Now, let's see just how innate pack hunting is. With any luck some part of his brain will recognize what he's in the right position for. I just have to make sure *I* move at the right time."

The time came quickly. No sooner had Amy finished her sentence than the wind shifted. Sensing the change, the great buck lifted its head to better sniff the air and, in so doing, fully exposed its long, warm neck. From his position behind the tree, Chottle flopped out onto the ground in full view. The buck, hearing the danger at practically the same time he sniffed it, not bothering to lower its head, rushed forward into a trap.

In a move so quick and deft it might have been considered humane, Amy leapt in the path of the huge creature. As her body passed in front of it, she lashed out with open mouth, snapped her jaws tight around its neck and tore out a section of its throat with her teeth. She landed two yards from the buck, a bloody piece of jugular still dangling from her mouth. Claws just watched in admiration.

As its lifeblood gurgled from the gaping wound, the buck staggered left, then right. Righting itself briefly, it lowered its head as if to attack with its antlers. Abruptly, as if the invisible string holding it aloft had been snipped by equally invisible shears, it collapsed to the ground. In moments, no longer pumped by an active heart, the blood began to trickle rather than gush from the wound. The doe and fawn were long gone.

Once certain it was dead, Amy bowed her head, in ritual thanks to the spirit of the great animal. After a moment, Claws—already back in his favored Glabro form—broke the silence with a rude, "Yum! Should we cook it?"

Before Amy could answer, there was a loud crunch of leaves and twigs. At first, they thought it was Chottle, but the metis was right beside them. Simultaneously, the trio turned to see a large black form, fifteen feet tall, rise from the thick brush.

"A grizzly bear?" Claws said, dumbfounded.

"Bear…bear…bear," Chottle repeated, beginning to shake.

"Don't be ridiculous. It couldn't be. There haven't been grizzlies this far south in two hundred,…" Amy began. Her sentence was cut off by a loud, long growl as the brown-furred hulk stood on its thick hindquarters, lifted its head and bellowed.

"Okay, so maybe it's a grizzly," Amy said. "Or maybe even a traveling Gurahl. But, if that's the case, we should just say hello and share the venison."

The Uktena had worked long and hard to repay the Kinfolk of the Bear for their part in the War of Rage, in which shapeshifters other than Garou were hunted and slaughtered. Though her tribe was the last to enter the war and the first to leave, Amy and all other Uktena bore both the guilt and the responsibility.

Stepping forward with her head down in a submissive posture, she barked a short greeting in the tongue of the werebear, asking if it wanted some, or even all, of the meal. Though she knew only a little Gurahl, she was certain she'd gotten both the words and the passive tone correctly, yet her offer seemed to elicit only rage. Foam flew from the thing's mouth. It reared savagely, ready to attack. It didn't even seem interested in the deer carcass. Amy was confused.

"Something's very wrong here," she whispered to Claws.

"No kidding. Back behind me," Claws said. As the pack's warrior, it was fitting he step up to lead the real battles. Amy was certainly not in the mood to argue, so she stepped lightly back. Without taking her eyes from the bear, or whatever it was, she shifted to Crinos and reached for her fetish bow.

Chottle, however, perhaps emboldened by his participation in the felling of the buck, didn't seem to understand the danger. Instead of pulling back, he flopped forward. Imitating the creature's roar and making some strange noises all his own, Chottle began to change. Fleshy ripples surged up and down his body. Bones stretched. Muscle massed. Limbs lengthened. Thick fur covered skin. But the end result was that Chottle looked much the same as he had when he began.

As if genuinely puzzled, the grizzly paused and stared, twisting its head. Chottle flopped forward in what may well have been an attack, only to meet the creature's paw as it swiped forward. With a pained whine, the metis flew a foot up in the air and landed ten feet away in a shaking, growling pile.

Now it was Amy's turn to twist her head sideways in wonder. A grizzly was strong, a Gurahl was stronger, but neither was that strong. Claws knew it, too. Any fear of offending their fellow shapeshifters began to fade.

"Notch a Bane arrow. I'll go in and tangle with it a bit. Wait for a clear shot at its eye and, whatever you do, don't miss! I've got a feeling we're going to take this thing down fast, or not at all," Claws said. Growing to Crinos, he wrapped his hand around the klaive he wore strapped to his blue Dockers and let his changing height pull it free from its sheathe.

"Claws, wait!" Amy said, but it was too late. He'd already taken an upright stance directly in front of the bear. A full seven feet shorter, even at his fully extended height, he growled at it and slashed the air with his blade. From appearances, speed was on the side of the Garou. The bear's lumbering movements seemed stilted, even for a creature that size.

Claws ducked the first paw swing, then leapt up over the back swing and flipped out of the way. The bear lunged left, exposing some hairy flesh beneath its left shoulder. Seeing the opening, Claws dove for it, klaive first, but the bear was too fast. Though the tip of the warrior's blade sliced some thick hide, the bear slammed into Claws with both arms and sent him to the ground. Lying on his back for a moment, Claws could see the six-inch wound he'd made in the creature, but no blood flowed from it. He didn't have much time to wonder why. In seconds the bear came down upon him, burying both paws into Claws' shoulders and pushing forward with his open mouth.

Dropping his weapon, Claws grabbed the bear's face with his hands and pushed up, giving Amy a perfect shot.

"*Now!*" Claws growled, but he didn't have to. Amy had already let the arrow fly—a perfect shot that would have pierced the bear's eye and lodged in its brain if it had completed its short arc. Instead, a massive bear claw swatted it out of midair. The fletching tumbled, front over back, before landing somewhere unseen in the brush. Neither Amy nor Claws had ever seen anything like that before, except on TV.

"I'm open to suggestions!" Claws screamed as he fought to keep the huge brown mountain of flesh and fur from bringing its full weight down on him. As it landed on all fours, Claws barely managed to roll out of the way. Simultaneously, bear and werewolf rose and faced each other on two feet again.

This time, though, with ungodly speed, the bear grabbed Claws' neck and waist and hoisted him up above its head. As it tossed the warrior down onto a rock, Amy could hear ribs crack. Before Claws could move, the bear, like a berserk mutant wrestler, lifted him again.

Sweet Gaia's Heart, it's going to kill him!

The words ran through Amy's head as she quickly reached into her rucksack, hoping that whatever weapon she pulled out first would be most useful. Her hand found the sphere. In an effort to pull it quickly out of the way, she sounded three notes on it.

fooooon ziiiiin weeeeeellll

The sound intoxicated her. Entranced and enchanted, with only the whites of her eyes visible, she dropped the singing sphere and the rucksack. Her limbs numb, she rolled her head and spine backward in mystic ecstasy. This time, it was no visionary experience. It felt as though the tone was actually pushing her physically, reshaping her, winding her like a coil. With Chottle unconscious and Claws fighting for his life, no one saw, but Amy continued to roll until, almost impossibly even for a supple Garou, the top of her brow touched the ground behind her feet.

Realizing his death was imminent, and wanting to see his own end, Claws forced his eyes half open. Just as the bear was about to lift him again, he saw Amy Hundred-Voices, in his estimation barely a songkeeper, perform an acrobatic series of maneuvers that would dizzy all but the best Uktena warrior. Still arched backward, her Crinos hands touched the ground on either side of her head. With a kick, her feet flew up and over. Spinning, she was airborne, playing the momentum of her body as if it were a harp. Twisting her spine as she dropped, she kicked Claws' klaive up into the air on one rotation, then snatched it in her left hand with the next.

With a growl that sounded more like a merry snicker, she leapt toward the bear. In midleap, she morphed into Glabro, closer to human. Her muscles thinned, her fur shortened. The great bear turned its head toward her and snarled as she, enjoying the momentum provided by the heavier form she had just shed, landed feet first on the bear's chest. In what seemed a defiance of gravity, she crouched there, making a handhold in the fur of the creature's pectoral muscle with her left hand. Then Amy shifted back to Crinos and slashed seven times, long and deep, before the bear could even position its claws to strike.

As it writhed, unable to decide which wound to grab at first, she dropped the blade, then flipped herself onto its back. Her own hairy back pressed against its matted fur, she reached around, wrapped her arms about its head and twisted until there was a loud CRACK. The bear stood long enough for Amy to reach the ground, then dropped.

His pain overwhelmed by wonder, Claws stared at her, wide eyed. Not noticing, Amy gingerly licked the scant blood on her paw with the tip of her tongue. She spat as if having tasted poison, then pointed toward the body.

"You're not even winded," Claws said, trying to get to his feet.

"Look at the wounds," she said. "That's no bear."

Claws turned and saw the cuts ooze black putrescence. Inky black larvae crawled from the largest gash. The skin nearest the tears fluttered as the grublike innards of the creature moved beneath its flesh.

"If it were human, I'd say it was a fomor," Amy said.

"What the hell?" Claws said, shaking his head. "A fifteen-foot Wyrm-tainted grizzly? In the middle of Nebraska? Why?"

"I…I…I," Chottle muttered as he shuffled to what may have been a standing position. He repeated the sound a few times, then fainted.

***

The trumpet still held the decades-old dent from the time Samantha knocked her younger brother in the head with it. Repairing it would have been a crime. Full of patches where the metal wore down, so tarnished it could hardly be called silver, the trumpet was more than an instrument, it was a piece of her history. She played for hours every day on the street. Jazz mostly, but sometimes some pop tunes. People liked it when she played the solo from Penny Lane. Tonight she'd hoped to catch some more change from some late moviegoers, but there'd been no such luck.

Instead she found herself staring at a tall, hairy nightmare. In a voice that was barely intelligible due to its rough tone and European (Russian?) accent, it demanded the instrument. One look into its dead eyes and Samantha realized that her life, despite any forgotten dreams and unfulfilled ambitions, was worth more than her history. Letting the prize clatter to the pavement, she ran.

Two blocks away, she turned and watched the garish monster try to make sense out of the treasure it had claimed. It twisted it this way and that, poked fingers and nose into it, and ultimately threw it away. As if hearing a distant sound, it turned and rushed off down an alleyway. She waited six hours after it left to walk back and reclaim the trumpet. Now it had a new dent, and a new story, but not one any would likely believe. By the next morning, even Samantha was convinced her "hairy nightmare" had been a crack addict or another mugger, amplified by her own fatigue.

With another signpost complete, Arkady trained his senses and honed his mind in preparation for the revelation of his next target. This time, when the sound reached him, he was prepared to embrace it. Even with his senses enhanced, or perhaps drenched, by the Spiral, this sound was dizzying—sharp, clear, folding in on itself in a way that threatened to suck all within earshot inside it forever. This time, even more exciting to the Silver Fang, it was also tinged with blood. An omen? A weapon? It seemed to speak as much of Malfeas as it did of Gaia—and that, perhaps, made it key to his journey.

And so again to the west, he turned his feet and watched for the splotches of silver he knew would rise to show him the way.

Chapter Four

"*We do not wish to destroy your religion. We only want to enjoy our own.*"

As the Indians began to approach the missionary, he rose hastily from his seat and replied that he could not take them by the hand; that there was no fellowship between the religion of God and the works of the devil. This being interpreted to the Indians, they smiled and retired in a peaceable manner.

—Chief Red Jacket and a missionary, as quoted in Wilcomb F. Washburn's *The Indian and the White Man*

Amy did her level best to explain what the sphere had shown her and how it made her feel, but her rapid volley of seemingly unconnected words and pictures scratched into the dirt only left Claws feeling more confused and agitated.

"Let me get this straight: The first time it put you in the Umbra. This time it made you a fighting machine," he said. "How did you even know which bones to flick?"

Amy shook her head, "I don't know. I just...I don't know."

She wondered why she hadn't asked herself the same question.

Claws' own mind, not used to contemplating such complexities, wavered from believing the sphere was Wyrm tainted and should be destroyed immediately to believing that it had no magic at all, and that Amy had completely snapped. Terrified he might try to take the sphere from her, she even suggested that no matter how false his former theory was, the latter might well be the case.

In the end, she agreed not to try further experiments and promised to present it to Johnny Sees the Wind, both for his opinion on what was obviously a relic of great power, and in the hope he would be able to provide a place of safety for it in his own cache of treasures. Delighted and uplifted though she was by the relic, Amy did not deceive herself that she was in any position to care for it properly.

"And?" Claws asked, prodding.

Amy, still wrapping the sphere and positioning it in the bottom of her rucksack with the greatest of care, pretended not to know what he was getting at.

"What? And what?"

"We'll go to the sept, give Sees the Wind the sphere *and?*..."

She pushed the rucksack closed and huffed.

"All right! I'll tell the story of Alaska! But...Claws..."

"Yeah?"

"There are some things I didn't tell you," she said sheepishly.

"No kidding," Claws said.

"Kidding...kidding," Chottle chimed in.

For a few hours they followed the Loup River east until it neared Columbus. There they crossed a patch of woods and followed Shell Creek upstream toward the village of Newman Grove. The woods lightened, exposing the fringes of a series of free-range poultry farms. From here it was due north to the

Willow Creek State Recreation Area, the patch of wilderness whose depths housed the sept.

The journey would be ending soon, but Amy wasn't the only one out of sorts. Though they had bonded as packmates more for the sake of seeking hidden knowledge than directly fighting the Wyrm or Weaver's legions, Amy and Claws had seen their share of combat, across five continents and among the ruins and desolate caves to which she was always dragging them. Hunting for food was all well and good, but the battle with the bear, quick and clean as it turned out to be, left Claws itching for a bit of action himself—especially since the last few weeks of travel had been so boring.

To lighten things up, he suggested raiding one of the chicken farms, just for fun. Amy hesitated, but realizing it would delay their arrival at the sept a bit more, she used a trick taught to her by a Gremlin spirit, the only prize from her single sojourn to Asia, to fry the circuits along a farm's electric fence. All three in the full-wolf Lupus form, they raced into one of the coops, sending the sleepy flightless birds into a mad tizzy. White feathers flew everywhere. Amy chuckled as Chottle galumphed after one of the slower birds. It was great fun for all except the chickens—until the revelry was ended by the blast of a twelve-gauge shotgun fired into the air. As he leapt back over the fence with the others, a laughing Claws caught a glimpse of a cursing farmer trying to sound dangerous as he shouted at them.

"I guess someone hasn't heard that wolves have been a protected species since 1973!" Claws laughed as they shifted to Homid for a rest a half mile away.

"Oh, I'm sure he was delighted to see wolves returning to the area," Amy said. "He did, after all, shoot into the air."

She sighed and lay down on the ground for a moment.

"We shouldn't have done that, you know. There's already a backlash in Yellowstone, where the wolves were reintroduced seven years ago. A few farmers have started shooting them again."

"Maybe we should pay them a visit," Claws suggested.

"Why? To give them heart attacks for defending their livelihood?"

"Hey! Whose side are you on?"

Amy rolled up and rested her head on Claws' shoulder. "Yours, of course," she said. "Maybe Chottle's. After that, it gets a little hard to tell."

"Better not repeat that to Johnny Sees the Wind," Claws cautioned.

"*I* won't," she answered with a pointed emphasis. "Will *you*?"

"Amy," Claws said, pulling back a bit in embarrassment. "Some of the places your heart goes, well, they're just beyond me, and they worry me. If there's help for you somewhere, I want you to have it."

Amy nodded. "Did you tell anyone about the sphere?"

"No. I thought it was a piece of junk or a toy…until tonight. Why? Are you having second thoughts about turning it over?"

"No. I just want to make sure no one *else* knows about it."

"Ah," Claws said with approval. "Now you're thinking like an Uktena."

A few hours later, in the supposed boundaries of a state recreation park, they reached a seemingly forgotten, terribly inhospitable area. Paths were overgrown, sometimes blocked by trees that had fallen so long ago they'd rotted to the center. Wherever they looked and sniffed, there were no signs of human campers. It was a small spot where the Wyld, it seemed, once more held sway.

As they walked deeper into the area, Amy found it odd that there was no bawn to speak of, no Garou patrolling the perimeter, no way to tell where the caern began. At first she thought the sept kept itself low key, to aid in its secrecy, but after a while, she started to wonder if it was there at all. Just as she was about to conclude they'd gotten the directions wrong or been tricked for some reason, they reached the flat top of a hill and saw what Claws and Amy assumed must be the Caern of the Hungry Flower.

The high, small open area, backlit by Luna in the gibbous phase that had marked Amy's birth, rose like a Native American silhouette cut with nimble fingers from black paper. In the center was what at first looked like a cross between a hogan and a shotgun shack, built from old wood, stolen metal sheathing and blankets. There were figures about it, one in Crinos wearing a ceremonial headdress, others in Homid and Glabro form. One of the human shapes had his head buried in the open hood of a pickup truck.

"Richard, this thing doesn't even *have* fuel injection!" it said.

"Then *you* take me home tonight," the wolfman replied in a rasping voice.

Each seemed practically a stereotype of the Pure Ones, as the indigenous North American Garou tribes called themselves. In the darkness, they all looked Native American, like the original Uktena, before the tribe's dwindling numbers led them to breed with other minorities. Self-consciousness gripped Amy. She'd met many people of many places, Garou of many tribes, but her encounters with her fellow Uktena had always been awkward, as if, despite the tribal tugs she felt, she herself were metis and did not quite belong. Her own patchwork heritage, part African, part Vietnamese, part German Jew, made her, in her own estimation, a poseur. She briefly wished the feeling were simply another demon-bear she could lash out at, but it would not fall so easily.

The headdressed wolfman, seemingly unconcerned with Amy and her pack, lodged his pinky in his ear and wiggled it furiously, trying to reach an itch that fell just shy of his nails. Shaman were eccentric. Could that be Sees the Wind?

A voice said "Shh!" loudly, and Claws realized that they'd been seen.

"Hey!" he whispered, nudging his silent companion. "Earth to Amy!"

She'd been standing there for quite some time, and her inaction was growing rude. So, Amy, with a final sigh of trepidation, inhaled and issued a howl of introduction.

Before any could answer, a trilling filled the air with the mechanized tones of a Bach cantata. A tall, lean female figure, human, turned away and fumbled for something in the folds of her clothing. Amy peered through the darkness, trying to figure out who was speaking to whom.

"Geez, Bandilack, you brought that thing *here?*" the human male by the pickup truck said.

"It's important," the woman Amy assumed was Bandilack answered. "I'll just be a second."

After a moment, the music stopped.

"Okay. Yes. Exactly as we discussed. You deposit the money with the charity and I destroy the files. Done," Bandilack said.

There was a slight chirp as the cell phone closed.

"*Ready now?*" the exasperated figure in Crinos, the one with the headdress, half barked.

"Yes. My apologies," Bandilack answered brusquely. She straightened and rejoined the group.

The strong male in Crinos lowered his hand toward a large shapeless mound on the ground. A small spark slipped from his lupine fingertips to a collected pile of twigs, dried brush and old newspapers. Amy might have thought it magic if she hadn't spotted the pack of matches in his hand. As the flames grew, she could see her initial impressions were a bit off. Though clearly these were Uktena who honored their history, with ceremonial symbols on their garb, there were also a few store-bought leather jackets and other fashionable items being worn. The largest had on sunglasses, no doubt purely for effect, and Amy caught a glimpse of the cell phone in the hand of a statuesque black woman in an Armani business suit.

In fact, now she could see that they were anything but homogenous. A burly Hispanic man with a gangland tattoo on his chest and dressed all in leather was pulling himself out from under the hood of the pickup. The tall one with the headdress, his arms impossibly thick, was still in Crinos, so his human ethnicity was difficult to determine, but his garb was Omaha, the human tribe that dwelled nearby. They all looked like pieces of Amy, a patchwork family themselves, which pleased her.

As for the hogan, aside from the blankets and trash, it was also composed of clean-cut, bolted lumber supports. Red dye identified the lumberyard from which it had been purchased. A roof of corrugated tin was also now visible. There was no door, just what seemed a curtain of strung beads that reflected the yellows and reds of the bonfire.

Without another word or motion, a glassy tinkling filled the air. At first Amy thought the sound was from chimes somewhere inside the structure, but it was too rough and atonal. No, it was the curtain. As it began to shift, she could see it was not made of beads at all, but small pieces of broken mirror slung together with string and strips of cloth, refuse collected from scrap heaps. Amy realized the significance at once: mirrors, reflective surfaces made it easier for Garou to pierce the Gauntlet that separated the physical earth from the spirit world. Johnny Sees the Wind spent more time in the Deep Umbra than he did in the world others might consider real. As the wall of broken glass fully parted, a short figure with long, white hair, wearing an old army jacket fraying at the seams, shuffled out among them.

Seeing his face, a familiar dread gripped Amy. Long before her First Change, she hated visiting her grandmother's house because of this very feeling. She realized her grandmother must have had some Garou blood that presented itself in odd, disconcerting ways, chief among which was her penchant for collecting and displaying dolls. They lined the walls, crowded the books off the shelves, filled every nook, corner and cranny with their flat plastic skin and near-human eyes. Their gaze seemed closer to imitating consciousness than Chottle's did, but unlike the blank stare of the metis, the dolls were horribly *other*.

The feeling was back: Sees the Wind, skin wrinkled like a dried brown apple, had doll's eyes. In fact, his facial skin hung so loosely upon his skull it curved around his eye sockets so that only the black pupils could be seen. His movements startled her. She expected him to be filled with cotton.

After another nudge from Claws, she remembered her manners and started the ritual introductions.

"I am Amy…"

Sees the Wind waved her to silence.

"I know who you are. You are Amy Hundred-Voices, so named because you spoke ten languages before your First Change and have tripled that number since. This is Claws with Teeth, so named because during his First Change, with his arms pinned by one of the three fomori who attacked him, he lashed out with his teeth and killed the other two. And the metis is Chottle, so named because you could not think of anything else to call him. Am I right?" Sees the Wind said with a wink.

Amy was flabbergasted. Reporting the pack's identity and lineage was her job. Sees the Wind had been unspeakably rude. Yet he was an elder. Was it a test? What should she do? Tickled by her discomfort, Sees the Wind cackled.

As his face grew taut from laughing, she became aware that it wasn't just the pupil she'd seen as black. The whole of his eyes, cornea and what was normally white, were all jet black, rendered that way, she guessed, from his long sojourns into the strange realms of the Deep Umbra, where dream and reality had no barrier between them.

Johnny snapped his fingers in the direction of the statuesque black woman. At once, she withdrew a long hollow stick from the folds of her Armani jacket.

"Are these the right ones?" he said to her.

"Of course," she replied. He nodded. Then, apparently recalling a bit of decorum, he made an effort at introductions.

"This is Kathy Bandilack. The tall Omaha who prefers to stand around puffed up in Crinos because his human arms embarrass him with their thinness is Richard Mountainside. The young Turk in the vest is Fits the Pieces. I will let the others introduce themselves to you later. They are my friends and packmates. And you are welcome here."

In response to Sees the Wind's seeming criticism, Mountainside shrank back down to Homid, revealing a dark-skinned Native American form that had obviously undergone a great deal of focused weight training. His thick arms and chest were almost comical, making his human form seem top heavy.

At first, Amy thought the item Johnny fingered was a ceremonial talking stick, normally reserved for more solemn occasions. He snapped the end off, tipped it toward his mouth and leaned back. Chewing loudly, he held the stick out to Amy.

"Choco-ball?" he offered. "I've always had a weakness for bittersweet. Brand doesn't really matter. Hershey's, Ghiraldi, no difference. Sometimes I eat bags of the Nestlé unsweetened stuff. Good for the heart, they say."

"No, thank you," Amy said.

Sees the Wind shook his head, "I should have figured you for a milk-chocolate type. No matter. We will discuss confections later."

He chewed a bit more then swallowed.

"You have entered one of the few caerns that have remained pure for centuries, despite the Wyrmcomers and the compromises our brothers had to endure," the elder said, now somber. He was referring to the arrival of the Europeans in North America and the subsequent insistence of the other Garou tribes that the Uktena "share" access to their powerful caerns for the sake of protecting them from the Wyrm. "It pleases me that this place is still pure Uktena, ever strengthened by new Uktena blood."

He motioned for them to step closer.

"Come sit with me," Johnny said. "Sure you don't want chocolate?"

Amy and Claws both shook their heads at the question but immediately obeyed the request. As the elder shaman sat a few feet from Amy, he cast Chottle an odd glance.

"Is he seated?"

Amy shrugged. "I believe so."

Johnny nodded. His knobby-kneed legs proved surprisingly supple as he folded them into a full lotus position. Then he stared into the fire for what seemed a long time. When he finally spoke, Amy wasn't sure if he was talking to the fire or her.

"What is your totem?" the old man asked.

Amy fumbled for a moment, then intoned solemnly: "We have communed with a great Frog in the bayou, a Roadrunner in Mexico, and…Claws believes that after killing a Scrag, he beheld a great serpent in Lake Champlain."

"I…uh…don't claim it was Uktena," Claws added sheepishly. Amy was relieved the first question was so simple. It wasn't unusual for a pack to have more than one totem. But Sees the Wind was clearly displeased. His ebony gaze hardened as if saying *perhaps you did not hear what I asked.*

Then he said again, "What is your totem?"

Amy put her head down and said, "We have none."

Sees the Wind laughed, "Sure you do! She has spoken to you at least three times now, but you don't hear her. Your ears must be clogged."

Then he leaned over and made a great show of looking inside Amy's ear.

"Hello! Hello!" he said. A few of his packmates chuckled. Sees the Wind waved them to silence and his face grew somber again.

"Fear makes us deaf. Fear makes us blind. There is much to fear in this world, much to be sad about. Our numbers grow fewer every day. The Wyld itself seems to be dying. But at my age, the spirit grows tired of its little fears and sadness—and shrugs at their coming."

To illustrate his point he stood and did a little dance. Miming a visit from his fears, he opened an invisible door and waved them in. "We have seen you so many times, old fears, have you nothing new to say?" he sang. Then he settled down with a bored sigh. "But no, it is always the same—so we entertain them but don't really listen as closely as we did in younger years. Do I still fear death? The pain or destruction of myself, my loved ones, my tribe, totem and Gaia? Yes, of course I do, but I no longer fear the things my heart believed would cause them."

Putting his hands on his knees, he bent down, bringing his coal-black eyes less than a foot from Amy's face. "You, Amy Hundred-Voices, are too young to be that familiar with your own heart, and your sadness has a depth which even your packmate fears."

Pack*mates*, Amy wanted to correct him. He'd forgotten about Chottle. Or perhaps he'd meant that only Claws feared for her? The furrow of her brow registered with the listeners. One filled the silence meant for Amy's response.

"Perhaps she is part Croatan and her melancholy is a desire to be with her true tribe?" Mountainside grunted. The Croatan were the third Pure tribe that occupied North America before the Europeans came. They all died destroying a great Bane at Roanoke. Many Wendigo, ostensibly the "younger brother" of the threesome, blamed the Uktena for not saving them.

"If she is Croatan, we should keep her here with us," Kathy Bandilack, the statuesque black woman, said, "for the sake of our lost middle brother."

Johnny shook his head. "We are not here to command. We are here to help. Once a soul's path has been found, you do not have to order it to follow it. To do so is its greatest wish."

He patted her on the shoulder, "So, tell me, with just one of your hundred voices, Amy, why, from your heart, you have so much trouble telling the stories of our people."

Staring at her own reflection in his black eyes, she spoke: "The words are easy enough to remember. It's the feeling behind them that is more difficult to recall, near impossible for me to conjure at will. As long as I fail at that, I will be no songkeeper." She was so surprised by her own forthrightness she had to wonder if the elder had cast some sort of spell over her.

Sees the Wind smiled warmly. "Good. You speak well when you believe what you're saying. There are plenty of bad songkeepers. I would rather crap out the thighbone of a horse than listen to some. But you, at least in your heart, know the difference between a good telling and a bad one. That is a wisdom only the best songkeepers possess."

He leaned forward and put his index finger to Amy's brow. "In there, you have a picture. A picture of the perfect tale. I want you to describe it to me now."

Amy nodded a few times, but the words would not come. As she felt everyone's gaze pressing upon her, she wanted to weep. Instead, she reached deep into her rucksack and withdrew the sphere. Still keeping her own fingers on it, she placed it in the elder's hand.

"Johnny Sees the Wind, I wish to give this to you as a gift, but first I would like to tell you how I found it."

Claws started as she broke her promise to him and gently flicked one of the bones. As the soft tone of the sphere filled the air, Amy's eyes rolled back into her head and she began to speak.

***

Starting with the end of an incision that had cut through an old scar on the scalp, Arkady gingerly peeled back the skin on the skull of the body on the table. A metal plate beneath, which patched the bone, caught some of the scant light from the windows of the hospital morgue. The color reflected back to his eyes as silver.

Silver again. Silver van. Silver trumpet. Silver skull. He was no fool; he knew the signposts were built in part by the pieces of his own history, and the parallel to the Silver Crown of his tribe was obvious, but what did the music mean? He held the skull as if trying to play it. He blew in the eyeholes, tapped on the top, trying to get it to sound.

An open file on the desk had a photo of the deceased. The human had been a music teacher. Upon reading that, Arkady sensed this signpost was complete.

The distant tone sounded again. East, west, north, south—it was so close now that one physical direction was the same as another. But this time, there was something strange mixed with it: words, whispered, shouted, at first too soft to make out any particulars save the measured shifts in pitch and volume. He followed, faster and faster, until the words became clearer—was it a ritual? A greeting? A conversation? No.

It was a story. Someone was telling a story.

Now, what kind of story would it be?

Quickening his pace, Arkady listened, wishing he could eat the details.

Chapter Five

When truth is buried, it grows, it chokes, it gathers such explosive force that on the day it breaks out, it blows everything up with it.
—Emile Zola, "J'accuse!" *L'Aurore*, 1898

Listen.

I'll tell you the secret of the universe. You could tell it to me, but I'm the one talking now. Wait a minute, you say? If we both know it, then what's the difference between us?

Well, that's part of the secret.

Here's another: in the beginning, though this thing that calls itself I hadn't yet learned to do so, everything I am, have been and will be was there. Just as all this was, and you were, too.

If all the pieces of then are here now, what's different?

Well, that's part of the secret.

Listen. I'll tell you. Because ever since I learned to talk, talking is what I do.

Two hundred years before the Wyrmcomers came to the Pure Lands, in ships that seemed like mountains on the sea, riding horses that made them seem like half men, half deer, carrying sticks that flashed lightning, the Mother that lived within these lands knew they would come. Gasping at what she knew they would do to her children, she inhaled, drawing in, out of fear, all her love, all her water. Rain did not fall from the sky. Riverbeds turned first to mud, then cracked dust. The dry earth

The dry earth

could no longer yield the plants that both the animals and the people ate. Many died.

The Hisatsinom, though wise, could not see what the Mother saw, but the shamans and songkeepers of the Uktena knew what these signs meant. Under their guidance, the Hisatsinom spread out from their cities to start new tribes. Before they departed, the Garou collected the greatest gifts Mother had given them and vowed they would be kept hidden until the days of greatest need.

Some hid them not far from the Kinfolk, but the most powerful gifts were carried by the strongest, farther and farther north, into the cold lands where the Wendigo dwelled, into the snow, into mountains where none would dare follow. There, far from even the eyes of their younger brothers, the Uktena built a city to remind them of happier times. And there the greatest gifts wait, for the days of greatest need.

***

"Do you *still* believe that, Amy?" Claws said, pounding his fur-covered hands together to keep them warm. The temperature was twenty below, with gale winds blowing at thirty miles an hour. He could only guess what the windchill made the temperature feel like.

"Let's just say it sounded a lot better back at the Greyrock Sept," she shouted back, straining to be heard over the blizzard.

"Really? I gave up back in the Yukon, myself!"

"Ha!" she called. "*You* never wanted to leave New Mexico!"

The tall, broad figure of the Wendigo that led them, though only five yards ahead, faded in and out of visibility. Tired of their patter, he stopped short, allowing the gray of his coat to peek from the shifting fields of falling snow.

"Conserve your strength. Even I don't know how far it is to shelter. Though I would willingly die fighting the Wyrm, I do not want one of Mother's storms to claim me. Follow in silence or risk being lost," Kusagak growled. He clearly resented the fact that even that much had to be said. He pivoted and plodded on again.

"*Ayungii! Atii!*" Amy said in Kusagak's native Inuit with a shrug.

"Yes, let's go," he snarled back, barely concealing a slight smile. He pivoted and plodded on again.

One could hardly blame him. He'd put up with their peculiarities and novice abilities for two weeks—all the while watching patiently as they found absolutely nothing. And now the blizzard he'd warned of was so bad that just a foot beyond his massive form, everything, everywhere was a whirl of white on white.

Amy, appreciating their guide's words, didn't bother to tell Claws yet again why they'd come to the Arctic National Wildlife Refuge to hunt among the rocks in search of Hisatsinom ruins. She found Kusagak broadminded for a Wendigo, and his sept, called simply Greyrock, unusually helpful. She had no wish to insult or push him. The Wendigo kindness was not without reason. It was clear upon Claws and Amy's arrival that the members of the caern were themselves terribly curious about the phantom city sightings that had been reported in the area for hundreds of years. This was a simple way to try to get some answers.

Amy's theories, she knew, had strong parallels with the Wendigo belief in the Ghost Dance, in which the participants built a great caern in the spirit world to hide their greatest treasures. While the Ghost Dancers had kept careful track of their own spirit caches, some of their elders thought that the legendary city sightings were one of their own ancient caerns, poking into the earth from a weak spot in the Gauntlet, the membrane that separated the realms. Indeed, sightings were more frequent during the aurora borealis, when the Gauntlet was weakest. To Amy's ear, the eye-witness descriptions of vast, complex structures carved seemingly out of the side of a mountain sounded more like the cities of the Hisatsinom than the simple villages of the Inuit.

In exchange for their help, Amy was forced to agree to share whatever she found with the Greyrock Sept leaders. Not quite trusting an Uktena to live up to a full disclosure agreement, they made her swear an oath three times. Living up to the oath would be simple enough. Despite several nights under the magical rainbow lights of the aurora, they'd seen nothing. At any rate, it wasn't the first time Kusagak had been on such an expedition, nor the first time such an expedition had failed.

The trio moved on in silence for the next hour, letting the wind howl for it. Upon climbing a sheer wall and reaching the flat top, a small, exposed plateau, Amy feared the wind would be even stronger, but, in fact, it died down a bit and briefly afforded a view of the peaks of the Philip Smith Mountains.

Kusagak grinned as he saw them. They were even closer than he'd hoped to the series of shelters and a small, simple Nissen hut that comprised Greyrock. In fact, the sheltered valley he called home was just on the other side of the plateau. He hand-signaled the information to Amy, who simply smiled and nodded at Claws. All he needed to know was that the news was good. With renewed strength of purpose they struggled through the deep snow across the flat area.

Weather notwithstanding, Amy's big concern was a young Inuit Kinfolk that lived at Greyrock named Marty Drumdancer. When she and Claws first arrived, she was asked, of course, to tell a story of her journey. Obliged to do so despite her lack of talent, she launched into a long, laborious detail of their trip to Tibet, and how the Stargazers there refused to speak to her. By the end, most of her audience had wandered off or fallen asleep, but young Marty, no more than ten, was fascinated. Born under the Gibbous Moon, if he turned out to be Garou, and the signs for that were promising, he'd be a songkeeper himself. The boy had long ago drained all the tales from the local Galliards, and visitors to Greyrock were rare. So, for the first time in her life, Amy was asked to tell a second tale. Flustered, she didn't know what to say, but she swore to the boy that upon her return she would convey every detail of their quest. Back in the present, as they started down a path on the other side, Amy wondered how interesting she could make two weeks of uneventful trudging, even to such a willing listener. As it turned out, she needn't have worried.

With the mountain now shielding them from the worst of the blizzard, aside from a gray mist that floated low over the valley, the whole area could clearly be seen. The big black patches that dotted the ground, like clumps of charcoal against a white sheet, struck her first. At a distance she thought they were woodpiles or maybe even ceremonial rings of some sort, but as they grew closer, she realized they were too large. About the size of Nissen huts, in fact. Then she and Claws both noticed that several of the splotches had red and yellow fires burning in the center. The cloudiness she'd mistaken for mist was black smoke from the fires mixing with falling snow.

By the time Amy and Claws realized they were looking at what remained of a war zone, Kusagak was already running, drawing his great warhammer. A series of burning craters was all that marked where Greyrock once stood.

Upon reaching what was his home, Kusagak growled, swung his hammer in the air and raced about the devastation for five minutes until he realized there was no longer any foe to fight. Whatever had destroyed the sept was no longer apparent, though it could easily be hiding just beyond the next snowy ridge. Quickly, the group moved from building to building, looking for survivors, and found only pieces of bodies. Marty Drumdancer, who would never even know if he were Garou now, and his mother were crushed by a caved-in roof.

The only thing still breathing, perhaps because the attackers confused him with one of the butchered dead, was the shapeless metis who couldn't even manage to retrieve fresh water for the caern.

Kusagak pulled at his misshapen form and demanded, "What happened here? What happened?"

"End…end…end," was all the frightened creature could manage. Amy thought he was crying.

Kusagak shook his head, gritted his teeth and was about to say something when his ears caught the sound of something living. Like a madman, he raced toward a group of trees away from the caern, where, pinned by a large sheet of ice and rock seemingly blasted from the side of the mountain, Ussak, the sept's warder, lay, his chest, arms and head free.

As Claws and Kusagak tried to leverage the huge debris away from the fallen Wendigo, Amy moved to make him more comfortable, an effort that seemed only to annoy the gruff old Garou.

"Don't waste your time. It doesn't matter. Grandmother calls me and I will answer soon. Just listen to me or I will have waited all this time for nothing."

Amy nodded.

"Eight days after you left, what we thought were oil surveyors made their way to the area just beyond the northern hills."

"This is a protected wildlife refuge! Drilling isn't legal!" Amy blurted

"You are naïve, older sister. Surveyors have been here before, but we manage to discourage them. Sensing no real threat, we sent three of our warriors to learn more. They did not return. It turns out, these surveyors did not frighten easily, nor was oil their target. Just as we had amassed a force to retrieve our septmates, we were bombarded with artillery shells. Artillery shells! After the shelling, fomori swarmed over the area to kill the wounded. They thought I was dead. At least they did not take the pathstone."

He opened his bloodied hand and revealed the small, smooth stone consecrated to the heart of the caern. As Amy took it from him, he coughed and a blotch of blood dribbled from his lips down the side of his face.

"Whose songs shall I sing?" she asked. "Tell me quickly, Ussak."

"Moonsinger and Brown Eagle," he began. He moaned loudly as Claws and Brunt managed to roll one of the larger boulders away, revealing his body. They all stared a moment in sad shock. Half of Ussak was virtually missing, crushed to pulp. Wondering what they were staring at, he turned toward where his lower torso should be. A strange grin came to his features, but he died before it could erupt into a final bitter laugh. Amy swore she heard it on the wind, though—and when she asked him later, Kusagak claimed to have heard it, too.

Inconsolable, Kusagak simply shouted, long and loud. Ussak was his mentor, his friend. And now, as the only member of his sept spared, aside from the metis, he bore the shame of being away during their final battle.

"Quiet, you fool! These bastards must know they're up against Garou! Your howl will bring them running!" Claws cried, but it was too late. He picked his ears up to the sound of a gasoline engine. Turning north, Claws saw a small hill of heavy gray metal. Sporting skis as well as treads, it burst through the snow cover and headed toward them. A red star was visible on the side.

"A tank?! They've got a tank?" he said.

"Old Soviet model. Anyone can buy them cheap on the black market," Kusagak responded. "We've seen them here before. Let's hope that's the worst of what they have."

With a high-pitched whine, the main gun whirled and locked onto their position. Kusagak tensed as if he wanted to face down the tank, but Amy and Claws grabbed him.

"Later!" Claws shouted, trying to pull the large Wendigo to cover. "Later!"

So full of rage that tears came to his eyes, Kusagak gritted his teeth and ran with them. As it was, they were nearly back at the top of the plateau before they lost their pursuer in a small series of caves. Amy gasped, realizing they'd left the metis behind.

Still, it was the next nightfall before they ventured out again. The weather had cleared and the edge of the plateau now afforded a view of a series of tents and temporary buildings pitched about a mile from the ruins of Greyrock.

"There must be fifty men there! It's a small army!" Amy gasped. "They came prepared for an assault."

"There's not much we can do against numbers like that," Claws said, shaking his head. Hearing what sounded like defeat, Kusagak exploded.

"Do not turn your back on me, older brother! Do not hide your sacred truths from me now!" he snarled. Amy grabbed him by the shoulders and stared deep into his eyes.

"We will not hide! We will pledge our blood to help you avenge your sept even if it means our own death! And we will hold back no secrets that can help us destroy these carrion followers of the Horned Serpent," Amy shouted, in her best imitation of Wendigo bravado. "But first we must mourn, then we must learn and then we must *plan!*"

Recognizing the wisdom of her words but unable to quell his rage, Kusagak stormed off and pounded the ground with his fists. At his prodding, they made their way back to the desecrated caern and by morning buried what they could find of the bodies. Unable to find the metis, they assumed he had been killed. In dawn's light they sang the Dirge for the Fallen. Once the last howl was sounded, Amy turned to Kusagak and pressed the caern's pathstone into his hand.

"I am certain Ussak meant for you to have this," she said. "Once we've cleared these creatures from the area, you will begin Greyrock anew."

Kusagak clenched the stone and nodded grimly.

They solemnly trudged along the valley as close to the enemy camp as they could get without being spotted.

Amy's estimate was quite correct. There were fifty-four armed mercenary soldiers visible within the camp. Six corporate types, with cell phones, clad in bright orange Gore-Tex, rounded out the mortal group. In the center of the encampment, a large warehouse had been constructed, with a metal skeleton holding it about a foot off the permafrost. Unused, unpacked drilling equipment lay alongside its exterior. Toward the southern perimeter, past where the tank and two large artillery guns were kept, some thirty fomori staggered about listlessly in the snow.

"They're Wyrm followers all right. But they wouldn't have brought all that drilling and blasting equipment if they weren't actually after oil. The sept may have just been a lucky find," Amy surmised.

"Now they will corrupt it and suck up Gaia's blood," Kusagak said.

Claws summed up what they were thinking: "And the question isn't whether we're going to die or not, but how much damage we can do before we go."

An odd metallic clink made Amy look toward the central building again. A group of mercenaries were unloading a truck full of bright, shiny barrels marked RDX. Puzzled, she rolled the three familiar letters over in her mind until, excited by her recollection, she swatted Claws on the side of his shoulder and laughed.

"That's Cyclanite! Explosives! Enough to bring down the whole area!"

"Hooray! But what good is it going to do us in the middle of their camp?" Claws asked.

"*Mene, mene, tekel, upharsin,*" she said with an odd smile.

"In English, please," Claws said, "or at least Garou, so Kusagak can understand."

Amy was more than happy to translate. "It's Aramaic. 'He has counted, weighed and they divide.' It means God has judged a city and is going to wipe it from the face of the earth." Now Claws was smiling, too.

ing of a child. Mercenaries came

to kill him, still in Crinos, Amy
her feet and started running. She
rcenaries shouting behind. Three
oward her on the left, ready to cut
at weren't bad enough, machine
he mercs churned ice and dirt up
ieces of snow and grit pelted her
ed in the snow, attempting to
ers not only about where she was
e she had been. On the latter, it
ccessful. No one was heading for

alized there was no chance of her
in time, the explosion occurred.
ed that there was no huge, colorful
movies. Instead, there was a bright
ght a glimpse of the thin walls of
hing outward as if it were a balloon
motion. The shock wave careened
, shredding most everything in its
was indeed a huge globe of red
as the blast hit the fuel dumps. But
s in midair herself, carried like a
d not in much of a position to
w.
ned by the initial explosion, now
umbling that threatened to shake
ns loose. Amy managed to look
before closing her eyes. The entire
built on seemed to be collapsing
le. Her rapid flight hit its zenith.

Late the next night, Amy found herself crouched down low behind one of the enemy's tents, staring at the central warehouse, waiting for the patrol to pass. As the two mercs rounded the corner and vanished from sight, she lunged forward. She was soon on her back beneath the metal floors of the temporary warehouse, pulling herself along hand over hand using the prefab metal support ribs that lined the floor. Sneaking in this far was easy enough. Entering the building would be more complicated. She only hoped Claws and Kusagak timed their distraction properly. Without realizing it, she'd rolled over a particularly large rock that lodged in the small of her back. Now it rolled with her, cutting past the fur of her Crinos form and drawing some blood. Clenching her teeth, she rolled over, trying to get off it, but ultimately found that pulling forward was the quickest way. The rock slid loose from her body but rolled under her rucksack and tore at the cloth.

She was just about in the center of the building, pushing up on the loose steel plates when Claws and Kusagak began their wild howling. With the sounds echoing off the nearby mountains, they sounded more like ten than two Garou—just the effect they'd hoped for. There was a flurry of shouted commands and speculative murmurs in the camp. The tank engine fired up. Amy turned to the side and saw booted feet rushing off. Finally in place herself, with a grunt she pushed up on the steel floor plate and lifted herself into the building.

As she scanned the prefab structure, she counted the canisters. Seventy-five—more than one for each of the enemy. Now all she needed were some detonators. Tearing open some crates also being stored here, she came upon another treasure—a laptop computer. Wondering what prizes it held, she lowered it into her rucksack and noticed that the tent pole had torn a small hole in the side. Not seeing anything missing, she returned to her search. Things were calming down in the camp. She heard the sound of tank shells exploding.

Though to her mind it was clear that Greyrock would have been attacked anyway, she found herself wishing she'd never dragged Claws up here. It was an embarrassing wish. Here, she had a chance to do some real good. But if they all died, as likely they would, just how real a good was it? No one would sing the songs or learn the lessons.

Swallowing her concerns, she returned to her search and, after examining a few boxes full of rations, finally came upon the detonators. Within ten minutes she had fifteen barrels wired and ready to blow. How long should she give herself? Too long, and if she was caught escaping, the detonators might be found and disarmed. Too short and she would not escape.

Four minutes, then. That would be just enough time for her to make it across the camp and clear the southern ridge. Not the safest place to be, given the size of the blast, but survival would be possible. She clicked the numbers in and set the timer off. Changing to Lupus, she dived under the building, wriggled the strap of the laptop around her neck and crawled quickly to the edge of the building.

She'd just cleared the structure and was making for the camp's edge when she spotted one of the Gore-

Tex clad
man, was
wrapped a
He was h
over in his
he held h
Professor
in her ba
there was

Still,
so made a
caught a
his tracks
"Am
muffled b
Shoo
stood.
"So s
you so m
He held
Amy
She had b
The
when she
tracks ba
whip out
leapt on
was still
unnotice
his prote
a powerfu
blood fro
out a shri

like the whimpe
running.

With no tim
pushed back ont
could hear the n
fomori shambled
off her path. If t
gun bullets from
in front of her.
eyes. She zigzag
confuse her purs
headed, but whe
seemed she was s
the warehouse.

Just as she re
clearing the ridg
She was disappoi
fireball, like in th
flash, and she ca
the warehouse ru
exploding in slow
through the cam
wake. Then the
and orange flame
by then Amy w
tumbling leaf a
appreciate the vi

Though deaf
she felt an awful
her internal org
down one last tim
area the camp w
into a huge sinkh

She knew she was about to tumble into the white abyss the Cyclanite had opened in the earth. Suddenly tired, she closed her eyes. After a moment, the rumbling faded, leaving only blackness followed by an odd sensation of warmth. When her body hit solid ground again, Amy wasn't in it.

Then there came a moment when the strangeness of the world bent down and kissed her on the forehead. With her Mother's warm, full lips pressed against her flat skin, a tingle ran down the length of her spine and she felt like a cradled child.

"Open your eyes," a voice whispered.

She did.

There, covered in icy ripples, glowing and glowering, encompassing the full field of vision and more, was a Hisatsinom metropolis, just like the biggest in Four Corners, Pueblo Bonito, in Chaco Canyon. Though covered and obscured by ice, the semicircular dwelling units, the great kivas, or holy centers, even the empty spaces meant for lush gardens were all clearly visible.

"Surprise!" the voice said, "For your birthday."

Amy had completely forgotten it was her birthday. But Mother never would. Still, remembering what the Gore-Tex-clad figure said, she didn't think she deserved any presents. The Wyrm had followed her here. She was responsible for the death of Kusagak's people, for the fact that Marty Drumdancer would never even know if he were a Garou. She lowered her head and wept.

"It's all right," the voice said. "You didn't know. Stand up."

Not wanting to disappoint her Mother, she obeyed. Standing was easier than she imagined. Almost floating up onto the balls of her feet, she reached out and tried to touch the city, but her hand was blocked by the cool ice. As a shiver made its way from her palm, up her spine and into the base of her skull, it carried another thought—was it a city at all? She looked again. This time the great buildings seemed little more than illusions formed by natural formations under the ice—geological strata revealed by the explosion.

Grasping for rationality, Amy recalled the sunken stone structures found off Okinawa, Japan, sixty to one hundred feet beneath the ocean surface. At first it was clear to the divers that they were the remains of a vast ancient city, until geologists shook their heads and pointed to dozens of similar, completely natural formations. Newer theories claimed that though they were partly natural, they were clearly modified by sentient builders. The truth of the place seemed to vibrate between acceptance and desire. But how much archeology was based on seeing shapes in the sand? How much on inventing them? What was the proof of *this* place? Again her eyes blinked and again she saw a city, proof positive that the Hisatsinom Garou fled far north to hide their treasures.

Her fingernail scratched the hard surface in front of her, leaving a jagged white line etched in the ice. Her eyes scanned left and right for some visceral, undeniable something. Lying at the base of what she imagined might be the central kiva, about a foot inside the icy cover, was what seemed to be a dark ball. Desperate for a tool, she began chipping away at the ice with the first thing she could pull from her rucksack, the laptop. Realizing how foolish that was, she fished around in her rucksack and tore apart a Bane arrow to get at its sharp stone head. The spirit inside, suddenly free, was confused that there was no blood.

After what seemed forever, she freed the edge of the sphere and touched its bony surface. Now there was no doubt. She chipped carefully at the sides, carving its shape as she went along, frightened she might bring the thing some harm. A low, deep creaking from within the ice didn't even make her hesitate. The world itself could explode around her, but she would not leave this place without the ball. At last she was able to wedge her hands on either side of it. She pulled, twisted, gritted her teeth and pulled again.

With a final tug, the sphere came free into her hands. The dream was real, but so was the precariously balanced mountain of ice that had contained it all these years. Weakened by the minor excavation, the glacier came crashing down. She wrapped herself around the ball as if it were a small child and told herself that at least, in dying, she had done something worthwhile; at least she'd finally held something real.

She awoke wrapped in blankets, feeling more like a big bruise than a person, to see Claws tending a fire nearby. Seeing her eyes open, he grinned and sat down beside her. Behind his head a million stars filled the sky.

"I lost you for two days, girl," Claws said. "I was sure that was it for you."

"How did you dig me out?" she asked, bewildered.

"Dig you out? Of what? You were hanging sideways in a big pine tree. That's what took me so long. I was busy looking down. Finally found your rucksack at the base of it. That stupid metis was still alive and started following me. He barked or something when he saw you up there."

"I was in a canyon. A city," Amy said, trying to sit up.

"Uh…okay. It was two days. I don't know where you were. But I found you in a tree, unconscious, and from the look of your wounds, you weren't in any shape to do much traveling."

She shook her head trying to get her bearings, then remembered the base.

"Did we win?" she asked.

"Big time," Claws nodded.

"Kusagak?" she whispered.

Claws shook his head. "With his people. We even lost the pathstone."

A sudden lump in her throat, Amy looked down. In her hands was the bone-sphere. She showed it to Claws and he shrugged. He sensed a bit of magic in it, but not much. Agreeing, Amy buried it in the bottom of her bag. At first she prayed the laptop would prove a more useful trophy. In Anchorage, they turned it over to a Glass Walker, who discovered that the data on the hard drive proved the expedition had been funded by the Pentex Corporation. Though they initially hoped this would lead to some legal difficulties for the megacorporation, days earlier Congress had passed legislation allowing drilling in the region. Pentex would only have to switch some of the dates to escape unscathed. Even the computer was useless.

Disgusted with her theories, too ashamed to tell Claws that the Wyrm had followed her, and now thinking the sphere yet another waste of time and energy, Amy sank into deep depression, wondering why she had ever come into being, forgetting that all of us are only part of the story.

Only arrogance assumes any of us is more than a reflection. Arrogance is fear. Fear is the turned Wyrm.

I ask again, if all the pieces of creation are here with us now, what is different between us? What is different between spirit and earth? What is the difference between you and me?

A song.

Just as the heart of each living thing dances between its images and its senses, the maps its mind creates and the terrain in which it lives, the universe sings a song. A song that shapes the dance of being, that gives it form, duration and meaning, allowing the Tellurian to vibrate in an ecstatic oscillation between oneness and uniqueness.

And what is the secret of the universe?

This: the music that forms the mind is the same as the music that forms the world.

Do not doubt this. I beg you.

Do not think of me as other.

Think of me as your own lips begging you to hear.

***

The story had caught them all off guard. They stared at Amy, still in its spell. But the sphere's tones in her own mind were fading, along with their effect, and countless desperate, disparate thoughts raced for the opening window of consciousness and battered their way into words.

She had them. She had them all. But she didn't know when to shut up.

"Don't you get it? In the Umbra, whole worlds are generated by our mythic traditions, the tales we tell here, the songs we sing. If whole realms, why not the whole Umbra, including the earth? If the whole Umbra, why not the Tellurium? Why not the Wyrm itself? Don't you see? If we find the right song, even the Wyrm can be healed. Corrupted, broken, sickly, the Wyrm is still one of the Triat that forms the All. Without Wyrm, there is nothing. He must be healed, and the path to healing him must be song. This ancient sphere, one of Mother's greatest gifts for a time of greatest need, is a clue to that. It is linked. I know it is."

Even the crickets were quiet after that.

Sees the Wind rolled the sphere from hand to hand, measuring its weight and balance. Making a grand gesture of the process, he perched it on the tips of his fingers and closed one eye, as if examining a rare gem.

Amy tensed. As much as she wanted him to confirm the sphere's value, she also, desperately, hungrily, wanted it back. Just seeing it in someone else's hands made her horribly uncomfortable. As he looked it over, he began to speak.

"Many other tribes, some Uktena as well, believe we hoard our knowledge out of avarice, arrogance or greed. Do you know the Western saying, *Do not hurl your pearls before swine?*"

"Yes, I do," Amy answered.

"What do you think it means?"

"That you should save the best part of yourself, or your spirit, for those who are worthy of it," Amy answered.

"Wrong. We Uktena do not hurl pearls before swine, not because it protects us from the imagined shame of their derision, but because it would be cruel to the swine. Through no fault of their own, pigs do not know what a pearl is and would perhaps try to eat it, thereby doing themselves great damage. That is why the Uktena keep their knowledge to themselves. Do you understand?"

Amy nodded.

"Then consider that even I might be a swine," he said with a wink." I see that your heart is full of sadness for the tragedy you feel, perhaps rightly, you caused. It wants with as powerful a longing as these eyes have ever seen, to provide some great meaning for the death of Greyrock. And that makes this pearl suspect. Is this the only thing that is true? No. But it is true, and it is what I see."

Then a broad grin doubled the wrinkles on the old one's face.

"You made this," he said, tossing the sphere back. "You keep it."

"What?" she wanted to say. He could not have meant it literally. Even if she was wrong about everything, even if it wasn't Hisatsinom, clearly it was ancient and not the product of some depressed low-level songkeeper. But the Uktena loved their cryptic declarations and, as an Uktena, it would be unspeakably rude for her to question his judgment on the dispensation of a relic, even, in some ways especially, to ask for a clarification.

Despite her unspoken disagreement with his decision, a tingle went up her arms the moment the sphere was in her hands again. Her sense of relief overwhelmed any other feelings she was having. Trying to conceal her secret pleasure, she laid the sphere gently next to her and immediately began ferreting through her bag.

"Well…uh…I also have this klaive…"

***

The Uktena songkeeper's words washed over Arkady, carving a picture of the relic in his soul. The more he thought on it, the more he became convinced that it was necessary to his quest.

A sea of relief, as great as Amy's, flooded him when the old one rejected it. The Uktena were simple in some ways, perhaps, but Arkady had no wish to face the shaman. His old, Umbra-warped eyes would see past any lies Arkady might have to devise, and his secretive, hoarding nature would almost certainly preclude him from offering any assistance to a Silver Fang.

After all, to those who did not see the world as Arkady saw it, he was on a fool's errand—following a dream. And that in itself gave him more in common with the younger one, Amy. She was the only one aside from him, he was convinced, who sensed the true value of the prize.

Yes, clearly, Arkady was far better off dealing with the girl when the time came to claim this great signpost on his path.

Chapter Six

I never want to leave this country; all my relatives are lying here in the ground. And when I fall to pieces I am going to fall to pieces here.

—Shunkaha Napin (Wolf Necklace)

"You lied to me," Claws said as they trotted along the open plain.

"I omitted details," Amy said, pleading in her voice for forgiveness. "Besides, I figured you sort of knew."

"I knew you *felt* responsible, Amy. I had no idea we were followed," Claws said.

"Owed…owed…owed," Chottle panted, as if offended himself.

"You said yourself everyone, everything was destroyed by the blast," Amy said. "So, we weren't in further danger."

"As far as we know, everything was destroyed. But people have phones, Amy. Whoever engineered it might not even have been in Alaska. They still might be out there, watching us."

"You're right. Absolutely. Unequivocally. I apologize. I am so sorry, Claws. I was just so embarrassed, confused. I couldn't even tell the tale without the help of the sphere,…" she began, but he cut her off angrily.

"We're lucky the Wendigo haven't killed us, for Gaia's sake! And another thing, you promised not to use it, but you did. That's not like you. That bone-sphere acts on you like some drug. I wouldn't be surprised if our fellow Uktena suspected us of Wyrm-taint by now," he snapped.

"But that's ridiculous!"

"Is it? Then why are you still being sent upstream to spawn?" he said in disgust.

For that, Amy had no answer.

Hours passed in silence. By noon the unshielded sun no longer felt safe, as if unable to find his quieter sister Luna anywhere in the sky, the fiery orb, like the Weaver itself, had gone utterly mad. From the moment they started their trek toward the small town of Dekane, Amy could feel the unfiltered rays burning her skin as if it were thin, oil-soaked paper on the verge of immolation. Dog days such as this, with the temperature tumbling over 110 degrees would make any Garou even more tense and irritable than usual. After all, it was an undeniable sign of the impossible truth, that Mother was sick and could soon be dying. All things considered, Claws was taking things pretty well.

"We could have at least waited until nightfall," he finally said, panting as he trotted beside her.

"Fall...fall...fall,..." Chottle begged.

"This *Kinfolk* has some kind of class he attends in Omaha and may be leaving tonight. They weren't sure how long he'd be in town. Did you want to stay here for another week?" Amy asked, her half-sneering pronunciation of "Kinfolk" revealing her disdain for Sees the Wind's request. "And, and, and," she added, "this morning it was thirty degrees cooler and I am loath to admit that, yet again, I am wrong."

Claws didn't bother answering, but she thought she saw him smile.

They traveled in Crinos, slower than the full wolf form and traditionally only for battle, but a compromise between evils. Wolves, like dogs and cats, only sweat from their paws and tongues— making travel in the heat difficult. The wolf-man form gave them the advantage of almost all their human sweat glands as well as thicker skin for greater protection from burning. And sweat they did. Amy and Claws' coats, dripping perspiration, matted down flat against their skin. Chottle seemed, as he always did, to simply suffer. Amy surmised his pain was probably made worse by his Wendigo bloodline, bred for arctic climes.

She did want to get this over with. She could have refused, but Amy's telling of the events in Alaska seemed to mollify some of Sees the Wind's concerns. Why not address them all?

Why not? Because now she had to drag her ass and her pack forty miles to Dekane and meet a young Kinfolk considered by the elder to be a potential mate. She found herself wishing the Uktena would just place personal ads, like some of the big city septs did, with their cute four-letter codes. SMFK for Single Male Fianna Kinfolk and so on.

"This is *not* my best destiny," Amy sighed. "Even if this boy is descended from Broken Medicine."

"Hey, it's not *my* destiny at all," Claws pointed out.

"Wooo! Wooo! Wooo!"

Amy snapped her head at the sound of Chottle's voice. Droplets of sweat flew around, one of which hits Claws in the eye.

"Wait a minute," she said. "I didn't say 'woo,' did you?"

"Nope," Claws answered, blinking his eye. "Listen."

Slowing her panting breath, she was able to hear what Chottle was imitating—the siren of a fire truck speeding along the nearby dirt road. As it passed, the trio ducked down behind some dried bushes to avoid being seen. Once certain they were alone again, Amy turned to the direction the truck had headed and caught a glimpse of jet-black smoke rising in thick, bilious clouds.

"Ychh," Claws muttered. "Can you imagine a fire today?"

"Welcome to Dekane," Amy said sadly. "Just outside the Omaha reservation, where, despite the best efforts to the contrary, arson and alcoholism run rampant."

As the small rows of 1950s government housing came into view and they realized they might soon be seen, Claws and Amy switched to Homid. The hard part was finding a shady spot to hide Chottle in. Eventually an abandoned barn near the main road seemed cool enough.

"Just for a while," Amy whispered, patting him on what she hoped was his head.

As the duo stepped out into the full view of human society for the first time in weeks, Amy felt as though she'd entered a third-world country. Small, dirty children played in dust on lifeless front lawns. The plywood doors on half the houses were smashed, gaping holed with frayed wood at the edges, and poorly covered by plastic and duct tape. The thin plasterboard walls visible inside one home had fist-sized holes smashed in alcohol-induced rages. Why repair houses that are not your own? When they were too far gone, they were abandoned. Eventually someone would set one on fire. Everyone would gather to watch, while the fire trucks, half an hour away, always arrived too late to save anything. Even now they poured water on steaming ruins.

"*Plus je vois les hommes, plus j'admire les chiens*," Amy intoned sadly.

"I know that one," said Claws. "French, right? Something about liking dogs more than men?"

Amy said nothing. A woman walked by, seemingly in her mid-fifties, with two teeth remaining in her mouth. She cackled, then praised Jesus for letting her go another day without drink. Amy was embarrassed to watch, yet equally ashamed to turn away. Though angry, she was also aware of her great distance from these people—what joys they shared, what dreams they followed, what despair haunted them. Though not Native American, she was Uktena—and insofar as these people were marginalized, occupied and ultimately dispossessed, she did find some sense of commonality.

There were other signs, too, more difficult to see. Signs of hope and humanity undefeated. A teen read Castenada. Two men painted the side of a house that was not their own. Colorful, handmade traditional signs announced a great community picnic this weekend. Perhaps even the most desperate were just waiting for the right story to inhabit, the right song to sing, before coming, once more, to life.

"That's him," Claws said, nodding toward a sunburnt teen in shorts and a torn Smashmouth T-shirt.

"That *boy*?"

"Think so." Claws called out, "Peter?"

As the boy turned, a smile made its way to Amy's lips. About seventeen, his face already had some deep character, with a chiseled Native American nose and deep-set eyes. He was skinny but muscled. And though he stood straight and tall, there was something quite unassuming about him, as though he somehow avoided the pressured, raw ego that plagued many poorer teens. But the first thing Amy felt was that he reminded her, very much, of Marty Drumdancer. The thought that the boy's features were still alive somewhere made her feel good.

Seeing the two newcomers, a puzzled look crept over his face.

"You know me?" he said, stepping up to them.

"We're friends of your Uncle Johnny," Claws said.

"Yes…friends," was all Amy could think to say.

Amused by the songkeeper's gift with words, Claws continued, "I'm…Casey and this is Amy. She's a little tired from the heat."

"So how is old apple face? Still think he's a shaman?" he said. Sees the Wind had yet to reveal his heritage to the boy, but he had given Amy and Claws permission to speak candidly if they felt it was appropriate.

"Wacky as ever," Amy ventured, smiling a little too much. What was wrong with her? She was acting like a schoolgirl in front of a boy at least eight years younger.

Peter nodded. "I kind of figured you two weren't from around here, given the clothes. Nice duds."

"So, Peter,..." Amy started.

After a while, he found himself forced to say, "Yeah?"

"What...uh...do you do?"

He made a face as if she were making fun of him. "*Do?* Eat. Sleep. Crap. Piss. Bay at the moon." Then in a voice of faux Injun Wisdom, he added, "Ask Raven why people ask stupid questions. What do you *do*, Amy?"

"I wonder what Raven says when you ask," Amy answered, feeling a bit more herself.

"Ha!" Peter smiled. "Okay. Mostly he asks why *my* questions are so stupid. So I guess we're even. You guys slumming or what? Not many people travel to Dekane for entertainment. As you can see, they haven't opened the new multiplex yet."

Peter eyed them again, as if trying to make up his mind, then, realizing they probably had some money and not much else was going on, said, "There's a bar down the road. Buy me a beer?"

A few hours later, as the sun went down and the day finally began to cool, the three sat in an old wooden booth sharing an icy pitcher of whatever was on tap in the dimly lit one-room saloon. The drunkenness would last only as long as they were in human form, so Amy decided to try and enjoy it.

"*Uisage beatha!*" she said, raising her glass. After a long draught, she wiped her mouth and said, "The

Irish usually say that with whiskey, but you get the idea."

After a few more sips, Amy was feeling a little freer with her tongue and soon tried to regale the boy with her borrowed tales. Painfully familiar with all her anecdotes, Claws rolled his eyes.

"Where today are the Pequot?" she quoted. "Where are the Narragansett, the Mohican, the Pokanoket and many other once powerful tribes of our people? They have vanished before the avarice and the oppression of the White Man, as snow before a summer sun. Will we let ourselves be destroyed in our turn without a struggle, give up our homes, our country bequeathed to us by the Great Spirit, the graves of our dead and everything that is dear and sacred to us? I know you will cry with me, 'Never! Never!'"

"Tecumseh," Peter nodded thoughtfully. "You know, we Omaha have the dubious distinction of being the only tribe in all North America that never raised its hand against the White Man."

"That would be a source of shame for me," Claws said, knocking down the frothy dregs of his plastic cup.

"And it is for many of us. Me, I figure hey, we're still here," Peter said, filling Claws' glass again. The warrior motioned for him to stop and caught his eye with a stern glare.

"So you just kind of hey, kick back and get assimilated?"

"Resistance is futile," Peter said with a bitter laugh.

"But sometimes you have to fight. You can't just lay down and die. And the Omaha did fight. They fought with the North in the Civil War," Amy said.

"For someone *else's* freedom," Claws said.

"Ah, what is life?" Peter said. "It is the flash of a firefly in the night. It is the breath of a buffalo in the wintertime. It is the little shadow which runs across the grass and loses itself in the sunset. See? Crowfoot. I know Native American quotes, too. And I know there are all *kinds* of wars. Were the Europeans genocidal maniacs who saw us as less than human? Sure! Are we currently oppressed by a cycle of poverty and a culture that was utterly overwhelmed two hundred years ago? You bet. Does that mean I should go bomb Exxon? No thanks. There's good and bad in everyone, everything. If you could just pry the bad part out, I'd be right there with you, trying to beat it to death. But, pshh! You can't."

"Be back," Claws said, excusing himself. I've got to check on Chottle…I mean, uh…take a leak."

"Chottle? I've never heard anyone call it *that* before," Peter said with a grin. Amy, who'd been curled up in the corner of the same side of the booth with Peter, sat up, moving a little closer. Seeing this, Peter whispered to her conspiratorially.

"My uncle always buys these crappy bittersweet chocolate balls, but I can't stand them. Do you like milk chocolate, Amy?"

"Uh, yeah, I guess so. Bittersweet's all right when it's in a cookie or something," she answered, more than a little amused at the similarity between uncle and nephew.

"In a cookie, yeah, that's it exactly," Peter said. Then he nodded toward the door Claws had exited from. "I think I offended him. Do *you* understand what I mean by a futile battle?"

"Yeah...I guess I feel the same way a lot of the time. But, I know something you don't. There is a way. Another war—and tools that can help you see the corruption," she said, beginning to feel a little proud of being a Garou.

"Oh yeah?"

"Yeah. And I can show it to you," she whispered.

"Then show me," Peter said softly.

Amy leaned closer; their lips were almost touching.

And then...

"Achoo!" Peter let off a huge sneeze. She pulled back to avoid the spray.

Before he could even grab a napkin, Peter sneezed again.

"Achoo!"

Padding his nose and watering eyes with the napkin, he waved Amy farther back.

"Wow! Do you, like, have a dog or a cat or something? Because I am incredibly allergic. It must be in your clothes. You know, the same thing happens whenever my uncle's around too long."

"I,..." Amy began, flabbergasted. She quickly rose and excused herself. "I'll be right back."

Seeing Claws on the street, she grabbed him and pulled him off to the side of a large building across from the bar. Once certain they were alone, she told him what had just happened. In seconds, they both fell to the floor in spasms of laughter.

"Allergic! Can you believe it? He's allergic to us!"

"No wonder there are more metis around! You think Sees the Wind knows?"

"He must! That old coot has one helluva sense of humor..."

As she sighed and collected herself, Amy's hand happened upon a smooth spot in the dust. Something was half-buried in the dirt. With furrowed brow, she did not look, but let her fingers pry the small thing free. Feeling it slip into her palm, she held it up and stared.

A parrot bone. She held in her hand a parrot bone.

"Do you see this?" she said, showing it to Claws, uncertain if it was part of a vision or real.

Claws nodded. "From KFC?"

"No. No. But it could be a pet," Amy said, then she began scraping the dirt from it, looking for some indication of its origin.

"Oh sure," Claws said, still laughing. "First Chottle, now a chicken bone. How many pets do you need?"

"Chottle is *not* a pet!" she snapped.

Then she saw them, quite clearly: Hisatsinom markings. She turned it over and over, quite stunned by how much it looked like the PVC duplicate she had carried with her in Alaska, until...

She grabbed a canteen from Claws and spilled the water onto the bone.

"Hey! Don't waste that! I don't trust the drinking water around here."

As the rest of the dirt fell away and the color of the bone shone through just a bit too white, Amy realized it *was* plastic. She flipped it over again and saw the scratch her own nail had made while climbing in Chaco Canyon. Her eyes went wide as she turned toward the small brick and mortar warehouselike structure they hid behind.

"What building is this?" she whispered.

"Hard to say…some kind of storage? I smell tobacco," Claws said. "What are you not telling me now?"

Amy popped up to her feet and started looking for a window. Claws tapped her on the shoulder.

"Hey, Peter Blows His Nose is back," he whispered, nodding toward the street. "But I want an explanation. Uktena secrecy shouldn't extend to packmates from the same tribe!"

The teen staggered out of the bar, still wiping viscous remains from his nose with a counter napkin. Amy and Claws met him in the middle of the road.

"Peter, what's this building?"

"Oh, used to be a daycare center. Few months back some tribe members got an idea for making some money, so they bought some old machines from the tobacco industry and turned it into a cigarette factory. You know, 'native' tobacco and all that crap. That stuff's about as native as Dan Quayle's ass. The real traditional tobacco is grown by a few staunch old-timers, and they only use it for rituals. This stuff is for the rubes," he explained.

The building reeked of Wyrm-taint. She could tell by the look on Claws' face that he was beginning to sense it, too. Was a cigarette factory enough to do that? And how did her parrot bone get here?

"They've been pretty successful, too," Peter said. "I saw some corporate types here last week, poking around. There's a rumor they want to buy the brand or something."

"Corporate types?" Amy said, some answers beginning to click in her head.

"Suits and cell phones. Hey, look, it's late, I'm a bit drunk and now I've got a snoot full. I've got to sober up, then take my antihistamines if I'm going to sleep tonight. Really nice meeting you, Amy," he said.

"Me, too," she said. Impulsively she leaned forward and gave him a quick kiss on the lips. "Hope we meet again sometime."

Peter's mouth twisted in what threatened to be a smile but turned out to be another massive sneeze. Covering his nose, he staggered back. He was about to say something, but he sneezed again, this time projecting a thick wad of mucus on his open palm. Rolling his eyes, he pivoted, quickened his pace and started off on the road back toward the center of Dekane.

"I think they have shots for that now," Amy called after him.

There was no answer.

Once he was out of site, Amy pulled Claws back behind the building, near a large metal garage door that graced the back wall.

"Chottle's in the woods over there. Want to tell me what's up?"

She showed him the resin bone, holding it between thumb and forefinger. "This is the replica

Hisatsinom bone I lost in Alaska. *Das ding an sich*. Our friends are still alive and nearby."

"Oh, crap! Don't tell me we've put the frigging Sept of the Hungry Flower in danger now, too?"

Appreciating his use of the word "we," she put her hand on his shoulder. "You go get Chottle. I'm going to step sideways, just to have a look."

The Gauntlet, the often impermeable membrane that separated the spirit from the physical world was strong here, and though a quick shift into Crinos eliminated any effects from the copious beer she'd shared with Peter, Amy couldn't make it through on her own. Deciding she'd need a visual aid, she began to look around for a mirror or other reflective surface.

Nebraska meant "flat water" in the native tribal tongue, and after a minute of poking around some wooded backyards, it was a simple matter for her to locate a small, still pond not far from the cigarette factory. It was in the backyard of a small construction company, with a small bulldozer and backhoe listing on the soft earth. More tools for scarring the Mother, she thought briefly. Looking into the pond, more of a puddle, really, she stared at the smooth Asian skin her human college mates had envied, then settled her concentration on the reflection of light in her own dark eyes. With a rush of sensation, not nearly as powerful as the feeling the sphere gave her, she pierced the Gauntlet and stepped into the Penumbra, the area of what the Wendigo called the Ghost World that was closest to earth and mirrored much of what was in it. Other than a few sad spirits going about their business, the area seemed mostly deserted.

The hair on the back of her neck stood up, as if she were being watched. She whirled and thought she caught a glimpse of a shadowy figure slipping off into the woods. Not sensing any immediate danger from it, she turned to the object of her journey—the cigarette factory.

Here in the Penumbra, the building glowed a sickly deep green. A black bilelike substance bled from the brick walls like drops of sweat. The mere fact that it was a cigarette factory wasn't enough to taint its spirit that much, but it may have been enough to draw the attention of some darker Banes. All the structure's openings, the doors and windows, pulsed in and out as if breathing. Their veiny surfaces stretched more with each pulse, as if ready to burst. A single pattern spider was trying to spread a web around one window, but every time the building expanded, a strand from its hard work snapped. Seeing Amy, it abandoned its efforts entirely and skittered off.

As Amy approached, her keen sense of smell was assaulted with a miasmic aroma that brought to mind the cancer ward where her grandmother died, surrounded in her bed by a hundred dolls. As Amy stepped up to the window, the spirit sounds of the place hit her ears. In the far background, she heard laughing children, a holdover, no doubt, from the building's days as a childcare center. Over and above that was a low, warbling drone that hit her nervous system like the sound of fingernails against a blackboard. A red balloon flitted by the window, only to be popped by a sharp, fast-moving shadow.

Pulling herself up to the windowsill for a full view, her worst fears were confirmed. The concrete floor, covered in runes and sigils visible only in the Umbra, was cracking from the strain of something very large trying to push its way up. They'd stumbled upon a lost Bane, the secret shame of the Uktena. The magics that kept whatever it was in check had held for years— but now the spirit of the place, corrupted perhaps by the cigarettes, was weakening the binding, and some great nightmare was on the verge of being free.

Tumbling backward from her perch, Amy fell out of the Umbra and at Claws' feet. Chottle shifted anxiously nearby. It was well past midnight in the middle of the week, so there was little fear any sober human would see him.

"Bad?" Claws asked.

"Bad," Amy answered, then described all she had seen.

"Tobacco isn't enough to cause what you described," Claws said. "Unless they're marketing it directly to children or something. I'll head inside to investigate and you cover the perimeter. I've got a feeling we're not going to be alone for long."

"Long...long...long..."

"No," Amy said. "Let me go inside. You cover the perimeter."

"This is my job," Claws said, shaking his head.

"This is my fault," Amy answered. "Don't take away my chance to make it right. Besides, it's empty and it looks like the sigils are holding, so, for now, it should be safer inside. Plus, I'm the one whose head is stuffed with all the lore. I might recognize something you don't."

"I don't know..." Claws hesitated.

"This place may be crawling with fomori any minute now. And you can warn me and save my life!"

Claws sniffed at Amy's efforts to mollify his ego. The streets and the woods were empty. There was no trouble to be seen.

"Take Chottle with you," he finally said. "I'm going to poke around. He'll just slow me down."

Amy nodded. As Claws shifted to Lupus and loped off to explore the area, Amy used one of the charms on her necklace to pick the lock on the rear service entrance next to the garage door. With Chottle shambling close behind, she entered the desecrated place.

The smell of fresh tobacco, not unpleasant, filled her nostrils. But there was another smell, too, acrid, not right. Scanning the well-maintained cigarette machines, the neat stacks of printed boxes and rolling paper, she wondered exactly what it was she was looking for. Heading toward the machines, she found the source of the smell in a powdery residue. With a little searching, she quickly located a few jars of whitish liquid, obviously being used to treat the tobacco. Pulling a vial from her rucksack, she filled it with some of the liquid. She was going through all the jars, looking for a label or some writing, when she heard Chottle let out a loud, pained whine.

Whirling, she saw the metis sprawled on the floor, bleeding profusely from a huge gash in his side. A shadowy figure stood above him. The long, sharp metal weapon in his hand hummed from some electrical power source.

"What on earth are you doing *here*? Did the sphere bring you?" a familiar voice said.

"You…you…you," Chottle whined.

The figure's foot came down on the wound. Chottle cried out, pain preventing him from moving. The metal stick was pointed at the center of his mass.

"I kept this from Alaska," the figure said to Amy. "We used it to blast five-foot-wide holes in the ice. Human form, now, or this factory-second beanie baby gets fried."

Amy obeyed. As the man stepped from the shadows, the terrible wound on the right side of his face, where Amy had slashed him, became visible. But more than that, without the obscuring Gore-Tex, scarf and goggles, his features were revealed. Salt and pepper hair clipped to a crew cut, he now wore a light blue short-sleeve button-down shirt that could've come from any bargain rack. The only sign that there was anything different about him now than when Amy knew him in college was a swollen patch on his abdomen, visible beneath the light blue thread. Without the scarf obscuring his speech, she could hear his familiar quasi-southern drawl, which Amy had always suspected was an affectation. Only now it was accompanied by odd flicks of an ochre-colored, sluglike tongue.

"Professor Stinton," Amy said sadly. "How long?"

"Precision, Amy! Precision! It's the key to a well-structured mind. What, exactly, do you mean? How long have I known about the Garou? Decades. I always knew you were a shapeshifter. Why do you think I cultivated our relationship back at the university? Why do you think I gave you just enough details about my theories to whet your amazingly predictable Uktena curiosity?" he said. Then he patted the swelling under his shirt. "Or, do you mean how long since the Great One entered me? Heh— you know, that sounds more like a homosexual encounter with Jackie Gleason than a spiritual awakening. Let's see…two years? I found his birthplace among some Mayan ruins. He sang to me from his prison here. He told me he doesn't belong. He told me how much he longs to go home and what he would do for anyone who helped him."

"You were in charge of the oil expedition in Alaska," Amy blurted out.

"In charge? I was *responsible* for it! When I told them I'd be following the trail of a Garou in search of lost artifacts, Pentex was only too happy to fund the expedition. With your access to the werewolf lore, I figured you had more to go on than I did. And, of course, I was right. Who knew we'd camped right on top of the damn city, especially when all the sightings occurred further north? Of course, that's the nature of a mirage, to project the appearance of something somewhere other than where it is."

Revelation crawled across her face like Luna eclipsing the sun.

"Ah, you understand. Such a good mind. And, like many of your species, you're often at your most reasonable when on the verge of Harano. You'll make a great addition when you fall."

"I'd sooner kill myself than join you," Amy said.

"Yes, I know!" he grinned. "But the fact of the matter is, you'll probably kill yourself anyway! Still, you've done so much for us already. Not one, but *two* caerns and their septs, signed, sealed and delivered. If you like, we'll be happy to let you continue believing you fight against us!"

"I won't listen to you."

"Yes, you will. In fact, if you so much as flinch without my say so, I'll kill this living throw rug." To emphasize his point, he pressed his foot down harder, digging his heel into the bloody wound. Chottle let out such a sad sound it brought a tear to Amy's eyes.

"Please, no tears! I know you better than you know yourself. Do you know why you adopted this pile of blood and fur? Did you ever consider the possibility it was because he was the *only* Garou you ever met more pathetic than yourself? That staring at *his* pain made you feel better?"

"No!" Amy shouted.

"Come, come. That was barely a growl. A real Garou would be unable to hold back after all the insults I've heaped upon you, after all the pain I've caused your kind."

Amy started panting, looking this way and that.

Can't go forward. Can't go back. Can't stay.

"Enough of this. I don't really care why you're here. Just give me the bone-sphere, or I'll kill Chottle."

There was a click in the back of her head as if the words had tripped a trapdoor in her psyche.

Can't go forward. Can't go back. Can't stay.

"Ah. You see? You *will* fall. Most likely Chottle will be the latest sacrifice to your grand unproven theories about the sphere, and his death may well push you over the edge. And even if you make the utterly mad choice of giving me the bone-sphere, well, that's just what the Great One wants. He's something of an artist himself, you see, and he's dying to play some new songs."

Can't go forward. Can't go back. Can't stay.

Dizzy, nauseated, Amy sank to her knees. Slowly, as if she were already drugged, her hands fumbled into the rucksack and made their way toward the sphere. She would use it now, and pray it would somehow magically enable her to free Chottle, and more, that even if what she did next meant the end of all of them, that it wasn't just the drug that Claws feared, that she wouldn't be dragged off to some corner of her dying mind where only dream was visible. She prayed that at least she would be able to see what *really* happened.

As her fingers curved around the sphere, she felt her mind refuse to function.

Can't go forward. Can't go back. Can't stay.

Stinton's lips had already turned up into a smile when the sudden sound of spinning tread against gravel made him turn toward the garage door. Before he could move, with a loud creak of bending metal, the garage door bent inward, tore free from its supports and caved in on Stinton. For good measure, the small bulldozer that had done the damage rolled in on top of him.

"Amy!" Claws screamed from the driver's seat. "We've got to get out of here! There are like twenty fomori and Gaia-knows-what-else heading up from the woods."

Amy was still on the floor, near tears, almost in a fugue state. As Stinton moaned beneath the fallen wall, Claws raced up and shook her.

"Amy! Amy! Where's Chottle!"

She looked at him for a moment, not quite sure who he was, when another whine from her packmate brought her back to the room.

"Under...the wall."

"Aw, cripes!" he screamed, then started trying to pull the wounded metis free. When Stinton shifted, still alive, Claws drove his fist into his skull, cutting bone and tendon. He withdrew it and found his claws covered with black ooze. Not only that, but Stinton's features began to reform. Coming somewhat back to her senses, Amy joined in and helped pull Chottle free. Then the trio dove outside, pulling the metis along.

"This way! This way!" Claws screamed, and he led them to an old Hyundai Excel parked on the grass nearby. Claws dived under the steering wheel and tore at the plastic cover to reach the wires beneath.

Amy rolled the wounded Chottle into the back seat, where his blood oozed out onto the vinyl interior. She was trying to think of some way to slow the bleeding, but looking out of the rear window, she saw three shadowy figures moving toward them. The engine revved and she hopped into the shotgun position.

The car lurched off onto the street, then with a screech sped off. The radio had been left on and a familiar piano hook, albeit quite tinny through the cheap speakers, filled the air. Amy moved to curtail the offending blare, but Claws, with a wild-eyed grin, one hand on the steering wheel, turned to her and said, "Are you kidding? Crank it!"

So she did, and Warren Zevon's "Werewolves of London" filled the night air.

*I saw a werewolf drinking a piña colada at Trader
Vic's*

His hair was perfect!

Amy stared in wonder as Claws, happy to be
alive, half shouted, half sang as the speeding Excel
laid down some miles between them and the fomori:

Arooo!

Werewolves of London.

Arooo!

"Arooo! Arooo!" Chottle imitated perfectly.
Sometimes he even hit it right on the beat.

***

*Having shredded his left arm in an effort to more
quickly free himself from the fallen door, Stinton staggered
out onto the road. The moans of the damned rose from
the woods as the fomori collected themselves behind him.
Black worms crawled from his bleeding skin and began
stitching the torn muscles.*

*It would be a simple matter to track them now. With
the metis so badly wounded, they'd have to return to the
legendary Sept of the Hungry Flower for help—finally
exposing the location of that rare cache of power. But
even that wouldn't be nearly as valuable to the Great
One as turning young Amy.*

*He trotted over to his own parked car. But before he
could unlock the door, an intentional rustling made him
turn. Smelling dog, Stinton grinned broadly.*

*"Another Garou! The evening is lousy with them!"
he said with a beatific smile. Turning to face his new
guest, his eyes filled with recognition. Even in the deep
shadows it was difficult for the tall figure to hide his perfect,
argent coat.*

"We know you. Is there something we can offer you? Anything at all?" Stinton asked.

"No thanks," the Silver Fang said.

Stinton felt a pinch at his neck and found himself staring at some terribly familiar shoes. With his foot, Arkady rolled the disembodied head over and stared down into the dying eyes.

"I already know what I want."

Chapter Seven

The cigarette should be conceived not as a product but as a package. The product is nicotine. Think of the cigarette pack as a storage container for a day's supply of nicotine....Think of the cigarette as the dispenser for a dose unit of nicotine....Smoke is beyond question the most optimized vehicle of nicotine and the cigarette the most optimized dispenser of smoke.

—Philip Morris, 1972

Sees the Wind held the vial with Amy's sample almost up against his right eye, as if the ebon organic orb were a microscope and by so doing he could see every molecule in the liquid.

"Nicotine, sure, and lots of it. Propylene Glyco, corn syrup, a bit of chocolate," he muttered almost as if speaking to himself.

When Amy furrowed her brow, the elder said, "That's no surprise. Some tobacco companies use chocolate and sugar to make the taste more appealing to kids."

"Ah, I know some grownups who like chocolate, too," Fits the Pieces reminded him, rolling an unlit cigarette back and forth in his mouth.

The Excel's arrival at the small clearing was met by the same group that had been there the first night. They were all sitting silently around the bonfire, as if waiting, when the car pulled up. Amy somehow knew they hadn't simply gathered for gossip on her first date, and in fact, no one had so much as mentioned Peter's name.

The old man's nostrils suddenly recoiled and he waved everyone to silence. "Wait, here it is…" he said.

Sees the Wind swirled the small vial and began chanting. After a few moments, the liquid seemed to expand and then separate. A thin layer, mottled olive in color, rose to the surface.

Kathy Bandilack whispered to Claws and Amy: "From what I've been able to learn, only a limited run of the cigarettes was being tainted. The tribesmen who made the deal knew nothing about it. They'll be furious when I tell them tomorrow. Stinton probably planned to have these 'special packs' given to various important people. Over time, smoking them would have corrupted most humans from the inside out."

Hearing that, Fits the Pieces pulled the cigarette from his mouth, tossed it to the ground and crushed it.

Still chanting, faster now, Sees the Wind started to bow and raise his head in a ceremonial gesture. As he did, in a practiced motion, he reached his free hand into one of the small pouches he wore, withdrew a pinch of powder and sprinkled it in the air around the vial. Though the powder did not enter the vial, the green portion of the liquid frothed, bubbled and rose to the rim. All at once, Sees the Wind fell silent. In response, the liquid dropped, and its entirety became clear, like water. As a final flourish, he knocked it back with a gulp.

"Hm! Managed to save some of the chocolate. Tasty," he said, raising his eyebrows and smacking his wrinkled lips in appreciation.

"Do you mock us?" Claws snapped. The weight of strange events, long hot days and near escapes had finally taken their toll on the warrior, and he was ready to rip out some throats.

Sees the Wind's response was utterly submissive: "No. I thank your pack for revealing this enemy, and apologize for the deception."

"Deception?" Amy said.

"Well, for starters, this isn't the Sept of the Hungry Flower," Kathy Bandilack said, stepping up. "Its true location and the cache of powerful fetishes and records it holds has been kept secret from you. It is not even in Nebraska."

Amy, her disappointment overshadowed by relief, asked, "Why?"

"Because I knew what the Wyrm would ask of you, but did not know what you would say," Sees the Wind explained. "When you throw a shadow up in front of yourself, you conceal both the bad and the good. You knew your refusal to tell of the destruction of Greyrock made you seem tainted, guilty. Many Wendigo wished to capture you, force the information from you and then kill you. Only the swift intervention of several Uktena elders delayed your fate at their hands. It was agreed that for a time, you would be left to me."

"We've felt as if we were being watched, from the moment I first did not tell the tale," Amy said.

"You were. By the Wendigo. By the Uktena. By the Wyrm. The creature you fought in the shape of a bear was a Bane that had followed you for days, having caught a familiar scent of corruption. It was terribly crowded around your pack when I first visited your dreams. Your spirit was complicated, confused, in many places at once, difficult to understand, difficult to help. Then I caught a whiff of my own secret shame upon you. The thing you saw in the cigarette factory, stretching itself to break its bonds, is one I myself trapped thirty years ago, Kwakiuktl. Among its terrible powers is the ability to shift reality itself."

"A Nexus Crawler?" Claws whispered.

"Once he could have been called that, but Kwakiuktl used his power to reshape himself into something even more horrible. Three decades ago, I fought him in Oregon. My own mentor, Stokes the Flame, threw himself at the creature, sacrificing himself just to allow me the twenty seconds to complete the binding. At the very moment I finished the rite, the creature shifted reality—and vanished. Though I knew he was trapped, I no longer knew where he was. And I was responsible for him. Since that day he has lived in the back of my mind, burdening my spirit with a tale I dare not share. Now he had reappeared, connected, somehow, to you. So I watched and waited. Then word came from the Wendigo pack sent to explore the remains of Greyrock. They'd found signs of a human survivor and tracked him back to Washington. His scent was picked up by our own Uktena scouts, who followed him here, to Nebraska, where, until now, the trail grew cold."

"And you brought us here, built this fake sept, to draw him out," Claws said.

"Yes. Only now do I know that the smell of Kwakiuktl did not come from you or from any of your pack, and that my true enemy waits in Dekane," he explained.

Sees the Wind could not help but smile at the thought. "Trapped beneath a daycare center. No wonder I could not see him. The laughter of the children hid him, but it must also have driven him mad."

"But what about your nephew? You knowingly put him in danger?" Amy asked.

"Peter? That rapscallion?" Sees the Wind laughed. He called out toward the curtain of broken glass. "Peter! Peter! Come here, will you?"

Sees the Wind hunched slightly and walked in place. His arm lifted as if to draw an invisible curtain. As he did, the teen emerged.

"Yes, Great Uncle?" he said, but Sees the Wind's lips moved as well.

Sees the Wind opened a small pouch and pointed to the darkness inside it.

"I'm done with you for now, little shadow. Back inside!"

"Yes, Great Uncle! Don't hesitate to call if you need me again!" Peter said. With that, he walked over, placed his foot in the tiny pouch, and began forcing himself inside it. Within a minute, he was gone.

"Kwakiuktl is not the only one who can play with reality," Sees the Wind said with a chuckle. A few of the others laughed as well. Amy shook her head and looked down, but Claws was not so submissive.

"This reeks of Wyrm-taint, old man!" Claws sneered.

Sees the Wind shook his head. "I merely asked a spirit to cast my reflection. Not unlike the mirage of the city you sought."

"But you used us!" Claws shouted, on the verge of rage. "You put us in the path of death and didn't even give us the respect to tell us why!"

He rose, shifted to Crinos and began snarling at the old man. Sees the Wind was unimpressed.

"Life is long, Claws with Teeth, and history is written by the winners. Perhaps one day it will be said that you used us. That is why so much depends on the tales that are told. So much depends on who tells the tales, who sings the songs." He walked over to Amy, put his hand beneath her chin and raised her head so they could see eye to eye.

"We are not so different, you and I. We both carried secrets, we both felt ashamed, we are both Uktena," he said softly.

"Is Kwakiuktl responsible for my sadness?" Amy asked.

"Attracted to it, more likely. And to the secrets you sought."

"Then I don't know why I fight," Amy whispered sadly.

The old man stood and shook his head. "Yes, you do. Amy, what is your totem?"

She met his ebony eyes with a furrowed brow.

"I don't know."

Sees the Wind stretched out his arms with open palms. As he stretched, he shifted to Crinos, but even that form showed his age, fur streaked with broad bands of white and gray, his lupine face deeply wrinkled and tired. His full eight feet swayed, as if the bearer's soul had but a tenuous grasp on the body it lived in. Like a puppet on a string, he lowered himself onto his knees beside Amy and rubbed her back with his still-strong hand.

It took a while before she realized this grand gesture of supplication was meant for her. In the High Tongue, he whispered, for her ears alone, "I go to face an old foe for what may be the last time. Will you join me, songkeeper?"

Amy glanced at Claws.

"It's your call. I follow you."

Her eyes danced briefly from face to face, then she simply nodded.

"Our efforts are blessed," Sees the Wind said.

"So all we have to do is head on over and fix those binding runes, right?" Claws said hopefully. Sees the Wind didn't answer.

"We will talk on the way. First, Kathy Bandilack will quickly tend your wounds and make you ready for the journey."

Kathy led the trio off toward a quiet area. As soon as they were out of earshot, Mountainside turned to Sees the Wind and said, "She may have refused the Wyrm this time, but remember her wild words the first time she was here. That bone-sphere is like a drug. She's still a danger." Then he added, laughing, "Imagine! Trying to sing the Wyrm to health!"

Sees the Wind cackled in response, "Yes! And you know the *really* funny thing?"

The old man turned slowly and somberly toward his packmate, careful to enunciate each word so that his feelings on the subject were plain.

"She may be right."

Chapter Eight

> How can the spirit of the earth like the White
> man?...Everywhere the White man has touched it, it is
> sore.
> —Wintu Woman, nineteenth century

With time crucial, the party traveled in the Umbra, where Sees the Wind could use his great experience in the Ghost World to cut the travel time to a third. Having in her journeys entered the shadow world often, Amy had seen everything from the spirits of city streets to suburbs and wilderness areas. In cities, the souls of old buildings would sometimes warp into earlier versions of themselves, revealing their history. In the wilderness, the souls of the flora and fauna, and the creatures that tended them, abounded. But here, strangely, there was little difference between one world and the other. On the horizon, she spotted a spectral stagecoach rolling along, carrying with it what seemed the ghosts of the Weaver's Spiders. Half an hour later in a wheat field, she heard the endless stalks of grain sing a single, shrill, monotonous note. But there wasn't much more.

As usual, Amy took a spot between the recovered Chottle and Claws, but en route, she began to wonder about the rest of Sees the Wind's packmates. Kathy Bandilack, proud, competent and severe, in particular fascinated her, so she slowed up a bit and began walking next to her.

"Thank you for healing Chottle," Amy said, smiling.

Bandilack didn't bother to turn as she answered.

"I did it because it is what Sees the Wind requested," she answered grimly.

"You don't like us much," Amy said.

"The first time you were here, we mocked you. But you did not rage. Now you learn we lied to you because we feared your weakness, and though I can see the hurt in your eyes, still you do not rage. I want to know,…" she said, but then her voice trailed off as she clicked her tongue in self-annoyance.

"What?" Amy asked.

For a moment, Bandilack let the silence hang, and weighed Amy with her eyes.

"Where is your rage?" she finally asked, half in disgust, half in genuine curiosity. "Why didn't you stand up for yourself in the face of those insults? Why did you stop your warrior from defending his pack?"

"Don't you think we have better things ahead to fight than each other?" Amy asked.

"Of course, but I watched you. I smelled you. Your blood didn't even boil. It's not even boiling now. The songkeepers I know have a harder time controlling themselves than any other auspice. It's as if you're tainted somehow, if not from the Wyrm than certainly from something. Even the mourning Garou, even those who fall to Harano, scream and wail their despair at sister Luna with the full force of their being. But you, it's as if you're unclean. How can you *stand* to be like that?"

Amy was about to give her a long-winded answer about how she had always tried to see the balance in things, how she was proud to be able to curb her tongue, but then her memory flitted back to her First

Change, during a rape assault. Even then, rather than attack her assailant, she just stopped, frozen in the alley, listening to her jackhammer heart, watching her strange new form as if she weren't quite in her body. It was a distance made greater by the death of the Greyrock Wendigo, but a distance that had always been there. Was she tainted somehow, even now working for Weaver or Wyrm? She wanted to defend herself. Bandilack wanted her to defend herself. Instead, grimly, she said bluntly, "I don't know. I've never had any choice."

Having learned nothing about Sees the Wind's packmates and too much about herself, she walked back up ahead to keep pace with Claws and Chottle.

"Making friends?" Claws asked.

"No. Apparently my reputation precedes me," she answered.

"They'll get over it," he said, trying to cheer her.

"*Cada cabelo faz sua sombra na terra,*" Amy muttered in Portuguese. "Every hair casts its own shadow on the ground."

She was grateful when, nearing the site of the building, Sees the Wind motioned for them to hide behind a small hill. He pointed his lean finger at the area surrounding the cigarette factory's spirit and spoke in a low voice. "Kwakiuktl and his prison punched a hole in the membrane that separates earth from the Umbra. All manner of Bane has been drawn to it, but none dare pass while Kwakiuktl remains. Even they fear him," he said.

"I don't see anything," Amy said. "And there was nothing around when I first visited the Umbra here."

"They hid from you, hoping you'd release Kwakiuktl for them. Look carefully, among the shapes, behind the webs, between the shades of color."

At first, she saw nothing, but then she spotted a dark figure crouching just out of sight, its color and texture providing camouflage. Then she noticed two more, then three. With a gasp she realized there must be sixty Scrags of various shapes and sizes and at least five Psychomachiae hiding near the cigarette factory, waiting for the great Nexus Crawler to free itself.

"If it's plugging up the hole, why not just leave it where it is?" Claws said.

"I cannot. The location is now too tainted to hold my old magics for long."

Indeed, the entire building was covered with an odd blur, and "breathing" much in the same way Amy had seen earlier. With every strain, the spirit terrain stretched, cracked and oozed that sickly green. One such vein on the far wall blistered, sending droplets of foul bile cascading into the spirit alley, where they landed with a hiss.

"We must hurry. Back to the earth. The tear must be sealed there."

Almost simultaneously, they slipped into what some might call the real world. Once there, Amy felt some peculiar trash at her feet that hadn't been in the Umbra. Without looking, she kicked it out of the way. Its nature obscured by shadow, it rolled like a lopsided ball. Thinking nothing of it, she made herself a silent promise not to use the sphere in this battle. On the one hand, if it did no more than drug her, it might somehow dull her senses to the fight.

On the other, if it was truly an item of power, she dare not reveal it, lest it fall to Stinton, Kwakiuktl or any other minion of the Wyrm. The promise made, she waited for a command from Sees the Wind. Instead, Claws tapped her on the shoulder.

"Uh, Amy? Look down, will you?"

Amy gasped and jumped backward, realizing what she had kicked: a human head. Looking closer, she said, with equal surprise, "That's Stinton!"

Mountainside crouched by the head, poked it with a stick and sniffed.

"Cut with a klaive," Mountainside said. Turning to Sees the Wind, he added, more than a little impressed, "One stroke. Nice and clean."

"een...een...een,..." Chottle said.

"We are not alone," Sees the Wind said, "but our ally does not wish to show himself. I do not have the patience to wonder why."

He turned back toward the building. The dim green glow previously visible only from the Umbra could now be seen here as well. Sees the Wind hunched his back and stretched his arms as if imitating a bird in flight. He whispered a few words, and a black raven flew down from the sky, landed on the windowsill and peered inside. Eyes closed, Sees the Wind shook his head. "Kwakiuktl is all but free. I will not be able to bind him again. I must kill him. It will take several years, but I will do it. Alone."

As the old man straightened and opened his eyes, the bird flew off. His packmates' protests folded over one another in exasperated outbursts.

"You cannot!"

"We live and die as one!"

"Are you nuts?"

Sees the Wind shushed them. "Foolish children! The battle to seal the rift will probably kill us all!"

He waved everyone close together, grabbed the stick from Mountainside and used it to scratch out a rectangle in the dirt. "This is the building," he said.

Then he took the disembodied head in both hands and plopped it in the center of the rectangle, saying, "And this is Kwakiuktl, only much prettier. The moment he sees me, he will grow angry and gain the extra strength he needs to be free. The longer I can conceal my presence from him, the better. So, I will become invisible."

Making a circle of Xs in the ground, he continued: "You will all surround me as I enter. When we are close enough, I will begin a ritual to call the necessary spirits to heal the rift in the Gauntlet. But to complete it, I must be seen—and he will break free. You must keep him from me until the spell is complete. Once the rift begins to seal, he and I will face each other again. Do not fear for me or try to follow, for at that moment *your* real battle begins. It will take time for the proper spirits to seal this gash, and in that time all manner of Bane, no longer needing human host, will make its way through to the earth. They must be stopped. And then, whoever survives, if any, must ensure that this place is cleansed."

When he saw that everyone understood, Sees the Wind pulled some powder from one of his many pouches and began chanting. Under Luna's glow he was tinged with white and blue, but as he chanted, even these cool colors faded to gray. The texture of his clothing and skin began to smooth until his very shape became more and more abstract. Its now-unfamiliar lines folded into each other until he disappeared completely. A calm, disembodied voice explained that while he was invisible he would have to move slowly to retain the magic. The Garou circled the spot where he last stood. Even Chottle took a place, with some help from Claws.

Amy felt a hand on her shoulder. Sees the Wind leaned forward and whispered in her ear, "Now, songkeeper, you will see with your own eyes how Kwakiuktl writes with the world."

Slowly, solemnly, as if in ritual procession, the group drew its weapons and made its way through the hole Claws had left with the bulldozer. The fomori Stinton had previously commanded lay about the corners of the room like listless extras from a low-budget zombie film. They shuffled when the Garou entered, but made no move to approach, torn between a desire to do them harm and a greater fear of what was trapped here. The concrete floor had new, spider-web cracks in it, the source of the green glow. Also now visible was a series of sigils carved in the midst of the pattern. But their shape was deteriorating at the edges, their very form giving way.

Satisfied he was close enough, Sees the Wind chanted rhythmically, slowly at first, but then faster and faster. Amy caught a whiff of some odd herbs in the air and realized the shaman had sprinkled them as part of his invocation. For a moment, she felt silly, as if on some Halloween quest, surrounded by children in costumes—but the sound of the old man's voice, even when so soft it was barely audible, carried with it such energy and passion that the solemnity of the moment hit home. It reminded her, however briefly, of the sound her sphere made—rich, enchanting, with edges that seemed to trace the outlines of the world before trailing off into forever.

His droning grew louder, his syllables harsher, percussive, as if the sounds themselves were driving stitches into either edge of the ethereal gap. Bandilack, Fits the Pieces and Mountainside tensed. Seeing this, Amy and Claws did likewise. Amy heard the old man inhale sharply, then shout. The exhale that accompanied this strident appeal to Gaia's ephemeral helpers seemed to suck all the color and shape back into his form. He was visible again, but, eyes closed, hands spread, he was so intent on what he was doing, he didn't seem to notice. As his hands rushed together and clapped, the floor rattled. Sees the Wind spoke faster and faster, the individual consonants he uttered meshing into a blur. He stamped his feet and flapped his elbows in a hurried dance.

A low droning filled the room. The hair on Amy's back stood up.

"It's laughing. It sees the old man," Bandilack said.

The concrete floor began to breathe, in and out, up and down, as the doors and windows had in the Umbra. The sigils stretched, swelled and began to lose its shape. As both the strange breathing and Sees the Wind's dance reached a frenzy, the thirty-year-old writing crumbled to the point where it looked more like an accident of dripping paint than the design of a practiced hand.

Then the floor shattered completely.

A great multisectioned, black-shelled insect, Kwakiuktl threw off the shackles of reality, rose full-bodied from the breach and at once set to work making manifest the tortured dreams of its unknowable mind. Below the sectioned shell, scores of flailing tentacles spread out into the room, a giant, grim, fanged mouth and a single yellow eye at their center.

"Sweet Gaia!" Claws said. "What are we supposed to do against that?"

"*Para todo hay remedio si no es para la muerte!*" Amy said, then quickly translated for the benefit of her companions: "There's a cure for everything except death."

Claws, Bandilack and Mountainside instantly shifted to Crinos and positioned themselves between Kwakiuktl and Sees the Wind. Chottle shuffled along with them. Fits the Pieces waved his hands and clasped them, intertwining his fingers as he prepared to call upon the help of some spirit. It was only as one of her fetish arrows glanced off the thing's thick armor plate that Amy realized she'd fired it at all.

A flash of green light erupted from the horrid central eye, spreading out in a series of concentric circles. All at once everything seemed blurry and distant. Amy recognized it immediately as a minor distortion, a nuisance at best. With each passing effort, its influence on reality would grow more far reaching.

She let fly a second arrow, this time aimed at the fleshy area near the eye. A satisfied rush washed over her as she saw it penetrate the skin. As the spirit within the arrow spread outward, a growing wound erupted, oozing black liquid. Her excitement was short lived, however, as a series of tentacles careened across the floor toward her. She soon found herself leaping and rolling out of their way, unable to stand let alone get another clear shot. A second wave of energy made things even blurrier.

With the long, black tentacles able to work their way around any obstacle, Claws and Bandilack, having apparently consulted with Mountainside, moved forward. Swinging their blades, they tried to clear a path toward the central body, knocking and slashing the vile arms as they came. Then, all at once, with another blast from the eye, the very concrete beneath them changed to liquid and they began to sink. Before he went under, Claws caught one of the tentacles and pulled himself free. Then he lifted Bandilack. Clinging to the creature's arms, they continued their attack.

Mountainside, meanwhile, made his way to the top of a pile of crates that had remained solid, if not secure. With a powerful leap, he launched himself toward the eye. As a human, his muscled arms made him look top heavy, almost comical, but in Crinos the same arms seemed impossible for the world. Using their strength, Mountainside grabbed a hold of the thing's eye and drove his head toward it, mouth open wide. He steeled himself against whatever he would taste, bit down and clamped his mouth shut. With the strength of will and body control taught him by a wolf-spirit, his mouth would not open again until Mountainside desired it, even if he died.

The bite had an immediate effect. Kwakiuktl's entire body rippled as its hundred tentacles all raced at once toward the source of the pain. His mouth still firmly clamped, Mountainside raised his powerful arms and ripped into the bilious flesh on either side, widening and lengthening the wound his teeth began.

Another ripple of energy flashed from the heart of the beast, hitting Mountainside directly, filling him with green light before cascading across the room. At first there seemed to be no effect. Mountainside raised both hands to strike again, his thick arms poised like trees. Then, all at once, a wave from the creature hit him and his form shifted shape and substance. His thick fur seared into nothing in a line across his body as the wave passed. Then his flesh began to boil and melt away. But still the thick cartilage in his Crinos jaws kept his teeth clamped. Then his bones began to vanish, each folding in on itself with sickening pops and cracks. Finally, for a moment, all that was left was his jaw until even it, clenched tight in the final moments of its existence, vanished.

Bandilack howled. A deep shiver went through the others. Eyes rolling into the back of her head, without even making an effort to contain herself, Bandilack abandoned herself to rage. Berserk, she tore at whatever was near, accidentally knocking Claws back in the process. Another burst from Kwakiuktl, and not only did the monster's wounds heal and lost arms regenerate, there were now four times as many tentacles.

Fits the Pieces, hands still clasped, about to finish his spirit call, didn't notice the change in Kwakiuktl until it was too late. Before he could move, tentacles had wrapped themselves tightly about all his limbs. As Fits the Pieces rose into the air, Claws rolled onto his feet, raced over and started slashing away at the base of the tentacles that gripped his fellow Garou. He quickly hacked through two, but that was not enough. In one swift contraction of the alien exoskeleton, Fits the Pieces was sundered into six different sections, his last howl cut off as his vocal chords separated from his lungs.

Amy realized she'd lost track of Chottle. Scanning the room, she spotted him nearly pressed against the wall, wrapping himself around one of the tentacles. Before she could determine who was winning, she spotted another tentacle rising up behind an unaware Bandilack. Amy notched an arrow and hit it dead on, sneering a bit as it shriveled in a pulpy husk. Though Amy knew it unlikely, given her berserk rage, she thought the powerful woman gave her an approving nod before going back to slashing at everything that moved. Claws, meanwhile, was taking a different approach, grabbing and holding onto as many of the swirling arms as he could—hoping to sever them off a batch at a time.

Just when it seemed impossible to speak or dance any faster, Sees the Wind did. Individual sounds and single moves in the dance were no longer discernable. A few more seconds was all he would need, just as it had been thirty years ago, with a different pack and a different spell. Sees the Wind's lips formed to utter the last syllable of the healing invocation that would seal the bleeding wound between worlds. He would have to say it four times, then he was done.

"Ah'n!" he shouted.

But then one of Kwakiuktl's tentacles broke free from Claws' grasp and dove straight into the old man's open mouth, cutting off the final sounds. Sees the Wind's eyes opened wide as he tried to breathe. In an instant, he was lifted by his mouth into the air, where he dangled helplessly. The old man shifted to Crinos and with one swipe of his claws slashed through the tentacle in his mouth.

He fell to the floor in a cloud of dust, pulling pieces of the severed tentacle from his mouth. With growing anger, he threw the pulpy chunks back at the beast, but one was firmly lodged deep in his throat and would not move. The old man coughed and choked, desperately trying to clear his windpipe and complete the spell. As he twisted and tried to force his fingers farther down his own throat, in spite of his years of experience, his frustration grew into anger, and an exploding rage overtook the elder. A mad beast, no longer able to speak at all, he ran, rolled, leapt and dived onto what must have been the thing's back, then drove both his claws through its armor, up to the palms of each hand, into the thick flesh.

Though the creature had no visible mouth, the building shook from an unearthly din. Kwakiuktl reared, rushing high into the tin roof, as if it were some strange whale that swam in earth rather than sea. Sees the Wind held on tight, digging his hands deeper into the corrupt flesh. With another howl, the creature dove back down into the breach, into the Umbra, carrying Sees the Wind with him.

The building rattled and sighed—or was it the earth?—and there before the onlookers was a gaping hole in reality. Peering through, Amy could see the two old foes. Johnny Sees the Wind looked like a cowboy riding a bucking bronco that was half mountain, half octopus. The duo vanished into the distance of the Umbra.

Amy, Claws and Bandilack looked at each other, panting. Chottle, pressed almost flat against the far wall, had been muttering something softly to himself, over and over, but Amy couldn't make out what it was. Amy was about to speak, but the tiny slice of silence was shattered by a rush of Banes as they raced for the gaping hole. With no spell to heal the breach, if they could quickly secure both sides, the Wyrm-creatures knew they would have a beachhead with which to begin Armageddon. Scrags began to flood the building. The fomori rose to help their spiritual cousins.

Seeing the mass of creatures emerge from the pit, a still-muttering Chottle rolled in an effort to make it to the exit. Though Amy was disappointed that he did not fight, she hoped he had at least a chance for survival.

Claws, meanwhile, entertained no such illusions. Spreading his legs akimbo for better balance, he waited for the rush to reach him. He kicked one and slashed at another. Amy shifted to Crinos, snapped the neck of the closest Scrag, then hurled it at two others. Three more came at her, another six at Claws. She swung at two, but the third pinned her arms.

Unable to move, Amy glanced over at Bandilack, who'd been nearest the hole. Scrags swarmed over her like insects until there was little of the Garou left visible. Amy saw a flash of steel, a rising claw. A few pieces of Scrag flew into the air, but then there was nothing more to be seen. There was a shape beneath the pile of Scrags that bore a slight resemblance to Bandilack, but it shifted, withered and after a few seconds was gone.

Chottle was almost to the exit when the Scrags fell upon him as well and began to tear at his already shapeless flesh. Feeling himself dying, unable to fight back, not knowing what else to do, his muttering rose in volume until it was a scream. He'd been instinctively repeating the last sound he'd heard, the final syllable uttered by Johnny Sees the Wind: "an...an...an..."

The voice of the metis, a perfect imitation of Sees the Wind's, now loud and clear, completed the Shaman's spell.

A hot, dry wind, its source roughly where the elder had stood, blew toward the rift. The great weeping sore in Gaia rolled, sighed and began to fade. Seeing their prize vanishing, the Banes pressed forward even faster, forcing themselves into the world as quickly as they could. As the rift all but completely sealed, a final unlucky Scrag found itself caught between worlds, pinned at the waist. It tried to pull itself into the earth but could not, and its exoskeleton proved no match for the returning Gauntlet. Its legs severed with a little pop, the half-thing pulled itself about briefly with its hands, like a novelty windup spider, until finally the loss of the black ichor that dribbled from its open waist became too great, and it collapsed.

Though pleased the rift had been sealed and Chottle had proven a hero, Amy felt a great sadness that no one would hear the story, no matter how badly told. Unable to free herself from the Scrags that held her, unable to reach a weapon or the sphere, there was little she could do. At least a hundred Scrags crowded into the cigarette factory, and some, though wanting their fair share of Garou flesh and blood, spilled out into the night for lack of room.

Just as she was about to vanish into the blackness of her own Harano, Amy felt a sudden easing of pressure at her shoulders. At first she thought her arms had both been broken. But no, she realized as she pulled her hands in front of her that she was free! Claws, still swinging, had used his blade to kill the two Scrags holding her. The time he spent freeing his packmate had cost him, though, and now he was being attacked en masse from the rear. In a howl of pain he went down, not unlike Bandilack. Unwilling to see that scene play out again, and knowing there was only one thing she could do, before she could recall her promise to herself, Amy had the sphere in her hands and was rapidly flicking the bones.

tooon tiiin toooong

The sounds pulsed through the room, this time rising rather than fading, until the collected tones became a thunderous, consuming symphony. The sounds crashed from the sphere, heedless of any air, flesh, bone or concrete they met along their way, as though their journey would not end until they cried out and were heard by the very heart of creation. This time, however, Amy was not the only one affected. In a great circle, at which the sphere was the center, the closest Banes and fomori grabbed their heads and shook. As the sounds emanated outward, so did the effect. By the time the creatures that had been pressed against the walls first heard the notes, those closest to the sphere were no more. The monsters did not die, they simply melted into air, as if the chord had met with whatever matrix gave them shape and being and somehow rendered it irrelevant. As the sounds pulsed farther into the world, a mile away, a man decided not to spend his last twenty dollars on liquor and instead purchased some food for his family. In a small apartment five miles distant, a young couple fell in love.

Amy, as the sounds washed her soul from top to bottom, desperately hoped it was all real.

Chapter Nine

Whoever saw such drunkards?
Barrels broken open, the ground and starry
ceilings soaked. And look,
this full glass in my hand.
—Jalalu'ddin Rumi, *Unseen Rain*

And what happened then? Well, with the earth-hole healed and Amy's mind still reeling from the tones of the sphere, the secret helper decided the time was perfect to make himself known. A full nine and a half feet tall, his fur the color of moonlight, Arkady stepped in through the breach in the back wall and bowed.

"Amy Hundred-Voices, I am Lord Arkady," he said with some difficulty.

If there were any question before, now she knew she was dreaming. She'd heard of the fallen Russian-born Silver Fang and the purity of his breeding, but this magnificent creature was too beautiful to behold. The perfect werewolf. If there were a Garou fashion magazine, Amy thought, half-delirious, Arkady would grace the cover. Even his scars were gorgeous. His wounded hand only added to the impression of great natural gifts honed by experience and strong character. Then again, the whole building seemed unusually lovely as well. In fact, Amy had never seen a building looking quite this good.

Ignoring the fact that she did not respond, he stepped closer and shifted to Homid to make the conversation easier.

"I am sorry I killed the fomor in your stead. Accept his head as a gift for the great service you've done us all. If you do nothing else, if by some tragic accident you die tonight, I promise you will always be remembered for finding the bone-sphere."

Amy shifted to Homid and returned the bow.

"*Ne stoit blagodarnost*," she answered formally in the Russian preferred by House Crescent Moon.

Despite, or perhaps because of, her own disorientation, she noticed that his form wavered, just a bit. There was a dull, unfocused look to his eyes, as if he were drunk, or stoned, or…

"Are you *here*?" she asked with a giggle.

"Yes. But not *only* here. Alongside the cursed Black Spiral that leads to Malfeas, the heart of the Wyrm, there is another path, a Silver Spiral. I walk it now, to bring our war back to the heart of the creature that began it."

"You're going to battle the Wyrm in Malfeas? And they think I'm crazy," Amy said with a dreamy chuckle.

"Don't mock me!" Arkady growled, making Amy take a step back. "While your soul still resonates with the music of the bone-sphere, our eyes are the same. Amy Hundred-Voices, listen to me. I am of House Crescent Moon. My appearance tells you how pure bred I am. One such as I appears once every twenty generations. There will not be another. Not before the end."

Amy blinked and furrowed her brow. "But what about after the end? I mean, suppose we lose. Suppose all the Garou and even Gaia die. Suppose Wyrm and Weaver no longer have Wyld with which to make themselves real, and there's absolutely nothing left. Don't you think that maybe, after a billion, scillion years of this dreaded absolute nothing, somehow, magically, mystically, some spark will rise again and eventually bring with it all this…this nonsense? Might there not be another of *you* then? In fact, I find it hard to believe that *any* world would be long without one such as you, *Al-ki*."

Arkady was genuinely taken aback. "I have not yet given up on *this* world, Uktena. Does the sphere make you speak this way? Has your battle with that Nexus Crawler left you mad?"

"No. Just annoyed. You want my sphere, but you hide your lust behind pretty words and desperate quests."

"My quest *is* desperate. As for my lusts, I didn't even know of your sphere until I heard it sing. Its tones resonate with the path I walk. They resonate with Malfeas, with the Wyrm."

"They resonate with *all* things, Lord Arkady."

"Then it is exactly what I need to succeed! Give it to me! It will give me the strength I need to crush the Wyrm in his lair!"

Amy shook her head.

"The trick is knowing what to play. You see, the Wyrm wants it, too, as badly as you. And if you fail, he'll use it to play his own twisted refrains, and then they will ring throughout the Tellurian. In a heartbeat, the war will be over. The Great Mother will perish and nothing remaining will remember her name. Until, of course, things start again."

"I'll take that chance!"

"You must not!"

Arkady whirled away and clamped his teeth, finding it increasingly difficult to conceal his anger.

"And what will you do with it? Bury it where none may ever find it? Or better yet, use it to play the melancholy whining of your own Harano?"

"Don't try to tell me Silver Fangs are immune to the sadness that stalks us all, Arkady. One of your own ruling families, the Winter Snow, all fell to Harano."

"I will not fall. I will not fail. Give it to me."

"No. It's mine," Amy said.

"You refuse me?"

"Last I checked, that's what 'no' means. Or would you like to hear it in all hundred voices?"

"Very well. I am deeply disappointed."

Arkady's blade sailed through the air and lodged in her shoulder. The bone-sphere went flying. Before she hit the floor, the artifact was in Arkady's good hand. She gasped. Without close proximity, the effect of its song was wearing off sooner. Her bravado was fading, taking with it her conviction. Shame and dread, for her more natural feelings, rose in her chest. Where *was* her rage?

"No. You can't," she half-mumbled.

Arkady sneered. He cupped the magnificent prize in his hand and tilted it this way and that, admiring the delicate craftsmanship he'd previously only imagined. Then he stepped close enough to Amy to retrieve his weapon, sheathed it, then twisted his head to listen for what only he could hear—the next step on the Spiral. Something distant, something silver, caught his attention. He smiled, shifted to Crinos and prepared to head for it.

Just as he was about to exit, a figure, previously obscured by the cigarette-making machines, lurched up to his feet with a groan and a sigh. Claws, blade drawn, hand shaking, myriad patches of wet redness on his fur, staggered toward Arkady.

"You heard what she said, Silver Fang," Claws said. "I believe the word was 'no.'"

Not waiting for a clever retort, Claws shifted to Crinos and swung the sharp end of his klaive toward Arkady's head. Even if the warrior hadn't been wounded, there would have been no contest. As it was, the only question was how merciful Arkady was willing to be. The answer to that was not at all.

The scion of House Crescent Moon ducked easily, spun and drove his healthy claws so deeply into Claws' gut, it would have been a simple matter for him to pull out the Uktena's liver. Claws' eyes rolled up into his head. He made a shrill whining like a wounded puppy. As Arkady withdrew his hand and Claws slumped to the floor, something inside Amy shattered.

"Is there no end to the fools that crawl upon this barren land?" Arkady thought. He shook his hand twice to clean it of the larger chunks of gore. A deep, low, vibrant sound from the floor, not unlike the heavy grating of concrete scraping against concrete, made him look toward Amy.

Arkady paused and forced a few English words through his thick vocal chords: "Growling now? Too late for that. Go study. Let the real werewolves fight the wars."

But the sound only grew louder. Once in his homeland, near the banks of the river Tisza, before it had been poisoned, Arkady saw a brown bear watch helplessly as one of its cubs was pinned and killed by a falling rock. The mother made a sound similar to the one he now heard rushing from Amy's open mouth, but not nearly as loud. He looked at her, puzzled.

"*Give me the sphere!*" Amy screamed, shifting to Crinos in midsentence.

A short, dismissive blast of air flew from Arkady's nose, a sign of the deepest disgust. Not bothering to answer, he turned his back and headed for the outdoors.

But then something on the floor snagged his foot. Arkady stumbled backward, briefly taken unawares. A hideous pile of fur and flesh on the floor, which Arkady had taken for a mangled corpse, was alive and daring to grab his foot!

"Chottle," Amy grinned in her growing, guttural rage, "you *are* a trickster." Claws fully extended, teeth bared, Amy gave herself more fully to the inferno that consumed her heart than she ever had to any lover, or even to the sphere. Her legs kicked at the floor to send her flying. She kicked again in midair, as if that would speed her more. In a flash, she propelled herself into Arkady's exposed side, a blade of grass driven into an oak by a sudden hurricane.

The great Silver Fang lord, already teetering from Chottle's attack, tumbled to the concrete. Amy slashed, ripped, tore and pulled at anything that remotely resembled her foe. The sphere rolled into a sidewall, making a sick sound like the thud of a damaged piano. Blood dripping from a wound in his side, Arkady turned and looked at Amy as though delighted to be surprised.

"Welcome to the Garou, pup," he snarled in the High Tongue. "What a shame your stay among us will be so short."

While Arkady spoke, Amy continued moving. She dove for the sphere as if into water. Her chest hit the ground hard. A rib broke from the impact, but now her fingers were laced around the most precious thing. She was pulling it toward her when she felt her ankles clench together in the grip of Arkady's hands. The Silver Fang, still on the floor, had stretched forward and grabbed both her feet. Now he was pulling her, and the sphere, toward him, embedding his claws in her calves, leaving long open welts in her skin.

With a second to decide, Amy flicked all the bones at once.

doon diiin jennn kaaa loooo miiiiii taaaa

The sounds dovetailed one another, rising above and burrowing below the range of Garou hearing. The resplendent chord rode her rage, then spread and enhanced it. Amy felt herself split in two, like the world itself, and felt a sudden kinship and pity for the beings that lived all their lives this way. She was half in the Umbra, standing before the spirit of the bone-sphere, half in the physical world, being pulled irrevocably toward Arkady.

In the Umbra, the spirit of the sphere, now a snake, now a frog, now a multiheaded mountain lion, warped in shapeshifting abandon, waiting for what she would do. Falling to her knees, she begged, no, prayed, to the creature.

"*What do I do? Can you help me kill him?*"

The great being simply shook its head.

Back in the physical building, Amy kicked herself free of Arkady's embrace and let loose a massive flurry of jabs, swipes and slashes. Arkady, rising to his feet under the barrage, was still amused, until a sharp sting and the feel of something wet and warm on his cheek made him realize the danger was real. Bracing himself to begin a full attack, his spirits soared—*if this is what the bone-sphere does for this whelp, imagine what it will do for me!*

In the Umbra, Amy searched the wise, warm eyes of the shifting being before her. Now a glowing bird of flame, it bared its chest to her rage and lowered its great head, once, twice, then three times. Though to some the meaning of the gesture may have been lost, to Amy it was plain. At first she was too terrified to admit the meaning to herself, then she realized it was the only way. Though now she decided, at last, that the sphere and all it showed her was real, even in her heightened state she was no match for Arkady. And even he, with the sphere, was no match for Malfeas.

In the Umbra, she plunged her claws into the fire bird's heart.

In the physical world, she plucked the final note of a long lost chord.

doooon looonn tuuuun

The bird of fire looked at her, pleased she was so quickly able to find its heart. It screamed in exquisite agony—then, in both worlds, in all worlds, the sphere exploded, hurling Amy and Arkady off their feet and into the opposite wall.

Amy, desperately sad and tired, tumbled into someplace else...

…that might just as well be called a dream. She and Chottle walked along a quiet beach that came right up against a lush, primal forest. Miles away, on the small strip of sand, she saw what looked like a horse and rider. As the image grew closer, she could see that it was Sees the Wind riding the back of the great Nexus Crawler, holding back its corruption with silver reins. He came to a halt before her and laughed.

"Kwakiuktl matches my eyes, don't you think?" the old one said, patting the creature's side. You know, I suppose I should mourn my packmates, but I've seen them in their mother's arms and know the use to which she will put them. Do not seek to know so much, little one, that you can no longer cry."

"We're alone now, no one to hear but you and I…" Amy began.

"And Chottle," the old man winked.

Amy smiled. "And Chottle. Tell me, what did you mean when you said I built the bone-sphere?"

With the unmarked, pointed stick he carried, bleached white from the sun, he made a little circle in the sand and poked a hole in its center. The spirit of the sand twinkled visibly in the air as he wrote.

"You said yourself that throughout the Tellurian things become real through song. You sang in your heart for a way for each of your voices to be part of a whole, yet still sing with its own true nature. Does that not describe your sphere? All your rage, all your being had been going into its creation for years, until finally you found it, and yourself. Do you understand?"

Amy nodded.

"Now tell me—what is your totem?" he asked.

Without hesitating, Amy answered, "Chimera—the many that is one."

Sees the Wind nodded.

"When the time comes, perhaps you'll build another bone-sphere, or something even more wonderful," he said. "And use it to trick the Wyrm into singing your song." Then he added in a hushed whisper, "Though on that day, I think it just as likely we'll all sit in a Grand Moot with the One Who Dreamed Us All."

Without another word, he bared his claws and drove them deep into the back of the Wyrm-thing. Johnny Sees the Wind cackled as it screamed, writhed and carried him off in the direction of the old man's choosing.

And in that moment, Amy realized that perhaps the pains and frustrations she'd been experiencing, the terrific gap between the daily internal battle she fought and the ones she felt she *should* be fighting was not some unique neurotic aspect of her psyche but, in fact, part and parcel of her spirit—the struggle she longed to be in was the one she'd taken part in all along. She just couldn't see it. And she knew that millions of others couldn't either.

Her heart cleared and a voice came to her, the one she so often wept for, the one that maybe came from deep within her or maybe came from somewhere beyond the ages, or both, the one she heard too seldom, the one that flowed quick, clean and certain, and it said:

Yes, that is the sadness of the world.

Though she could feel the realness of the forms around her, and the air against her skin, for the longest time, there wasn't any sound at all. Even the cicadas were still. Eventually, Arkady rose to his feet. Still dizzy, he walked over to Amy's prone form and hovered there. It was over. Everything was over. He could no longer feel the signs. He was no longer on the Silver Spiral and feared he had been knocked onto the Black.

He lowered his head close to hers and watched as her eyelids fluttered open. A few bits of saliva dripped from the tips of his incisors to her face as he spoke, the wetness bringing her more fully to consciousness.

"Tell me quickly why I shouldn't kill you."

She met his gaze unwavering.

"Because I'm the only one who carries an understanding of the sphere. You know in the end it may save us all—and you are no fool, Lord Arkady."

He huffed and he puffed. Bits of whitish mucus flared in the circles of his nostrils. Amy felt the power of his lineage in his hot, blasting breath. Almost like the spirit of the sphere itself, Lord Arkady was a naked godhead. As he moved his head closer, so close it threatened to touch, she feared his very being might dissipate the paltry illusion of her life.

Then he sneered and walked away.

An hour later, as dawn threatened once more to turn truth into dream, Amy could still hear his distant, pained howl, carried to her by winds so deep, dry and harsh, they, at least, must have been sympathetic to him.

"Hmmm. I liked that one," Claws said, nodding. "Has heft."

Though the stomach wound was slow to heal, it hadn't interfered much with his appetite. Nevertheless, he'd stopped gnawing on the bone to listen more carefully. He hadn't even noticed he was no longer chewing. But Amy did. In fact, everyone at the newly reformed Greyrock Sept had listened with rapt attention to the story of their birth and now rolled the details over quietly in their mind, except for Chottle, who was nearby in the snow, practicing his new camouflage abilities on an uncooperative arctic rabbit.

Claws watched with a smile as Amy stood proudly, wrapped her recently finished Kente cloth around her shoulders and exited the circle, humming to herself. The tune sounded familiar, and it was terribly catchy, but it took Claws several minutes before he realized she was making it up as she went along.

About the Author

Stefan Petrucha is the writer of Topp's acclaimed *X-Files* comic. His work on that series has been republished in six trade paperbacks in the United States and abroad. He also writes the adventures of Mickey Mouse & Co. for Egmont Publishing in Denmark. His first published short story appears in White Wolf's **Inherit the Earth** anthology. His first novel, *Making God*, was published in 1997.

Sometimes a novelist, sometimes a video director, sometimes a shared illusion, he has a gaggle of eclectic, top-notch writing assignments, in comics, prose and other fields, under his belt and slightly to the right of his loose change. He currently works for Westchester-based PBI Media Inc., the publisher of such notable periodicals as *Film & Video* and *AV Video Multimedia Producer*, as a feature writer, associate editor and web guru.

THE RAGE CONTINUES...

Tribe Novels 6: Silver Fangs and Glass Walkers

The Garou war against the savage Wyrm-beast in Bosnia continues.

In Tribe Novel: Silver Fangs, King Albrecht joins the fray at last, only to clash with his old nemesis Margrave Konietzko.

In Tribe Novel: Glass Walkers, the young Theurge Julia Spencer tries to unravel the secrets of the dread Lore Banes who steal the Garou's very history.

August 2002